THE EARL'S SCANDALOUS BARGAIN

MERRY FARMER

THE EARL'S SCANDALOUS BARGAIN

Copyright ©2019 by Merry Farmer

This book is licensed for your personal enjoyment only. This book may not be re-sold or given away to other people. If you would like to share this book with another person, please purchase an additional copy for each recipient. If you're reading this book and did not purchase it, or it was not purchased for your use only, then please return to your digital retailer and purchase your own copy. Thank you for respecting the hard work of this author.

This book is a work of fiction. Names, characters, places, and incidents are products of the author's imagination or are used fictitiously. Any resemblance to actual events or locales or persons, living or dead, is entirely coincidental.

Cover design by Erin Dameron-Hill (the miracle-worker)

ASIN: B07XH2HBT5

Paperback ISBN: 9781670814432

Click here for a complete list of other works by Merry Farmer.

If you'd like to be the first to learn about when the next books in the series come out and more, please sign up for my newsletter here: http://eepurl.com/RQ-KX

 Created with Vellum

CHAPTER 1

ST. ALBANS, ENGLAND – SUMMER, 1886

*L*ord Frederick Herrington was lost. He'd stepped off the morning train from London and onto the St. Alban's platform with the sudden, strange sensation that he didn't know which direction was which or where the way out was. Which was absurd, considering how many times he'd made the journey to visit his good friend—his best friend, really—Lord Reese Howsden. But as he exited the train, he was met with the anxious sensation that nothing around him was familiar, that he was treading on foreign shores.

"This way, my lord," the station porter called to him, gesturing both toward the luggage that was being unloaded from the train's final car and the stairs that led down the platform to the walkway that he'd be able to cross as soon as the train moved on.

"Many thanks," he told the porter, touching the brim of his hat and marching on to collect his suitcase.

He'd only brought the one suitcase, and not out of any sense of frugality in visiting his friend. He didn't have much left to his name. The number of personal belongings that he'd found it necessary to sell to pay off his late father's mountainous debt was staggering. It was a blessing that modern clothing didn't require the assistance of a valet to dress in, because he couldn't afford one in any case. It was pure luck that he was able to afford the salaries of the remaining staff at his ancestral home, Silverstone Castle, but even that wouldn't be his to worry about much longer. The one thing that had occupied nearly all of his waking moments since he'd returned home from military service upon his father's death, the purpose behind his education and the activity of his formative years, was one sale away from slipping out of his hands.

"Thank you." He tipped the baggage handler a shilling, grateful that the man would have no idea how dear even that small amount was to him, and stepped back as the train chugged into motion once more, moving on to its next stop. St. Albans wasn't a large enough station for a prolonged stop, just as Freddy felt his life wasn't significant enough for the world to stop spinning long enough for him to find his equilibrium again.

Once the path was cleared, Freddy started across the

tracks to the station house and the waiting area out front where, he hoped, Reese's carriage would be waiting for him. He pulled up short halfway across at the sight of a vaguely familiar face on the opposite platform.

"It's Lord Gregory, isn't it?" he asked, stepping up to the inbound platform.

The finely-dressed young man who stood waiting, his face pinched into a troubled frown, blinked and glanced Freddy's way. For a split-second, the man looked terrified. He let out a breath as recognition dawned in his features.

"Lord Herrington." He stepped forward to meet Freddy with an outstretched hand and a smile. "What a pleasant surprise."

"Likewise." Freddy returned the smile and shifted his suitcase to his left hand so he could offer his right in greeting. "What brings you up to this lovely town, Lord Gregory?"

The anxious, hunted look returned to Lord Gregory's eyes. "Call me Sebastian, please."

"Sebastian it is. And do call me Freddy."

The young man seemed far more grateful for the simple courtesy than Freddy would have expected. He went on with, "I've just come up to have a word with Reese Howsden about...a certain matter."

"Oh?" A flash of unaccountable jealousy rushed through Freddy. Sebastian was handsome and refined. A little too refined. And his mannerisms gave him away just a bit too much. All the same, Freddy swallowed and reminded himself that Reese was just his friend, nothing more, and that he himself wasn't.... Well, he didn't know what he was. "Is there anything I can help with?" he asked, determined to let courtesy win out over confusion.

"No, no," Sebastian waved away the offer, relaxing into a smile. "Though I do appreciate your kindness. It's so difficult to find friends we can trust," he added in a quiet voice.

Prickles raced down Freddy's back. The instinct to deny what Sebastian was implying warred with an odd sort of relief to know that he wasn't alone. The intensity of the emotions only made him feel more disoriented, so he blurted, "I'm on my way to Albany Court myself."

Sebastian brightened. "Ah, so that's why the driver insisted on staying."

"He's here?" Freddy glanced past Sebastian to the station gate, eager to move on, but also strangely compelled to talk to Sebastian longer.

"Mmm." Sebastian turned to nod at the gate, then faced Freddy again. "You're a lucky man," he said with a wistful smile.

Freddy's face went hot. "Yes, I'm grateful to have such a good friend in Reese, especially when everything is falling down around me." He sensed that wasn't what Sebastian meant, but he needed to pretend he hadn't understood.

Sebastian's expression shifted to concern. "Everything all right?"

The simple show of kindness, coupled with the depth

of confusion within him, had Freddy blowing out a breath and rubbing a hand over his face. "I suppose everyone in the empire knows about my father's debts."

Sebastian had the good grace to look sympathetic.

"Well, I've finally gone and done it," Freddy went on. "I put Silverstone Castle on the market."

"I'm so sorry." Sebastian reached out to touch Freddy's arm in solidarity, his expression genuinely sad. "It wasn't entailed?" he asked.

Freddy shook his head. "No, thank God. I don't know what I would have done if the whole thing had been tied up in legal ropes. At least this way, the tenants will have a new owner and hopefully they and the staff will be able to stay on. But still," he added, not certain where he wanted to go with the sentence.

"It's hard," Sebastian said. "I can imagine. You're not the first man I've known to lose an ancient, family estate because of bad investments and debts. It's happening all over these days."

"At least I still have the title," Freddy sighed, though that, too, had a distinct possibility of dying out when he died, unless he produced an heir. And deep in his heart, he knew that wasn't likely. He had yet to meet a single member of the fairer sex that he could imagine himself going through the process of procreation with. There simply wasn't a lick of interest in that direction for him.

"Well," Sebastian said after the silence between them lingered on too long, "I wish you the best. I'm certain you'll land on your feet."

5

"Are you?" Freddy sighed. "Because I'm not."

"You just said you're headed to Reese's," Sebastian said with a shrug. "You've got the very best of men battling in your corner." He paused, and his mouth pulled into a wistful, lopsided smile. "I envy you, really."

Freddy barked an uncomfortable laugh, pretending once again that he didn't understand exactly what Sebastian was implying. "Don't envy a man who stands on the brink of losing everything and being humiliated for it."

To his surprise, Sebastian turned deadly serious, the light going out of his eyes. "Losing one's money and legacy is not the worst kind of loss out there. "Pray that is all you lose."

Freddy frowned, well and truly confused, but he didn't have time to ask what Sebastian meant. The train whistle that had sounded in the distance a moment before blared louder as the London-bound train rolled into the station, its brakes squealing. Sebastian reached for Freddy's hand once more, and Freddy shook it.

"Wish me luck," Sebastian said, his expression dour, as the train stopped and its doors opened. He let go of Freddy's hand and headed for the first-class car.

"Good luck," Freddy called after him, unsettled and wondering what Sebastian needed luck for.

If felt awkward to wait on the platform for the train to leave so that he could wave off a man he barely knew, so he turned and headed out through the gate and into the street. As Sebastian had said, Reese's carriage was waiting off to one side, along the road. The driver, Mr. York, recognized Freddy and waved.

"I hope you weren't waiting long," Freddy told him, handing over his meager suitcase when he reached the carriage. "I ran into Lord Gregory and had a chat with him."

"It's no problem at all, sir," York said with a smile. "It's a fine day, and I rather like watching trains."

Freddy nodded and stepped into the carriage, shutting the door behind him. He let out a breath, relieved to be alone and protected from the outside world, and comforted by the faint scent of Reese that pervaded the carriage's interior. He closed his eyes and sat back, letting that scent fill him. Images of Reese's kind smile, his flashing blue eyes and sandy hair, his broad shoulders and narrow hips, flooded him.

The smile that the Reese of his imagination wore turned sultry and beckoning. Heat flooded Freddy, and his groin tightened. He snapped his eyes open, grateful that the carriage jerked forward at exactly that moment. What was he up to, letting his thoughts wander like that? Reese was his friend. He didn't want to muddy the waters by getting into...into one of *those* arrangements with him. Memories of things he'd seen in school and abuses he'd witnessed in the army flooded him, dousing whatever embers had started to glow within him. He knew full well everything that a relationship with another man entailed, the humiliation and the degradation, and he knew it was the last thing he wanted or needed at a time like this.

The ride to Albany Court was pleasant and short, once he adjusted his thinking and concentrated on the beautiful countryside and quaint villages they passed instead of his own, disturbing thoughts. Rolling through the gates of Reese's estate felt like coming home as much as returning to Silverstone Castle ever did. The massive, Jacobean façade of Reese's ancestral home greeted Freddy like an old friend. He was certain that Reese would be able to help him cope with the loss of everything he should have been able to preserve, including the loss of his pride.

"I'll see that your things are taken up to your room, my lord," York said as he positioned the step for Freddy to climb out of the carriage.

"Thanks." Freddy took a deep breath as he stepped down.

"They're all in the conservatory, or they were when I left," York went on.

Freddy's breath caught in his lungs, nearly causing him to cough. "They?" he asked.

"Lord Howsden and his guests, my lord," York explained. "His brother has come over from America with his wife, of course, and Lord Henry—Mr. Howsden, as he insists we call him now—has brought a friend from Wyoming. They've been here for more than a fortnight. And the usual lot is here as well."

Freddy's mouth fell open, but he didn't know what to

say. Reese hadn't told him he was in the middle of hosting a house party. He'd expected to find Reese alone at Albany Court. He'd expected the two of them could commiserate about his losses together, privately. He hadn't known he was walking into an event. If felt like... like he had been robbed of something.

As fast as he could, he smoothed his expression. "Thank you, York," he said, moving on into the house with a whole new kind of trepidation in his heart.

REESE HOWSDEN COULDN'T KEEP HIS FEET OR HIS heart still. He paced the length of the conservatory, pulling his pocket watch out of his waistcoat and checking the time yet again. At the far end of the room, the bulk of his house guests were clustered around the shiny, new grand piano he'd just had delivered, singing a rousing rendition of the latest popular tunes.

"You play surprisingly well, Miss Garrett," John Darrow complimented the dashing Miss Lenore Garrett as she added an expert cadenza to the popular tune.

"Thank you, my lord." Lenore returned the compliment with a smile, then launched into a rousing Stephen Foster tune.

"Don't act surprised, Lord Whitlock," Lady Diana Pickwick scolded John with an arch look. "Just because Miss Garrett is an American from Wyoming doesn't mean she's a heathen."

"I never implied such a thing," John replied with a

teasing grin. "We have heathens enough here in England as well."

Diana huffed at his wheedling comment and the wink that followed it.

"Poor Miss Garrett," Henry, Reese's brother, laughed as Reese finished the length of his pacing by his side. "She's not going to get much interest from Whitlock, I'm afraid."

Reese hummed in agreement, forcing himself to stop and stand sedately at his brother's side. "Yes, John and Diana have been dancing around some sort of flirtation for a year now," he said. "Though I'm reasonably certain Diana is convinced she hates everything about him."

"Isn't that always the way it starts?" Henry's wife, Ellie, laughed.

"Not with the two of you," Reese answered her with a smile. "As I seem to recall, you fancied each other right off the bat."

Ellie laughed and blushed, and Henry gazed adoringly at her. Anyone with eyes could see that Reese's brother was madly in love with his American wife, and by more than just the bump of her belly that created telling lines on her gown. They'd brought their two other young children with them as well, which had pleased Reese's own son, Harry, named after his uncle, to bits. Harry adored having cousins to play with up in the nursery.

"Love stories like ours don't come around every day," Henry agreed, leaning in to steal a quick kiss from his wife. He then turned to Reese, arched a brow, and said, "Or do they?"

Self-consciousness flooded Reese, and he had a horrible idea that it showed on his face. "How is your friend, Mr. Charlie Garrett, enjoying England so far?" he asked, praying Henry would take the hint and change the subject.

Henry paused for a moment, his grin sly, but cleared his throat and said, "He's enjoying it, though he wishes he'd brought his wife with him. He misses Olivia desperately."

"As every man should miss his wife when she isn't with him," Ellie added.

A quick pang of longing for Freddy struck deep in Reese's gut. He pulled out his watch and checked the time again. Where was the man?

"But Olivia had oodles of things that needed her attention back in Haskell," Ellie went on. "Which is why Lenore came with him instead."

As if on cue, Lenore turned away from the piano keys and called, "Ellie, come here. You know that show tune far better than I do." She stood from the seat and gestured for Ellie to join them. Two weeks under his roof and Lenore was already treating the place as her own. Not that Reese minded. He liked Lenore and the two of them had become fast friends.

"Excuse me, my lord." Ellie laughed and left to join the others.

"Mrs. Howsden, please stop my daughter from

making an exhibition of herself," Mr. Garrett greeted her as she reached the piano, though he looked as proud as a father could be over the attention his daughter was getting.

"They seem a lively duo, whether Mr. Garrett misses his wife or not," Reese said as Henry closed ranks with him.

Henry laughed. "Charlie was a card player and a scoundrel in his early days. He and Olivia met on the Oregon Trail years ago, when everyone was rushing out to stake a claim on the frontier. It appears as though Lenore has taken after him, and in more than just looks."

Reese glanced back to the dark-haired beauty. "She does favor her father," he said. "Does she have the same business sense?"

Henry's answering grin said almost as much as his words. "Charlie is here to look for investors for his growing hotel empire. Lenore is here to find a titled husband. I have a feeling they're both going to be successful beyond the wildest dreams of most Brits." He paused, then added, "Watch out for Lenore and her schemes, by the way. A widower marquess is akin to the holy grail for dollar princesses, like Lenore."

Reese chuckled, shaking his head. "I won't marry again," he said. "I was lucky enough to find a woman who understood who I was and what I am about in Ethel. And since we managed to generate Harry, I've no need to go through that again."

"Not to mention the fact that you're madly in love

with someone already," Henry added, lowering his voice so that not a soul in the room could hear him. When Reese sent a telling glance to him, Henry went on with, "He's the one, isn't he? This object of desire who you told me about all those years ago?"

Reese's chest squeezed tight, making his heart feel as though it were bound in a cage of uncertainty. He nodded, but couldn't bring himself to speak.

"And he still doesn't know how you feel about him?" Henry asked, quieter still.

Reese puffed out a breath. "Oh, I think he knows."

"But?" Henry prompted.

Reese was saved from having to explain the entire, confusing tangle of doubt and affection as Freddy himself walked into the room. It was as though the curtains had been thrust open, flooding Reese's insides with heat and light. In a flash, he felt lighter than air, in spite of the concerned look on Freddy's face as his eyes went straight to the scrum of guests around the piano. He'd failed to tell Freddy that he had a house full of people, mostly out of fear that Freddy wouldn't come if he knew. But now that he was here, it was as though the world could start moving again.

Then Freddy glanced his way, met his eyes, broke into that sheepish smile he had that drove Reese to distraction, and it was all Reese could do to keep from running to him.

"That answers that question," Henry said under his

breath as Freddy changed direction and marched toward them.

"Reese," Freddy said with a crisp nod by way of greeting.

"Freddy," Reese replied, clasping his hands behind his back to keep from throwing his arms around him and kissing him senseless. It was a poor greeting, but Reese didn't trust himself to do or say more. "I'd love for you to meet my brother, Mr. Henry Howsden of Haskell, Wyoming."

Freddy extended a hand and Henry took it, saying, "I've heard so much about you. It's a pleasure to meet you at last."

Freddy's face flushed and his eyes darted about for a moment, as if he'd arrived in the conservatory naked and had just realized it. "I've heard wonderful stories about you as well," he said, glancing anxiously to Reese as if to ask how much he'd revealed.

"Henry and his wife are here with a Mr. Charlie Garrett and his daughter from Haskell. Mr. Garrett has come on business," Reese explained, his words coming out in an overeager rush. He wanted Henry to think the world of Freddy, just as he did.

"Are you here on business as well?" Freddy asked Henry.

"No, I'm here to visit the ancestral home," Henry answered. "Reese has taken quite good care of the place."

Freddy's face pinched with anxiety once more. That brought all the things Reese knew Freddy was suffering through back to the surface. "How is everything?" he asked with a cautious lift of one eyebrow. The question might have seemed polite to anyone not in the know, but Reese knew everything.

Freddy pressed his lips together tightly for a moment, sadness and anxiety in his eyes. "Could we speak in private?" he asked in a soft voice.

Reese's heart felt as though it were about to explode. Other parts of him were in serious danger of exploding as well, if he didn't rein himself in. "You don't mind, do you, Henry?" he asked his brother.

"No, by all means," Henry said with a smile that was both teasing and overjoyed. "It looks like Ellie is about to take center stage anyhow, and I should be there for it." He clapped Reese's arm, nodded to Freddy, then walked off to join the others.

"We can speak in the library," Reese said, switching to the gentle tone of voice that he couldn't help but use when it was just him and Freddy.

He started for the door, Freddy following him, a buzz of electricity surging through him that said at last, they might just have reached the point where something was about to happen between them.

CHAPTER 2

Freddy's nerves bristled as he followed Reese out of the conservatory and down the hall to the library. The shock of finding a full-blown house party where he had expected to find only Reese was beginning to wear off, but that only brought his problems back to the center of his attention.

All the same, as they entered the cozy, quiet library, he opened with, "Your brother seems like a nice chap."

"He's the very best of men," Reese said with a smile.

"And what is this York tells me about your brother and guests arriving two weeks ago?" Freddy asked, doing his best not to sound put out.

Reese looked sheepish as he headed straight to a small table holding a variety of decanters. Sunlight poured in through tall, clean windows, casting a cheery light on what felt to Freddy like a gloomy scene. "I should have told you they were coming, but you've been so busy with the business of your estate. I miss Henry terribly, but he enjoys his life out there in the Wild West." He reached the table and turned to say, "I know it's early, but would you like a tipple?"

Freddy held up his hand. "No, thank you. The way things have been lately, I'm afraid that if I start, I won't stop."

Reese pulled back from reaching for a decanter and turned to study Freddy with a concerned frown. "It can't be that bad, can it?"

Freddy sighed, rubbing his temples with one hand. He crossed to the fireplace and stared at the old carriage clock that made up the center of a display of various antique time pieces. "I've taken the plunge," he said in a melancholy voice. "I've given up all hope of salvation and put Silverstone Castle on the market."

"Oh, Freddy, I'm so sorry." Reese marched straight toward him, sympathy deep in the lines of his face. "I know you were hoping to avoid it."

"It was unavoidable," Freddy said with a shrug. "I can admit that now. Father's debts continued to grow after his death, what with the ridiculous rates of interest he agreed to. No improvements to the land or shrewd investments after the fact were ever going to be able to keep up with the payments. It's sell Silverstone now, while I can, or end up declaring bankruptcy in a few years' time."

"Bankruptcy is not an option," Reese said in a somber

tone. He shifted his weight, fixed Freddy with a worried stare, then asked, "Could you ask Henrietta for the money to shore things up? It was her home as well."

Freddy shook his head, rejecting the idea. "I am not going to beg my sister for financial salvation." The very idea was abhorrent. "And besides, her money belongs to Ricky. She cannot very well spend the Tavistock fortune saving Herrington property."

"I suppose not." Reese paused before going on with, "Will the price of the sale cover the amount of the debts?"

Freddy nodded. "Barely. There will be just enough left over for me to purchase a modest flat in London. Though I should be wiser about my expenditures and buy a flat in York or Winchester, someplace less costly, instead."

"You can always stay with me," Reese said, inching closer. "For as long as you'd like."

The hair on the back of Freddy's neck stood up. He glanced slowly up to meet Reese's eyes. There was more than just casual friendship there. Reese cared about him, perhaps more deeply than anyone other than his sister, Henrietta, and had since they'd met at university. A warmth seemed to radiate from him that pulled Freddy in. His heart sped up, and his cock stirred to life.

He sucked in a breath and took a half step back, then cleared his throat and strode away toward one of the windows to stare out at Reese's perfectly kept gardens. "I'm sure Henny will offer to let me live at Tavistock

House," he said, his voice hoarser than he wanted it to be. "Though with her and Fergus newly married and expecting, I'm not sure I'd be entirely comfortable there."

He glanced out the window. The jolly party that had been singing their hearts out when he and Reese had left the conservatory were all now flooding out onto the sunlit lawn, where a badminton net, croquet set, and a variety of chairs had been set up against a background of colorful, summer blooms.

"As I understand it, you wouldn't be the only one abiding under that roof," Reese said, seemingly as cool as a spring breeze, as he walked slowly to join Freddy. "Linus Townsend is set to move in as soon as your sister and Fergus return from Ireland."

Freddy hummed, picking out Dr. Townsend among Reese's other guests. He seemed to be attempting to convince Lady Natalia Marlowe to play croquet with him. "I suppose that makes sense. He is Fergus's personal physician, after all."

"I'm surprised he didn't go with them to Ireland," Reese said, standing shoulder to shoulder with Freddy. "Although who would want even a physician to accompany him on a honeymoon?"

His voice dropped to a soft purr, and when Freddy peeked to the side, Reese was watching him with soft eyes and a slight flush. The scent of his cologne filled more than just Freddy's nose. It seemed to sink into his bones, whispering forbidden things.

"I don't know why I feel so gloomy about selling

Silverstone," he said, breaking away from Reese once more and crossing to the glass-topped table where Reese displayed his most valuable books. "I knew it was inevitable even before Father died. All the letters he wrote to me when I was in South Africa were like prophecies. I believe he encouraged me to join the army —to make a man of me, as he said—so that I would be thousands of miles away when he spilled out the whole truth to me."

"Knowing something is inevitable and coming face to face with it are two entirely different things," Reese said, following him.

His words had an electric effect on Freddy, particularly when Reese stopped mere inches away from him. Freddy's lungs seemed caught in a vise, and his legs threatened to give out from under him. One slight sway, one flicker of his wrist, and he would be able to touch Reese, if he dared.

"Just know that you'll never have to go it alone," Reese said, his voice so gentle it could have been a caress. "I will always be here for you, no matter what slings and arrows life throws at you."

He lifted a hand, resting it on the side of Freddy's face. Deep, swirling longing poured through Freddy. It felt so astoundingly wonderful to have someone there for him, offering him unconditional support. In his heart, he knew every word Reese spoke was genuine, that he would never truly fail as long as Reese existed. But comfort came with a cost.

Reese swayed closer, his gaze dropping to Freddy's mouth. His thumb followed, swiping tenderly across his bottom lip. Freddy's lips parted, and Reese moved in, his eyes closing.

"I met Lord Gregory at the train station," Freddy blurted. Fear at his overwhelmingly sensual response to Reese pulled him back. He cleared his throat and marched toward the table of decanters, picking one and yanking out the stopper with a little too much enthusiasm. "What was he doing up here?"

Reese remained where he was for a moment as if frozen, his eyes still closed. He winced slightly, drew in a breath, and headed for the table as though nothing out of the ordinary had happened. "Poor Sebastian. He thinks he's about to find himself in a spot of bother."

Freddy sloshed brandy into a snifter, replaced the stopper, then grabbed the glass for a quick swig that left him gasping for breath. "Spot of bother?" he managed to wheeze out as alcohol burned his throat.

Reese reached the table, took the glass from him, and put it down with a look that was almost admonishing. "Nothing to worry about. Some photographs...." He shook his head instead of finishing his sentence. "He came to me looking for advice and I gave it."

"Did he stay long?" Freddy cursed himself for asking and for the prickling jealousy that welled up in him, as it had at the train station. It was stupid to be jealous. Reese was his friend. What he did with the rest of his life was his own business.

"Overnight," Reese said. Freddy's jealousy flared hot for a moment as he imagined where Sebastian might have slept, but Reese went on with, "My brother insisted he stay and join in the fun and games yesterday." He nodded to the window. "We should probably join in ourselves."

"An excellent idea," Freddy said with a rush of breath. He and Reese headed for the door. He wasn't certain how much longer he could have endured being alone in a cozy room with Reese and his dangerous feelings in any case.

"Everything will turn out all right, Freddy," Reese said as they reached the door. "You'll see."

He was close enough to touch Freddy's hand, brushing their fingers together. Something primal within Freddy wanted to twine their hands together, to revel in the touch. But he couldn't. It was wrong. Every example he'd ever had of men who chased those feelings had ended in disaster.

They broke apart just before crossing outside through the conservatory door. The other guests seemed to be having a perfectly delightful time. It truly was a beautiful day—sunny but not too hot—and the ladies had abandoned all thoughts of parasols and decorum to dash about the lawn in pursuit of the games on offer.

"Mr. Garrett," Reese spoke up, taking a step ahead of Freddy toward a grey-haired gentleman with a western-style hat and a broad smile. The man glanced Reese's way. "I'd like to introduce you to a good friend, Lord Frederick Herrington."

"Lord Herrington." Mr. Garrett strode toward them, stretching out his hand. Behind him, in the cluster of ladies, the young woman who must have been his daughter broke away and scurried to join them as well. "Reese here has told us so much about you," Mr. Garrett went on, shaking Freddy's hand.

"Good things, I hope," Freddy said, heat rising to his face and neck. He must have looked like a right ninny, blushing away as he was.

"Very good things," the young woman said, inviting herself into the introduction. She smiled at Freddy with a particularly interested light in her eyes.

"Freddy, may I introduce Mr. Charlie Garrett of Haskell, Wyoming and his daughter, Miss Lenore Garrett," Reese made the introductions.

Freddy let go of Mr. Garrett's hand and took Miss Garrett's, bowing over it. "The pleasure is all mine."

"I must say," Miss Garrett went on. "I do so enjoy the way men introduce themselves to women in England. It makes me feel quite like a princess. I don't think I'm ever going to want to go back."

Something tickled at the back of Freddy's mind. He took in the expensive cut of Mr. Garrett's suit and the fashionable style of Miss Garrett's day dress. The term "dollar princess" instantly sprang to his mind.

"Do they not treat women with decorum and respect

in Wyoming?" he asked, hoping he was being droll and not rude.

Fortunately, Miss Garrett laughed. "Not in the manner that English gentlemen have. Which is why I like you all so much." She hadn't let go of his hand and squeezed it tighter before asking. "Would you like to be my partner for badminton?"

"Um." Freddy glanced to Reese, no idea what to make of Miss Garrett's American boldness.

Reese laughed and nodded toward Miss Garret. "Don't look at me. I'm perfectly all right with Miss Garrett choosing whomever she'd like for her partner."

The comment left Freddy with an uneasy feeling, but he forced himself to smile and focus on Miss Garrett. "I'd love to," he said, starting toward the badminton net with her. "But I must warn you, badminton is not my sport."

"Nonsense," Miss Garrett said, swaying closer to him as they walked. "You look fit as a fiddle. And Reese told me earlier that you used to be a soldier."

"Reese?" Freddy's brow went up at the familiar way Miss Garrett addressed him as Reese and not the more proper Lord Howsden.

"Yes, he has been singing your praises since we arrived," Miss Garrett laughed. "Reese and I have become great friends." Clearly, she hadn't understood why Freddy was surprised. Though it was somewhat of a breath of fresh air to spend time with a wild American who didn't understand the protocol of who should be called what and when. "Here," she said as they reached the edge of the marked-off court, bending to retrieve a racquet from the ground. "What you don't know, I will teach you."

Freddy certainly thought she was capable of that. "Who are we playing against?" he asked.

"Us," Linus Townsend said as he and Natalia took their places on the other side of the net. "And I can assure you, you will lose."

"Not if I have anything to do about it," Miss Garrett said.

The game began with Miss Garrett winning the serve and demonstrating that she was far more skilled in badminton than any woman Freddy had yet seen. She attacked the shuttlecock with gusto, lunging when she needed to and running to hit the shots that were out of Freddy's reach. Townsend and Lady Natalia weren't half bad themselves, which made for a lively game.

"I'm so glad you aren't one of those men who thinks that women should be pretty ornaments and nothing more," Miss Garrett said, panting, as they switched sides, preparing for the next volley.

"How do you know I'm not?" Freddy asked with a grin, settling into attack position as they waited for Townsend to serve.

"You wouldn't be playing this hard if you were," Miss Garrett told him. "You would be flattering and teasing me, but you wouldn't have your heart in the game." She lifted her eyebrows in an impish flicker, then poured all of her concentration into the game.

Freddy found himself laughing. He liked Miss Garrett, and there were few people that he liked so instantly. He glanced to the side, to the game's spectators, and caught sight of Reese in discussion with Mr. Garrett and his brother. Reese saw instantly that Freddy was looking his way and treated him to a wide smile, as if to say thank you and well done for entertaining his guest so well. Or perhaps the smile was simply pride and affection.

"Lord Herrington!" Miss Garrett cried out as the shot Townsend served sailed right past him.

"Sorry, sorry." Freddy faked a laugh as he straightened, then jogged back to collect the birdie. "My attention wandered for a moment there."

"I could see that," Miss Garrett said. She marched up to him with a scolding look, mirth sparkling in her eyes, and took the shuttlecock from him. She lingered for a moment, their hands touching. "I'm not sure that my poor, delicate pride could handle you paying attention to anything but me right now," she said, fluttering her lashes.

Freddy laughed and surrendered the shuttlecock. "Forgive me, Miss Garrett. I don't know how I could possibly find anything as fascinating as you are."

Her smile widened and she stepped back with a pleased laugh. A moment later, she hit the birdie back over the net so that Townsend could serve again.

Freddy sank into a ready position again, but his shoulders bunched, and an odd thought gripped him.

Miss Garrett was flirting with him and he was flirting right back. But there was something hollow in it, something that didn't quite fit. Their hands had touched, but that was all. He hadn't felt even a fraction of the electricity that just being near Reese shot through him. It was certainly enjoyable to be playful, even to touch someone else. Heaven only knew how little touch he'd had in his life. But it wasn't the same. It wasn't terrifying and magical all at once.

"Nice shot, Lord Herrington," Miss Garrett called as Freddy dove after a particularly tricky serve.

The game continued at a quick pace with nail-biting volley after volley. Freddy found that he played better than he assumed he could, but he ascribed all the credit to Miss Garrett. Townsend and Natalia seemed to be having a grand time as well and flirted up a storm. They were certainly a couple, or would be soon if they weren't already. Which made Freddy wonder if people were saying the same thing about him and Miss Garrett, even though they'd only met five minutes before.

It struck him as his muscles flexed in exertion that a dollar princess might be just the solution to his woes. Miss Garrett was likely worth a fortune. Men all over England were marrying American heiresses to save their flagging estates. He wouldn't be doing anything a dozen other men weren't doing by courting her.

Except that everything within him rebelled at the idea of giving anyone a place in his heart and in his life.

That place was already firmly taken, whether he wanted it to be or not.

The stray thought distracted him again, only this time, instead of missing a shot, he failed to see that Miss Garrett was headed straight for it as well. They collided with a force that knocked both of them off their feet and into the grass. Freddy was completely disoriented for a moment as he crumpled to his side, Miss Garrett tangled underneath him.

Fortunately for them both, Miss Garrett burst into laughter. "Oh, dear, Lord Herrington. This is a muddle."

She was flat on her back beneath him, her arms circling him for support. Her skirt had flown up, revealing trim ankles and silk stockings. Her chest heaved with laughter against his, and she wore a delighted smile.

And Freddy didn't feel a thing. Not a hint of lust, not a modicum of temptation. He felt horrible over the fact that he might be hurting her, but that was it.

"I'm so sorry," he laughed, even though the laughter had a panicked edge to it. He muscled himself to a sitting position, taking her with him. "How unforgivably clumsy of me. It was all my fault."

"Accidents happen every day," she said, settling in his arms, her hands on his shoulders, smiling broadly at him as though he met her approval and then some. "I forgive you." She leaned in closer and added, "Provided we continue on to win the match."

He liked her. He couldn't and wouldn't deny it. Miss Lenore Garrett was just the sort of person that could be a good friend. She reminded him of his sister. "We shall win, Miss Garrett," he said.

"Oh, please call me Lenore," she said.

"And you must call me Freddy, as all my friends do," Freddy said.

She grinned from ear to ear. "I shall, then, Freddy," she said. "Now, let's get up and win this game."

CHAPTER 3

The sound of Lenore Garrett's laughter ringing up from the badminton court set Reese's teeth on edge. As much as he knew he had to, he couldn't pull his eyes away from the tangle of limbs and skirts that she and Freddy made as they attempted to right themselves. It was clear to him that Miss Garrett was doing her best to prolong the process. Her hands were all over Freddy, a fact that brought acidic stabs of jealousy to Reese's gut. He couldn't blame her really, knowing how much she longed to snag a British husband, but what he wouldn't give to play with Freddy that way, to handle him so casually without anyone around them batting an eyelash.

"Reese."

Diana's call only barely cut through Reese's thoughts. He turned his head slightly to her, but his eyes remained fixed on Freddy and Miss Garrett as they stood, brushed each other off, and resumed their places on the court.

"Reese, hello." Diana's call was closer.

Reese finally managed to drag his attention away from the bittersweet scene of Freddy laughing, pink-faced and happy, to turn to Diana. "Sorry," he told her. "I don't know where my mind is."

Diana fixed him with a knowing grin and came to a stop, resting a hand on one hip. "I was going to ask if you'd care to come join us for croquet, but if you're otherwise occupied...."

"No, no, I'll join you." Reese faced Diana fully, deliberately not looking back to the badminton court. "Are you coming, Henry?" he called over his shoulder to his brother, who was standing shoulder to shoulder with Mr. Garrett, watching the games with a grin, Ellie by his side.

"I'm fine watching, thanks," Henry called back to him. As Reese walked on, he could have sworn he heard his brother add, "This is all about matchmaker's games anyhow."

Reese clenched his jaw, hoping Diana would see it as a smile and not the grimace it was. Another trill of laughter from Miss Garrett only made things worse. It was ridiculous for him to let something so trivial affect him so deeply. Except that it didn't feel trivial at all. It felt as though his life were at stake.

"What color do you want?" Diana asked as they reached the croquet set, where John, Harrison and Beatrice were already selecting mallets and balls.

"I'll take whatever's left," Reese said, feigning casualness so that he could glance back over his shoulder at the game. They were in the middle of another volley. Townsend was attacking the shuttlecock and Freddy and Miss Garrett were working well together to return it.

"There are only five of us playing, so you have a choice," John said, yanking his attention back to where it should be.

"Blue then," Reese said, moving to pick up the mallet.

"Then I'll be red." Diana moved in to collect her mallet and ball.

"Not black?" John asked, an impish glint in his eyes. "I would have thought you'd choose a color to match your heart."

Diana glared at him, then let out a frustrated breath. "If we're choosing colors to match our hearts, then yours should be yellow, you coward."

John laughed outright and selected the yellow mallet. "Anything you say, my sweet."

Diana's chin went up sharply as she marched away from John to the start of the course.

"You won't win her by tweaking her nose, you know," Harrison chuckled, slapping John on the back, then selecting the green mallet for himself.

"I will in the end," John grinned. "And I'll have the most delightful time doing it."

On any other day, Reese would have rolled his eyes and laughed at his friend. He was clearly besotted by Diana, even more so since she had taken over the leadership of the May Flowers women's political group. John played the braggart whenever he could, but Reese suspected he liked a powerful woman who could run rough-shod over him.

But then, he supposed that everyone liked playing the submissive role now and then. He glanced back to Freddy—still hot in pursuit of a badminton victory—as he made his way to join Diana. He wanted nothing more than to rescue Freddy from his financial situation and to take care of him the way he deserved to be taken care of. Reese's own rank and fortune were greater than Freddy's, after all, and he had no doubt his level of experience in matters of the heart—or rather, matters of the cock—far outstripped his. But the fantasies that kept him up late at night and accompanied his most satisfying sessions of self-abuse were those that involved Freddy taking the lead and buggering him senseless.

"What a curious expression you're wearing, Reese," Diana said, teasing in her eyes, her expressive mouth pulled into a lopsided grin. Her expression cracked and she laughed a moment later. "I still can't get used to calling you and everyone else by your Christian names."

"We're all friends," Reese said with a shrug, grateful that she'd changed the subject before he had to. "What we do in our own, private circles is none of society's business."

"Too true," she agreed, then took her first shot. "I do so love living in a modern age," she added with a happy sigh.

Reese came along after her, hitting his ball through the wickets and on to within a few feet of hers. John was supposed to come next, but he and Harrison had fallen into some sort of distracting discussion instead.

Unfortunately, that gave Diana time to pick up her previous topic of conversation.

"I've seen looks like the one you've been wearing today on a man's face before," she said.

"Oh?" Reese pretended innocence. He was unable to resist peeking at the badminton game as the players changed sides.

"I would say that you're besotted," Diana went on, assuming a teasingly formal air. "But I rather think there are baser forces at work, Lord Howsden."

Reese fought not to wince as he turned back to her. "Good heavens, Lady Pickwick. What would you know about baser forces?" he asked, imitating her formality.

His ploy seemed to work. Diana laughed. "I am a woman living in a progressive era, Lord Howsden," she said, striking an elegant pose. "We know far, far more than our mothers knew about these things."

"Perish the thought." Reese shared her grin.

"Coming through," John shouted as he hit his ball toward Reese and Diana. He was lucky enough—or perhaps something more nefarious was involved—to connect with Diana's ball. "Oh, dear," he said as though he were having the time of his life. "I suppose I'll just have to send you off to the edges of the game."

"You beast," Diana growled as she stepped back and was forced to watch John line up, then send her ball sailing across to the far side of the lawn. Once the damage was done, she huffed, then marched off to stand by her now remote ball.

"I've seen cleverer ways of wooing a woman," Reese told John with a laugh and a shake of his head.

"I'll win her in the end, of course," John replied with a wink.

The game progressed. Reese was a fairly good shot and got ahead of the others in short order. Harrison and Beatrice seemed more interested in keeping their balls close to each other, which made perfect sense, considering Lady Beatrice was the sweetest woman Reese knew and Harrison was a puppy in her wake. Diana seemed determined to get back in the game, and before long, they were standing within feet of each other again.

"I swear," she said, shaking her mallet. "If he gets close enough to me...." She let her threat drop, took a breath, then turned to Reese with a tight smile, as if she were determined to think of something other than John. "Of course, we all know you have different tastes," she said.

The comment felt so out of the blue that Reese worried the color drained from his face. "I beg your pardon?" he asked.

"In matters of love," she went on, looking as though she believed she'd guessed right. "We all knew that the standard society beauty wasn't going to do it for you."

"I...I can't possibly know what you mean." Damn him, but after all these years, even though Diana was a friend, he still panicked every time he sensed so much as a threat of being exposed for who he was. Exposure was dangerous, as too many of his friends had learned.

"I mean," Diana went on, sidling closer to him, "that we all knew it would take someone like an American heiress to turn your head."

Relief spilled through Reese, making him momentarily giddy. "I can assure you, I have no romantic interest in Miss Garrett."

Diana raised her brow. "No? Then why have you been staring at her like a man whose heart is on fire since you came outside?"

Thank God for Miss Garrett!

"You are mistaken," Reese laughed. "I'm afraid my heart is the sort that can only be given away once." That much was the truth.

"How noble and romantic," Diana said, a little less teasing. "I'm sorry that I never met Lady Howsden."

Reese's wistful smile was genuine. "She was special, my Edith," he said, his heart squeezing in grief for a moment. "We understood each other on a level that, I fear, married couples seldom do. I miss her."

He wasn't lying either. He had been damned lucky to find a woman like Edith, a woman who understood what it was like to feel a passion for the same sex. They'd discovered each other's secrets by chance, or perhaps it was by fate, and become fast friends. She was the daughter of a viscount and knew her own mind. He admired her beyond telling for her willingness to do what was necessary to create Harry, and supported her efforts to find a truer kind of love and companionship, in spite of their marriage vows, as she supported him. And he'd stayed by her side through every, bitter day of the cancer that took her.

"Yes, I can see how much you loved her," Diana said in a far quieter voice when he was silent for too long. "Forgive me for suggesting you are in search of a replacement for her."

"It's nothing," he said, pulling himself together. "I understand completely how society believes a widowed marquess in possession of a fortune must be in want of a wife."

Diana smiled with him, at least until John called, "Stop wool-gathering and play your ball, Lady Pickwick." She then let out a gruff breath, frowned, and continued with the game.

Reese found himself in a slightly melancholy state of mind as he waited for his next turn, then hit his ball on, coming closer to winning the game. He truly did miss Edith. She'd known all about Freddy and encouraged him to make a move. He hadn't had the courage all those years ago. Then Freddy had gone off to South Africa and Edith had become ill. Things were different now. For years, he'd been too distracted with his losses to feel as though he'd missed an opportunity, but lately, things had changed.

He glanced across the lawn to where the badminton game had ended and the players were all shaking hands as they headed up to the tables the servants had set with tea. Edith would be goading him mercilessly to do something bold, something worthy of a heroic lover, if she were there now.

"Wake up, Reese! You're inches away from winning the game," Harrison called.

"I am at that," Reese called back, pretending to be in as jolly a mood as everyone else.

He took his next shot, play continued, and within minutes, he'd won. He held back, waiting for some of the others to finish, cheering them on. And when they had all reached the end of the course, after a round of congratulations, they headed up to the tea tables as a group.

"And what is this I hear about another election?" Mr. Garrett was in the middle of asking Henry as they joined the others. "Didn't you just have one last year?"

"We did," Diana said, jumping right into the conversation.

"Why another one so soon?" Miss Garrett asked, her eyes shining with interest. She stood close by Freddy's side and glanced up at him, eyes bright.

But it was Diana again who answered with, "There was a horrible scandal involving Mr. Parnell," she said with a scowl. "And then Gladstone's Irish Home Rule bill was defeated."

"It led to a vote of no confidence," Beatrice added, proving that she was as much a May Flower as Diana was. "Not to mention a split in the Liberal Party."

"It's widely feared that the Liberal Unionists will

join ranks with the Conservatives and that this election will be a rout," Diana sighed.

"Goodness me," Miss Garrett said, blinking rapidly. "You all seem to be quite involved in politics."

"The ladies are more informed and politically savvy than we are," Harrison said, smiling at Beatrice.

"Is that so?" Mr. Garrett asked, leaning back and slipping his hands into his pockets as he studied everyone with a smile. "And here I thought that our young ladies in Wyoming were the most politically savvy in the world."

"Women have had the vote in Wyoming since eighteen sixty-nine," Miss Garrett said proudly.

"How wonderful," Natalia said, her eyes alight.

"Although we still cannot vote in federal elections," Ellie added.

"You must work to change that," Diana insisted. "We must all work so that women everywhere can vote."

"I agree," Reese said. He stepped away from Diana to circle around the outer edge of the group, ostensibly heading to the table to fix himself a cup of tea, but really so that he could stand closer to Freddy.

"Women have so many more opportunities these days than our mothers had," Natalia went on. "As my mother is constantly telling me. Women can attend universities now and work in certain professions. My step-father and his friends fought to expand their rights a few years ago."

"What noble men," Miss Garrett said. She inched closer to the other ladies, who seemed to be swaying closer together into a knot of female empowerment, leaving the men on the outskirts of the conversation. "And are they still championing the cause of women?" she asked.

"They're trying to," Diana said. "But Irish Home Rule has taken up nearly every parliamentary debate in the last few years."

"And what is Irish Home Rule?" Ellie asked, smoothing a hand over her stomach.

Freddy stepped subtly back from the ladies as Diana launched into an explanation of the Irish Problem. Reese caught his movement out of the corner of his eye and tensed, praying Freddy would join him at the tea table.

By some blissful stroke of divine luck, that was exactly what Freddy did. He sent Reese a cautious smile as he came to a stop next to him, reaching for the teapot that Reese had just put down.

"I hope the rights of women do expand," he said, pouring.

"I'm sure they will," Reese said, adding cream and sugar to his cup. "Especially with this lot on the front lines." He wanted to hand the spoon he'd used to Freddy. He was mad for thinking it, but there was something borderline erotic about Freddy stirring his tea with the same spoon.

"Everything is modernizing, so I don't see why women shouldn't as well," Diana continued behind them. "We need to fight for progress in order to keep it."

"I couldn't agree more," Miss Garrett said.

Freddy reached for a clean spoon before Reese could

offer his, so Reese put his down, cursing himself for a fool. "It's only a shame there are no rights for our kind," he said in a low voice.

"I beg your pardon?" Freddy glanced anxiously at him.

Reese shrugged. "What with the Labouchere Amendment that passed last year."

"I don't see what acts of gross indecency have to do with me," Freddy whispered back, his face going bright pink.

Reese took a sip of his tea, turning to study Freddy as he did. He shouldn't have dropped such an unsubtle hint. Most men like them knew the shorthand well enough to communicate without saying much. Freddy was clearly out of the loop. Of course, Reese had known he was, but that didn't make him feel better. Not when it was so obvious that they were standing on the edge of a precipice, about to fall.

"Modern transportation is a wonder as well," Beatrice said, drawing Reese's attention back to the conversation. How they had moved from elections to women's rights to transportation was a mystery to him.

"It is amazing," Miss Garrett said. "Why, it took less than two weeks for us to steam our way here from New York, and only a matter of days to reach New York from Haskell by rail."

"The railroad here in Britain astounds me sometimes," Natalia agreed. "Mama always tells me how difficult it was to get from here to there when she was a girl, but now, why, we could all be up in Scotland by the end of the day."

"We should take advantage of this miraculous rail system while we're here," Mr. Garrett said. "There are so many places I've read about that I'd like to see in this beautiful country."

"Which places are those?" Henry asked with a smile.

"Tons of them," Miss Garrett answered for him. "I'd love to see Gretna Green, of course, because I've read about it in so many novels." She glanced around until she spotted Freddy, then smiled.

"It's not much to look at," John said with a laugh.

"You would say that because you don't have a romantic bone in your body," Diana snapped.

"Or the battlefield of Hastings," Mr. Garrett went on. "And a dozen other places. Stonehenge, Winchester Cathedral, or Canterbury Cathedral, or York Minster."

"Papa has a fascination with cathedrals," Miss Garrett said with a laugh.

"York Minster is beautiful," Beatrice said. "I've been told its east window is made from over a million pieces of stained glass."

"Surely not a million," Miss Garrett said, blinking in wonder.

"The only way to find out is to count them," Harrison joked.

"Why don't we go there, then?" Henry said, turning to Reese as though asking what he thought of the idea.

"The line that passes through St. Albans heads all the way up to York, doesn't it?"

"It does," Reese answered with a nod.

"Then let's make a day of it, say, tomorrow," Henry suggested.

"I'm game if the rest of you are," Reese said. He turned to Freddy to see what he thought.

"I'm not certain about the train fare," Freddy murmured.

"Don't worry about it," Reese told him quietly. "Consider it my gift to you."

"Are you certain?" The look Freddy sent him, full of gratitude and desperation, made Reese want to wrap him in his arms and never let go.

"Of course," he answered softly.

"We'll make a day of it, then," Henry declared. The conversation had gone on amongst the rest of them, and the decision had been made. "I'm certain a grand time will be had by all," he said. He punctuated his comment by turning to Reese with a sly look that seemed to hint he knew just what kind of mischief people in love could get up to on a day trip.

CHAPTER 4

*Y*ork was only a few hours away from Albany Court by train. Every one of Reese's guests who had marveled about the speed and convenience of modern transportation was perfectly right, as proved by the fact that they all arrived en masse in the picturesque, northern town shortly after breakfast. Though Reese wasn't certain the other train passengers appreciated a dozen, loud aristocrats and their guests chattering away as they took up most of one of the first-class cars.

"Frankly, I find it charming that tea is served on the train," Miss Garrett said as she fell into step with Reese as they made their way from the train station to the old city wall. Freddy was already dashing up the narrow steps that led to the walkway atop the wall with Harry, a sight that squeezed Reese's heart in his chest.

"They don't serve tea on trains in America?" Reese

asked, offering her his arm as they prepared to cross the busy street.

"They do," she admitted, "but not the way they do here. There's something so...so refined about a traveling tea service."

Reese grinned at her, steering up onto the curb on the opposite side of the street and on to the stairs the rest of their party was climbing. The old city wall had once protected the city, but now it was a path for tourists and pedestrians that provided some of the most spectacular views of the ancient city. "Perhaps it is more than simply the tea you enjoy about British society?" he suggested.

She glanced up at him and laughed, a knowing look in her eyes. "You see right through me, don't you, Lord Howsden?"

"I thought we agreed you'd call me Reese," he said with a sideways smirk, knowing full well she was flirting with him.

"Did we?" She inched closer as they started up the narrow stairs but didn't let go of his arm. If anything, she held it tighter. "Am I considered a friend?"

"Of course, you are," he said. She was teasing him, perhaps even baiting him, but he didn't mind. He'd encountered American buccaneers in search of titled husbands before, but Lenore Garrett was a thousand times less conniving than any of them.

"I'm glad to hear it," she said as they reached the top of the wall. She paused, sucking in a breath, surveying the quaint rooftops, the winding river, and the country-side beyond, and saying, "What a magnificent view."

"It is rather nice," Reese admitted, gazing straight down the length of the wall toward where Freddy had a firm grip on Harry as he stood atop the edge of the wall, arms outstretched as though he commanded all that he saw. The two got along so well together.

"Don't lollygag," John called from much farther down the wall, looking straight at Diana, but speaking to them all. "This walkway is narrow and we're not the only ones trying to get from here to there."

Diana muttered something that Reese couldn't quite make out, but he laughed all the same and escorted Miss Garrett on. "If there's not a wedding by the end of the year for those two, I'll be a monkey's uncle."

"I couldn't imagine you as a monkey's uncle," Miss Garrett laughed, sticking almost scandalously close to his side as they walked. "Although I suppose Mr. Darwin implied that's what we all are."

"I'm not sure that's an accurate interpretation of *Origin of Species*," Reese grinned. "But close enough."

Miss Garrett hummed as though impressed, her brow lifting. "Handsome, titled, wealthy, and intelligent." Embarrassed heat rushed up Reese's neck to his face. It doubled when Miss Garrett went on with, "It's a wonder you never remarried."

He peeked sideways at her, finding exactly the sort of look he imagined he might in her shrewd eyes. He cleared his throat and said, "I hope you will not find it indelicate of me, but I am not on the marriage market. Not at any price."

"Ah, I see." To her credit, she didn't loosen her hold on his arm or march away upon discovering he wasn't an option for her. "Your heart belongs to someone else then?" she asked, her cheeks pink with interest.

Up ahead, Harry let out a peal of laughter as Freddy swung him into the air. The brilliant morning sunlight caught the highlights in Freddy's dark hair and lit his face with a healthy glow. Harry was as happy as Reese had ever seen him and danced around Freddy once his feet were on the ground again, begging for another swing. Freddy obliged, then lifted Harry to ride on his back.

Only when Miss Garrett cleared her throat slightly did Reese realize he'd let the silence go on too long. She had a curious look in her eyes, as if she'd just put together pieces of a puzzle and seen the picture it made. But that couldn't possibly be true. A young woman from America couldn't possibly have the sophistication to understand those sorts of things, could she?

"I suppose you could say my heart belongs to someone else," he said in a rush, wishing he hadn't let his mind wander. It was happening more and more lately, which wasn't a good sign. "Harry's mother was a special woman," he finished.

"I'm sure she was," Miss Garrett said with a charming amount of reverence. "I believe I saw her portrait in one of the galleries at Albany Court."

"Yes, she had it painted shortly after we were married," Reese said.

"She was lovely. I can see the resemblance in Harry."

Their conversation lulled as they reached the bridge over the River Ouse. Freddy and Harry stood right in the center of the bridge. Freddy was pointing something out to Harry upriver. The sight was so beautiful that it took Reese's breath away. It gave him so much peace to see that the two people he loved most in the world enjoyed each other's company.

"Look, Papa, there's a fair over there," Harry shouted as Reese and Miss Garrett reached them. "Uncle Freddy says he sees ponies and dragons."

"Dragons?" Reese's brow shot up. He exchanged a glance with Freddy.

"Absolutely dragons," Freddy said with a solemn nod, though mirth sparkled in his expression. It was clear to Reese Freddy was teasing his son.

"Can we go see the dragons, Papa? Can we?" Harry hopped down from Freddy's back and rushed over to Reese, grabbing his free hand and tugging it.

"I wouldn't mind seeing a few dragons," Henry spoke up from the edge of the pack of the rest of their friends.

"Nor would I," Natalia added.

"Then by all means," Reese said. "Let's go see some dragons."

"Hoorah!" Harry dashed back to Freddy. "Papa says we can go to the fair."

That seemed to decide things. Rather than heading

on directly toward the minster, they descended to the river's edge and followed the path that led to the field where the fair was set up.

"Freddy seems to truly enjoy Harry's company," Miss Garrett said, starting up their conversation again once they were on their way.

"And Harry enjoys his." A tiny part of Reese wondered what she was getting at, if she really had managed to guess his secret. Perhaps Freddy said something during the badminton game the day before.

"I'm glad Freddy has such good friends at such a difficult time," Miss Garrett went on.

Reese frowned slightly. "Did he tell you about his financial situation?"

"My father did," she admitted. "Papa tells me that a great many British nobles are losing everything these days, that the great estates of legend and lore are completely out of money. Worse still, he tells me that most of the old families have no one to help them." She smiled up at him. "I'm glad that Freddy has you."

"I don't know if I am much help to him, really," Reese said, anxious over how true the simple statement felt. "All I can do is offer him a place to stay when he needs it and someone to talk to about his troubles." Although, if given half a chance, he would offer so much more.

As if she could hear a part of his thoughts, Miss Garrett said, "I'm sure there's more you can offer than tea and sympathy."

Again, the uneasy feeling that the woman was far

more perceptive than was safe for him sent prickles down his back. "He's my friend," he said. "My closest friend. I would do anything for him."

Miss Garrett's grin turned lopsided. "Would that we all had a friend like that. A handsome, titled, *wealthy*, intelligent man with the power to solve all our problems."

Reese wasn't certain why she emphasized his wealth. "I don't know if I have the means to solve all his problems," he began. "Wealthy as I am. My fortune—"

He stopped, mouth open, when the answer hit him. He was wealthy. His father might have been a perfect ass, but he'd managed Albany Court well, in the end. He himself had made even more improvements, not to mention his wise investments, and he'd accumulated a healthy sum that sat in a bank, collecting interest. Did he have enough to truly come to Freddy's rescue? Did he have enough to purchase Silverstone Castle? If he shuffled a few things around, liquefied a few assets, it was entirely possible.

"Do you know, Miss Garrett," he said as they walked on, a feeling of renewed purpose filling him. "I think I need to speak to my solicitor as soon as we arrive back in St. Albans."

Miss Garrett laughed. "Please do call me Lenore," she said. "And I'm glad if I've said something that helps the situation."

"You may have." Reese sent her the sort of smile he usually reserved for his inner circle. He found himself hoping that Lenore did find a husband in England. He rather liked the idea of keeping her around as a friend and ally.

"Reese, can I have a word with you?" Henry asked, approaching with Mr. Garrett at his side. "I've had an idea."

"By all means," Reese said, changing direction to meet them.

Lenore let go of his arm. "I'll let you men speak," she said, starting off toward Freddy and Harry. "I think I see more lively company anyhow."

"Don't say we've chased you off," Henry said, pausing to watch her go.

"Nothing chases my daughter away from where she wants to be," Mr. Garrett laughed. "She has a mind of her own, that one."

"I believe you're right," Reese said, smiling. And he might just owe a great deal to that mind. The prospect of being able to save Freddy the misery of losing his ancestral home filled him with excitement. The maudlin part of him believed it was an ideal expression of everything he felt for Freddy. And he wasn't lying when he said he would have to contact his solicitor as soon as they got home that night.

"WHERE ARE THE DRAGONS, UNCLE FREDDY? YOU said there would be dragons." Harry practically bounced as he dragged Freddy deeper into the tents and booths that made up the fair.

"We might have come upon them right at their naptime," Freddy said. Perhaps it wasn't the best idea to promise magical creatures to Reese's son when he couldn't deliver on them. He'd hoped there would be some sort of painted dragon at the fair somewhere. But whether there was or not, the boy was a ray of sunshine, and he would have chased down a real dragon for him if he could.

"I think I saw them over there."

The cheery voice of Lenore filled Freddy with relief. He paused, twisting toward her and waiting for her to catch up.

"Did you hear that, Harry? Miss Garrett knows where the dragons are," he said.

Harry lit up. "Where? Where?" He obviously adored Lenore, which Freddy found easy to believe. She was pretty, engaging, and full of energy.

"Right this way, young Lord Harry," she said, taking Harry's other hand.

"Where are we going?" Freddy whispered to her over Harry's head.

Lenore glanced back at him with mischief in her eyes. "You'll see."

They walked on. Now that he was holding two people's hands, Harry leapt every few steps, using their arms as a swing. Lenore was a good enough sport to lift the lad into the air along with him, causing Harry to laugh like a cherub.

"I do hope to have children of my own one of these

days," Lenore said as they approached a tent with a shingle over the entrance that said "Hall of Mirrors", so seemingly out of the blue that sweat broke out down Freddy's back.

"Children?" Freddy choked. He could feel his face go red.

"Don't you want children?" she asked with a pointed look.

"I...um...I hadn't thought...." He was glad she wasn't holding his hand directly, because he was certain his had gone clammy. Children were wonderful, but getting them was another story.

"I think you would make an excellent father," Lenore said. "You're so good with Harry."

"Harry is special," Freddy said, his smile returning.

"And so is his father?"

The slight uptick in her tone had Freddy sweating all over again. She couldn't possibly know. She was only twenty if she was a day, and she was American to boot. And he wasn't anything anyhow. At least, he didn't think he was. Except, perhaps his feelings did run in a backward direction. But he wasn't what Reese had implied yesterday in his comment about their kind. He wasn't what he'd seen in the army barracks of South Africa, or in the dormitories of Oxford, for that matter.

"Reese is a trusted friend," he managed to say before things turned too awkward.

Lenore hummed. Her eyes narrowed slightly and her grin sparkled with cunning. "What about Lord Whitlock?" she asked, nodding across the crowded tables and booths to where John was accepting a handful of tickets of some sort from Reese. Henry and Mr. Garrett were handing out tickets to their group as well.

"Yes, John is a friend as well," Freddy said. "And once he corners Diana and wears down her resistance, he probably will make a good father."

"Ah," Lenore said. She nodded her head as though crossing a name off a checklist. "I see. And Lord Landsbury?"

A grin spread across Freddy's face as he caught on to what she was about. "I'm certain Lady Beatrice believes he will make an excellent father," he said. "Though you never know what tomorrow will bring."

"Point taken." Lenore exchanged a grin with him. "I would ask about Dr. Townsend, but the way he and Lady Natalia have been circling around each other makes me wonder whether fatherhood is already in the offing."

Freddy's brow shot up. He had underestimated Lenore entirely if she could pick up on sexual undercurrents without blinking an eye. Perhaps things in Wyoming weren't as backwater as he assumed.

"Natalia comes from a thoroughly unconventional family," he said. "Her mother is a powerful woman with just a hint of a reputation."

"How exciting." Lenore's eyes lit up.

"And her sister married a Scotland Yard inspector under, er, unusual circumstances."

"Even better," Lenore went on.

"Their brother, the current Earl of Stanhope, is a dear friend of mine." Freddy's shoulders relaxed. It was so much easier to talk about other people than himself. "We served in the Transvaal together, but before that we knew each other at Oxford. Reese as well."

"And this Lord Stanhope. He is...." She arched a brow in question.

"Married to the love of his life," Freddy finished with a laugh. "But don't worry, we'll find a titled husband for you if it's the last thing we ever do." It felt somehow freeing to speak openly about the elephant in the room.

Lenore laughed. "I see you've found me out."

"It wasn't that difficult," Freddy confessed.

"Difficult or not, I have no intention of returning to Wyoming. At least, not without a wedding ring and a lovely, titled man on my arm," she said, every ounce of cunning back in her eyes. She went on with, "What about Reese?"

"Reese?" Freddy's voice squeaked on the name.

"Papa said I can see the dragon," Harry said, tugging on both his and Lenore's hands.

Freddy winced. He'd entirely forgotten Harry was there, and the boy was yanking on his hand. "We'll see it in a moment, my boy."

"Can we hurry?" he asked.

"Of course." Freddy glanced back to Lenore.

"What do you think of Reese?" she asked outright. "As a husband?"

The question had a startling effect on him. It sent

sparks through his veins and filled him with a strange sort of lightness. Images of Reese dressed to the nines, the way he had been for his wedding to Edith, jumped to his mind, but the look he wore wasn't for Edith at all. It was the sort of look that accompanied the way their hands brushed when no one was looking, the way Reese nudged his leg under the table when they were seated next to each other. It sped his heart and made him uncomfortable in a tantalizing way.

"Come on," Harry sighed, pulling his hands out of Freddy's and Lenore's.

"Reese is my closest friend," Freddy said, as if by rote. "I think he would make an ideal husband for anyone."

"What do you think his best qualities are?" Lenore asked, tilting her head to one side.

"His qualities?" Freddy shrugged and squirmed, feeling as though he were on the spot. "He's kind and he's compassionate. He's been through a lot and he knows how to treat all people with the respect they deserve, whether they are royalty or working-class." His shoulders relaxed and something warm and soft settled in his gut. "He is true and loyal. He's the kind of man who would be there for you, without you having to ask, if you needed support or a shoulder to cry on. And he's also jolly good fun. He can make me laugh like no one else. And I can tell him anything, anything at all, and he'll listen, without judgment or complaint. He makes me feel—"

He stopped abruptly, too aware that he was blushing.

He'd said far, far too much, and he'd said it like a lovesick fool.

Strangely, Lenore looked as though she approved of every word and then some. "Has Reese ever told you about a man from my hometown of Haskell? A man named Theophilus Gunn?"

Freddy frowned. The odd question shook him out of the rapture he'd worked himself into. "I don't believe so."

"Well," Lenore said, stepping closer to him. "Theophilus Gunn is American, but he used to serve as valet to a Lord Stephen Leonard before and during the Crimean War. They were more than just master and servant, though. They were—"

She was cut off as a high-pitched scream and the sound of crashing and shattering sounded from the Hall of Mirrors tent a few yards away. Freddy blinked, suddenly realizing that Harry was missing.

"Harry?" he called, looking around.

Reese had notice something was wrong and started toward them. "Harry!" he called as well.

"Oh, dear," Lenore said as all three of them dashed toward the tent.

CHAPTER 5

From the moment he caught sight of Harry stomping impatiently away from Freddy and Lenore and making his way toward the Hall of Mirrors, Reese's paternal senses went into high alert. He broke away from Henry and Mr. Garrett in the middle of a sentence to stride after him. And as soon as he heard the shattering crash from inside the tent, he shifted into a run.

"Harry!" he shouted, passing Freddy and Lenore and ducking into the tent, his heart in his throat.

The interior of the tent was lit by a combination of lamps and mesh holes in the canvas roof that let in the sunlight. All the same, the space was cramped and hot. It was a confusing mass of carefully-placed mirrors, many of them warped to make the viewer appear taller or fatter than they were. Or at least they would have been placed that way. Three of the tall mirrors closest to the door had fallen over and shattered into silver shards in the grass.

Harry sat to one side of the pile of glass shards, his knees drawn up to his chest, bawling his eyes out.

"Harry." Reese rushed to him, swooping to lift his son into his arms and to hug him tight. His heart pounded so hard against his ribs that the edges of his vision went black for a moment. "What happened, son?" he asked, trying to keep his voice even. He fumbled with Harry's hands and legs to determine if the shards of mirror had cut him at all.

"The dragon scared me," Harry wailed, wriggling to squeeze his arms and legs around Reese. His tears instantly dried up now that he felt he was safe, and a wide-eyed look of wonder replaced his terror. "I saw it, Papa. I really saw it."

Freddy and Lenore dashed into the tent, but stopped at the destruction that met them.

"Is he hurt?" Freddy asked, rushing to Reese's side. "Harry, are you hurt?"

Harry shook his head. "I saw the dragon, Uncle Freddy, I did!"

Freddy stared at Harry, then glanced to Reese, face pale, mouth open in confusion. "I'm so sorry, Reese," he blurted. "I shouldn't have let him out of my sight."

"There's no harm done," Reese said. The relief spilling through him was so intense that he would have forgiven anyone anything, much less Freddy letting a lively and curious boy out of his sight. He glanced back to Harry. "Did you cut yourself at all, tiger?"

Harry shook his head. "I pushed the dragon."

Slowly, Reese became aware of the rest of the details of the scene. A paunchy man with a straw hat and his tall, thin assistant had dodged their way around the other mirrors and now stood at the edges of the shattered glass, staring at the devastation with red faces. The paunchy man looked ready to explode.

"What've you done?" he boomed, turning to Reese. "My mirrors."

"I'm terribly sorry," Reese said, as defensive as he was regretful. It wasn't going to be a pleasant confrontation. "My son was frightened and, I believe, pushed one of the mirrors over."

"Pushed it over?" the paunchy man bellowed, proving Reese's fears. He turned to the tall man. "Reg, clean this up. And as for you," he whipped back to Reese and Harry. "Who the hell do you think you are, letting your brat march in here and destroy property?"

"It was a dragon," Harry whimpered before burying his face against Reese's shoulder.

"I beg your pardon. He's just a child," Freddy said at the same time.

"I don't care if he's the king of the moon," the paunchy man growled on. "Them mirrors cost loads, they do."

Reese grasped Harry as best he could while

attempting to reach past him to his inside jacket pocket. "Let me pay for—"

"A child could have been hurt, thanks to your negligence," Lenore cut in, taking a step forward and staring down the paunchy man as though she were about to instigate a shoot-out in the style of her frontier home. "How could you be so careless as to set up your mirrors in such a way that a boy of five could topple one and cause two others to fall and shatter as well? What if he had been hurt?"

"I—" the paunchy man backed up, stepping on a corner of glass with a crunch. He blinked, then came back at Lenore with, "Now see here, missy—"

"I will not see here." Lenore raised her voice. "Thanks to your negligence, a child could have been hurt or maimed or worse. He could have been cut in a thousand places. He could be lying here in the grass bleeding to death, and you would be to blame. How do you think the York police would feel about that?" She took a step closer to him as the man's mouth flapped in shock. "And do you have a proper permit for this display? For this entire fair? How do you think the town would react if they knew your shoddy workmanship nearly caused the death of a well-born boy? Do you think they would ask you back again? Do you think they would allow you to set up your show anywhere in the county?"

"But I—"

Lenore rested her weight on one leg, crossing her arms. "No. I thought not." She took a step back, glancing to Reese and Freddy. "I think we're done here, gentlemen," she said before turning and marching out of the tent.

Freddy stared after her with wide eyes, then glanced to Reese. Reese had a hard time not laughing. He cleared his throat and handed Harry over to Freddy. Harry seemed perfectly at ease wrapping himself around Freddy and hiding against his neck. Reese reached into his pocket, took out his wallet, and handed the paunchy man a sum that should have more than paid for the mirrors.

"Again," he said, his mouth twitching as he tried to look solemn in the wake of the tidal wave that was Lenore Garrett. "We're very sorry."

The paunchy man muttered something that didn't quite form into words as he swiped the money away from Reese. In the end, he touched the brim of his hat and said, "Many thanks, guv'nor."

Reese turned to Freddy, lifting his brows slightly, and gestured for him to leave the tent.

As soon as they were out in the sunshine again, walking swiftly away from the whole thing, Harry lifted his head from Freddy's shoulder and said, "Uncle Freddy, I think Miss Garrett is the dragon."

It was too much. Reese burst into laughter that shook him from the top of his head down to his toes.

Freddy laughed as well. "I think you're right, my boy."

Harry cocked his head to the side and asked, "Do you think we could ask her to breathe fire?"

Reese's laughter doubled. He reached for Freddy's arm, gripping it for support, before he managed to say, "I think she just did."

They continued laughing. Freddy swayed closer to Reese until their arms bumped. Rather than jerking away, he stayed close to Reese's side as they reached the far end of the fair. Only then did Harry work up the courage to wriggle out of Freddy's arms. That, out of necessity, separated them.

"What has the two of you laughing so hard?" Harrison asked as he and Lady Beatrice spotted them. They were playing a ring toss game, but stopped and came to join them, smiling in expectation.

"Harry got into a bit of trouble in the Hall of Mirrors," Reese explained. "And Miss Garrett got him out of it."

"Miss Garrett?" Lady Beatrice asked. Her grin turned knowing as she glanced between Reese and Freddy, as if attempting to figure out which one of them had their sights set on Lenore. "Where is she now?"

They all turned to search through the fair. Their group was spread out amongst the various games and booths, spending the tickets Mr. Garrett had purchased for everyone after consulting with Reese and Henry. Lenore had joined her father, and the two of them were laughing over Mr. Garrett's attempts to test his strength by hitting a platform with a mallet to ring a bell.

"Looks like she's occupied," Freddy said. "Should we go back and join her?"

"I don't want to go back," Harry said, grabbing Reese's hand and squeezing close to him.

"We don't have to, tiger," Reese told him. He glanced to Freddy. "We could always go on ahead to the minster." In fact, the thought of having a bit of time alone with Freddy—and Harry, of course—thrilled him in a thousand ways.

"I'd like to move on to the minster myself," Lady Beatrice confessed, glancing to Harrison. "Would you mind?"

"Not at all." Harrison smiled at her, then glanced to Reese. His expression turned thoughtful for a moment as he studied Reese. Harrison knew everything, of course. All of Reese's close male friends did, even if they never spoke of it. A blink of an eye later, Harrison turned back to Lady Beatrice and said, "Let's just go tell the others where we're heading." He nodded to Reese and Freddy. "You two go on ahead. We'll all catch up."

Reese was tempted to open his wallet and pay Harrison for his kind service the way he'd paid off the paunchy man. "We'll let the minster know you're all coming," he said, adding a wink.

Harrison and Lady Beatrice headed back into the fair as Reese and Freddy turned to walk up toward the street that would take them the rest of the way to York Minster.

"I wonder what that man will tell his wife about the whole thing tonight over supper," Freddy chuckled as they reached the busy thoroughfare of the street, swinging Harry between them.

Reese didn't need to ask what he was talking about, he just knew, as if their thoughts were in tune. "If he even has a wife," he said.

"Oh, men like that always have wives," Freddy laughed, rolling his eyes. "Though whether she's happy with her circumstances is another story."

Reese made a wry sound of agreement. "And yet, everyone seems so hell-bent on rushing into marriages that will only make them miserable."

"Not everyone is rushing," Freddy said with a shrug. "And we've got friends who have rushed into marriages that have made them blissfully happy."

"True," Reese agreed as they reached the top of the street and crossed over a small green to the entrance of York Minster. "There are more ways for people to be happy together than marriage, though."

Freddy glanced sideways at him, giving Reese the impression that he'd stepped over a line or said more than he intended to. The furtive look shot straight through Reese's heart like an arrow. The day was so beautiful, so sunny, inside and out, that he hated to think he'd caused Freddy any upset.

Then again, perhaps upset was just what Freddy needed to jolt him out of the limbo Reese could see he was living in. It was time for change, time for them to get on with things.

"People can be happy in a marriage without loving

each other the way poets and artists say they should," he went on, casually glancing up at the massive stained-glass windows. "Like Edith and I were happy."

"Were you?" Freddy asked, lowering his voice.

Reese dragged his eyes down from the windows to study him. There was a tender sort of desperation in Freddy's eyes, like he was an animal trapped in a cage, just waiting to break free and join his pack in the wild. That anxious look of yearning did things to Reese's insides that certainly weren't appropriate for a church. Or perhaps they were. Perhaps a church of the magnitude of York Minster was exactly the right scale of setting for the depth and sacredness of everything he felt for Freddy and always had.

"We were," he admitted at last, shrugging. "Edith and I were friends. We had an understanding. That's more than a lot of married couples can say."

"Papa." Harry tugged at Reese's hand. He danced impatiently, as though standing in the nave of a grand cathedral, staring up at stained-glass windows was the most boring thing ever.

Reese let go of his hand. "Lead the way, tiger. We'll follow. But be careful, and be quiet," he dropped his voice into a whisper.

"Yes, Papa," Harry whispered, then darted off toward the front of the nave.

"You're going to regret letting him off the leash," Freddy said with a lopsided grin that plucked at Reese's heartstrings.

"Probably," Reese chuckled. "Though I think his run-in with the mirrors has subdued him a little."

He was partially right. Harry dashed up the aisle to the front of the nave, but slowed his pace as he glanced around at the sheer magnitude of everything around him. Reese also suspected that he needed a nap—which would either make him calmer or three times as obstreperous.

They were silent for a moment as they took in the grandeur of the building. York Minster had withstood the test of time not only from the thirteenth century, but dating back hundreds of years before that, when various incarnations of the building were constructed and destroyed or damaged, only to be rebuilt. In fact, as Reese had once learned, the site had been home to a Roman garrison a millennium and a half before. Bits and pieces of the ancient fort's foundations could still be seen here and there across the footprint of the cathedral. It was encouraging to think that something so significant continued to exist, if in a different form, through trials and change.

"Papa, there are stairs," Harry exclaimed in wonder off to one side, then immediately dashed down into the crypt.

Reese picked up his pace and followed, Freddy falling into step beside him.

"Are you certain he won't get into trouble?" Freddy asked with a wry laugh.

"Trouble is a relative term," Reese chuckled,

descending into the cool darkness. "Harry has a love-hate relationship with the dark."

Sure enough, Harry was waiting at the bottom of the steps, glancing around at the low ceiling and thick columns of the crypt. There were lamps set up at intervals, casting enough light for tourists and pilgrims to see their way through to whichever famous resident of the past they wished to pay their respects to. Those lamps sent eerie shadows flickering across the walls and tombs as well. Crypts and shadowy places had always given Reese a morbid thrill, a thrill which Harry seemed to have inherited, so he moved on, stepping carefully into the underground world.

"It's spooky, Papa," Harry whispered, a note of delight in his voice.

"Fun, isn't it?" Reese laughed, reaching for Harry's hand.

Harry nodded and took Reese's hand, but only for a moment. They hadn't gone more than five yards into the crypt before he let go and charged ahead into the shadows, asking, "Does it go all the way back?"

"I'm certain it does," Reese called after him. "But, tiger, do be careful."

"I will," Harry said as he stopped to look at the carving on a tomb off to one side. He ran on again in seconds.

"Papa and Uncle Freddy will be right behind you if you get too scared," Reese called.

"I will not get scared," Harry huffed and dashed on.

Freddy chuckled, matching Reese's sedate pace as they wound their way through tombs and memorials of men long dead and gone. "He's very much like you, you know."

"Unfortunately," Reese laughed.

Freddy paused, following Reese off to one side, where a particularly old tomb caught his eye. "Did you and Edith ever think about having another one?" he asked in an uncomfortable voice.

Reese glanced to him, wondering if the slight pinch to Freddy's brow was jealousy or some puzzling form of regret. "We did talk about it," he said. "We both loved children. I continue to love children, and if things were different, I'm certain I'd have a family to rival our queen's." He paused for a moment, contemplating the strangeness of a world where those who wanted children couldn't have them and those who abhorred them had too many. It didn't bear thinking about for long, though. "I believe we would have had more, if Edith hadn't gotten sick."

"Do...do you still want more children?" Freddy asked, softer and more anxious than ever.

They'd reached the far side of the crypt, where only faint fingers of light illuminated the corners. Reese paused beside a stout pillar, worn with age. He knew the real question Freddy was asking, whether he would marry again for the sake of offspring. He faced Freddy, heart thumping, blood pumping, captivated by the impossible idea of the two of them having a child together somehow.

"If the opportunity arose," he said in a hushed voice, fighting his body's urge to sway closer to him.

"So, you are looking to remarry, then?" Freddy asked, lowering his eyes. His shoulders sank in disappointment.

"No," Reese confessed, raising a hand to rest on Freddy's shoulder. "I won't find a woman as understanding as Edith ever again. And besides...." He lifted his hand to cradle Freddy's cheek. "I want other things. I want you."

The admission slipped out before he could think to stop it. With it, his inhibitions dropped. He leaned in, sliding an arm around Freddy's waist and drawing him close. With a quick intake of breath, he slanted his mouth over Freddy's, capturing him with a sudden kiss.

The contrast of hard and soft as Freddy attempted to gasp in shock, parting his lips under Reese's, was intoxicating. The scent of Freddy's skin and the heat rippling from him made Reese giddy and reckless. He deepened their kiss, brushing his tongue across Freddy's lower lip for a moment before daring to slide it alongside his. Freddy's answering sound of surprise turned into a long, deep moan. His arms snaked around Reese's torso, fingertips digging into his back.

It was more than Reese ever could have asked for, and he lost his mind to the powerful sensation of victory. He threaded his fingers through Freddy's hair, taking a short breath before diving in for a second delicious kiss. Freddy didn't fight him. On the contrary, he clung to

Reese, kissing him back with desperate, unpracticed hunger. Reese lowered his hand from Freddy's back to his backside, pressing his throbbing erection against Freddy's hips. He nearly died of bliss when he found Freddy just as hard as he was.

The urge to move against him in a mad quest for release was too much for Reese to resist. With their mouths locked together in passion, he jerked against Freddy, not thinking, not wanting to think. He only knew that if he didn't grab the fleeting moment they had, he would regret it forever. All he wanted was to feel pleasure, and for Freddy to feel it too. All he wanted was—

"Papa?"

Harry's plaintive call from several yards away, nearer the center of the crypt, slammed reality back into Reese. He stepped back, panting, eyes wide. In the dim light, he caught Freddy's startled, flushed expression. Freddy's eyes were hazy with passion, and he, too, was having a hard time catching his breath.

"This isn't the best place for this," Reese whispered, not sure if he wanted to burst into laughter or drop to his knees to beg Freddy for forgiveness. Then again, dropping to his knees in front of Freddy when they were both in a state would create more problems than it would solve.

He took a long step back, tugged at the bottom of his jacket to be sure it covered enough to give him the time he needed to settle, and cleared his throat.

"Papa? Where are you?" Harry called again, clearly more upset.

"We're just over here, tiger," he called, stepping away from Freddy with a final, significant look. Harry stood under one of the lamps, his lower lip quivering. "I'm so sorry, son," he said, rushing to Harry and dropping to an uncomfortable crouch to hug him. It would be a few more minutes before he could risk picking him up and squeezing him without embarrassment. "Uncle Freddy and I just wanted to see one of the tombs over to the side."

Harry's smile returned, and when Reese stood, he gladly took his hand. "Did you see it?" he asked Freddy as he emerged from the shadows.

"Yes, I did," Freddy said, his voice hoarse and strange. He met Reese's eyes. All the passion and acceptance that had been there moments before was gone, replaced by stiff confusion. "We should go back upstairs to see if the others have arrived."

Reese couldn't help but wince. "Yes, that sounds like a wise plan."

He steered Harry toward the stairs they'd come down, squeezing his hand. Freddy walked ahead of them, outpacing them in no time and disappearing up the stairs before Reese reached the bottom. It stung, he couldn't deny it. But at the same time, it didn't feel like a complete rejection. Something was most definitely alive between them, and more than ever, Reese was determined to pursue it.

CHAPTER 6

reddy felt as though his skin had suddenly grown too tight to contain his body, as if he would go mad trapped inside of himself. How Reese could emerge from the crypt to greet their friends with a casual smile, as though the world hadn't just tilted off its axis, was baffling. He laughed and chatted with Henry and pointed out the magnificence of the minster's east window to Mr. Garrett and Lenore. Their entire group tried to count the pieces of glass, dissolving into hilarity in the process, but Freddy held back. He watched as Reese joined in the conversation with John and Harrison once they'd finished with the minster and headed back into town to have tea at a small shop that somehow managed to accommodate them all. And all the while, he smiled as though the skies had opened and the Holy Spirit had showered him with blessings.

Freddy could barely put one foot in front of the

other. He couldn't gather his thoughts into complete sentences as he trailed behind the rest of their group. He thanked God that he could use an increasingly sleepy Harry as his excuse not to participate with the others and ended up carrying the boy to the train station and letting him sleep on his lap as they made their way back to Albany Court. He pretended to sleep himself, but his mind was anything but quiet.

Reese had kissed him. And it hadn't been just any kiss either. It had been hot and consuming. His whole body had reacted to Reese's closeness and his assertiveness. Reese's tongue had been in his mouth, for heaven's sake. More than that, Reese had held him in such a way that Freddy could feel the hardness of his cock as it rubbed against his through their trousers. And, God help him, he'd loved every second of it. Not just loved it, he'd adored it. The intimacy, the carnality, the pure, physical sensation of it. But above all that, he'd loved the emotion of it. He loved the way, for just a fleeting moment, his soul had felt completely at peace with who he was and what he desired. He knew. Denial would be impossible forevermore. It was Reese. It'd always been Reese. The way he wanted him was exquisite torture. Now more than ever.

"Freddy," Lenore whispered close to him, yanking him out of his increasingly disturbing thoughts. "Freddy, we're here. Wake up."

Freddy sucked in a sharp breath and blinked his eyes open. He hadn't exactly fallen asleep, but his riot of thought had pulled him into a trance-like state of otherness.

"We're here?" he asked, adjusting Harry in his arms and straightening.

"Just now," Reese said, using the tender voice that made Freddy's heart feel a thousand times too big for his feeble chest.

Freddy blinked again, looking around. The train compartment's door stood open and only Reese and Lenore were left inside. Reese sent him a sympathetic look and scooped Harry into his arms before stepping down to the platform.

"Do you want me to carry you to the carriage as well?" Lenore asked, a sparkle in her eyes.

That was enough to jolt Freddy into full wakefulness. He laughed and stood, gesturing for her to step down first. "Something tells me you probably could if you wanted to," he said, following her.

"Of course I could," Lenore laughed over her shoulder. "We grow women strong in Wyoming."

Freddy felt better walking by her side out of the station, to the carriages Reese had arranged to pick them all up and take them back to Albany Court. He had the uncanny feeling that Lenore was, indeed, stronger than most of the women he knew. Specifically, that she wouldn't shriek in disgust if she knew what had happened between him and Reese in the crypt. He deliberately sat beside her in the carriage, and he was uncomfortably relieved when Reese chose to ride to the house in another carriage.

The brief reprieve was only that, though. Brief.

"I can take Harry up to the nursery," Henry said as their group wandered blearily into Albany Court's front hall. "You need to go take care of that matter you mentioned to me at the fair."

It was late, but in spite of Freddy's exhaustion and confusion, he raised his eyebrows at the comment. "What matter?" He glanced curiously at Reese.

"It's...." Reese paused, biting his lip. The simple gesture sent a tidal wave of unexpected lust through Freddy. He could still remember what Reese's lips tasted like. Even more, judging by the warmth that overtook Reese's expression, Freddy had a feeling his emotions were written all over his face. "Maybe we should talk about this in the library," Reese finished.

"I can't believe you're not going straight to bed," Natalia said with a wide yawn as she headed for the stairs, along with nearly everyone else. "I'm knackered."

"Do you need me to carry you up to the nursery, Lady Natalia?" Townsend asked, mounting the steps behind Natalia with a mischievous grin.

Freddy would have laughed at the fact that Townsend made the same joke to Natalia that Lenore made to him, but his nerves were already bristling too much at the thought of speaking to Reese alone.

Natalia did laugh, though. "Dr. Townsend, you are bad."

"Only when I'm exhausted after a long day of frolicking," he said.

The two of them laughed as though sharing a private joke and continued up the stairs. Indeed, all of their friends seemed to be floating on a cloud of contentment and sharing personal tidbits from what was, by all appearances, a wildly successful outing. Not one of them glanced back down the stairs with censure or took any notice of Reese gesturing for Freddy to follow him down the hall at all.

That didn't stop Freddy's nerves from prickling with expectation or his blood from pumping harder as he strode after Reese, down a darkened, empty hall and around a corner into the library. It was alarming enough to be alone with Reese when the magic of what had happened between them in the crypt still crackled in the air, but when Reese shut the library door behind them, Freddy's knees went weak.

"What did you want to talk to me about?" he asked, his voice barely more than a whisper.

Reese remained perfectly still for a moment, his hand still on the door handle. The fire in his eyes as he studied Freddy was enough to send the banked embers in the fireplace roaring back to a full blaze. They were close enough that Freddy caught the scent of Reese's fading cologne mingled with the scent of his skin. He should have moved away, should have done what he could to avoid temptation, but his feet were rooted to the floor, and he could barely breathe. He could hear his heartbeat thumping in his ears.

It was Reese who moved away first, drawing in a breath as he passed Freddy and walked on to the table that held decanters. "I had a thought this afternoon about...." His words failed as he stared at the decanters. He reached for one, grasped its neck, then let go, as if having second thoughts. From there, he shook his head and stepped away from the table, pacing toward one of the bookshelves and fiddling with the buttons of his jacket.

"About what?" Freddy asked, finally able to coax himself into motion. He crossed the room like a moth drawn to the flame of Reese, meeting him at the bookshelf. Before he could steady himself, he was standing far too close to Reese.

Reese raised his eyes slowly to meet Freddy's, a flush painting his cheeks. "About how much I love you," he said in a rush.

Freddy was certain it wasn't what he'd started out saying, but that was all the thought he had time for as Reese reached for him. In a flash, they were back in the crypt, back in the safe, dark space where no one would see them. Reese slanted his mouth over Freddy's and, God help him, Freddy gave in to the kiss instantly. He groaned deep in his throat as their lips met and parted and as Reese thrust his tongue against Freddy's.

Desire and long-denied need rushed through Freddy as he kissed Reese in return, pressing his fingertips into the firm muscles of Reese's back. His body reacted to Reese's with carnal splendor. Heat infused him, and his prick strained against the confines of his trousers. As sternly as his mind tried to tell him what they were doing was wrong, his soul shouted victoriously that it was so very right.

For a moment, Reese broke their kiss, panting as he rested his forehead against Freddy's. He squirmed, struggling to shrug out of his jacket, then unbutton his waistcoat. The heady thought that Reese might take off all of his clothes and show off his firm, fit body brought Freddy near to the point of shaking. He had only just entertained the idea when Reese's arms were around him again and their lips brushed once more.

Freddy felt himself at a complete disadvantage. He didn't know what he was doing. He'd never kissed anyone before, not like that. As delicious as it was, he quickly felt himself sinking into unfamiliar territory. Reese fumbled with the buttons of his jacket, pushing it off Freddy's shoulders and letting it drop to the floor, all the while managing to keep their mouths more or less joined.

"I've wanted you for so long," Reese panted, undoing the buttons of Freddy's waistcoat, then tugging his shirt out of his waistband. "So long."

Freddy's cock jumped as Reese smoothed his hands over the bare skin of his torso. It felt so good to be touched that way that he let out a deep moan of satisfaction. That evidently wasn't enough for Reese, though. Still managing to kiss his lips, his cheek, and the top of his neck, he pulled his own shirt from his trousers and guided Freddy's hands to spread across his skin.

It was new and wonderful. Freddy had always known Reese was fit, but feeling that for himself drove Freddy to the edge of madness. He wanted to explore every part of Reese, to learn his body as well as he knew his own. And Reese seemed to sense that as well. He fumbled with the fastenings of his trousers, and when they were loose, he nudged Freddy's hands down.

Freddy gasped as Reese's cock jumped free, right into his hands. Reese was thick and long and hot. Most of all, he was hard. Desperately hard. Freddy inched his hand down to his base, cupping his balls. They were pulled up tight, and Freddy's own balls responded in kind. He handled them lightly, then drew his hand up, intending to pull away.

"Yes," Reese stopped him, closing his hand over Freddy's and guiding him up and down his shaft. "God, yes."

Reese rested his forehead against Freddy's again, breathing heavily as he prompted Freddy to stroke him. Need like nothing Freddy had ever known overtook him, and even after Reese moved his hand away, bracing his hands on the bookshelf over Freddy's shoulders as Freddy's back pressed into the books, he kept stroking. More than that, he closed his hand around Reese's cock, brushing his thumb over its tip and gathering the moisture forming there before working him with increasing intensity.

Reese groaned in response, his body rippling with

tension as it partially surrounded Freddy's. His breath came in increasingly ragged gasps punctuated with sounds of pleasure. It was so erotic that pleasure pounded through Freddy, building steadily in his groin, even though he was the one touching Reese and not the other way around.

The sounds Reese made grew more desperate, and he started to jerk into Freddy's hand, giving in to pleasure. It was fascinating and powerful, and Freddy closed his eyes, so he could focus on the sounds and the feel. He worked faster, and Reese's cries became deeper and stronger, until they focused in one, deep groan as a warm jet of cum spilled across Freddy's wrist.

Freddy gasped, his eyes flying wide, his mouth dropping into an "O". He'd made Reese come. Not only that, he'd reveled in every moment of the process. His own prick was so hard he feared the slightest friction would cause him to spill as well. Reese sagged against him, suddenly limp as he worked to catch his breath. It was a sharp contrast to the raging tension and unfulfilled lust that still pulsed through him.

At last, Reese pushed back from the bookshelf, meeting Freddy's eyes with wickedness. "And now you," he said, breathless. He dropped to his knees, reaching for the fastenings of Freddy's trousers.

Fear hit Freddy like a bolt of lightning. In the back of his mind, sick memories of a boy in their Eton dormitory being forced to do what Reese was proposing to one of the head boys hit him.

"No," he gasped, batting Reese's hands away and stumbling to the side and out of his reach. He cleared his throat and straightened his unbuttoned waistcoat. "I mean, no, thank you," he fumbled. The stricken look on Reese's flushed face was far too much for Freddy to bear. "I...I have to go to bed," he blurted out, then turned and ran.

It was a coward's move. The harsh ache in his groin as he threw open the library door and dashed into the hall and the awkwardness of running with a throbbing erection wasn't nearly punishment enough for the hurt he knew he was causing. He couldn't face it, though. He couldn't face that last stumbling leap off a cliff that he could never rest on again.

He tore into his guest room, then shut and locked the door behind him. In his heart, he knew Reese wouldn't barge into his room and demand humiliating favors, as he'd seen happen not only at school, but in the army too. But he needed that safety.

With the door locked, he wriggled out of his waistcoat and then his shirt. The sleeve of his shirt was still damp and the musky scent of Reese lingered. He tossed the shirt aside, but that wasn't enough. He undid his trousers, then stepped over to his bed to yank off his shoes. His trousers, socks, and drawers were next until he was completely naked. Even that didn't alleviate the feeling that he was trapped inside of himself, ready to explode from the inside out. And it did nothing to dampen the scent of Reese's musk that he knew he would never be able to forget now.

He flopped back on his bed, groaning with a heady mixture of desire that hadn't ebbed one bit, guilt for abandoning Reese, and longing to be with him again. His cock was still as hard as steel and stood straight up against his abdomen. The only hint of relief he felt from the maelstrom inside of him came when he closed his hand around himself the way he had Reese and let himself feel the pleasure.

He was already primed and ready, but stroking himself while imagining Reese's mouth closed around him—as Reese had clearly been about to do—was wonderful. He got himself off on a regular basis as it was, but always with vague images that he was too afraid to examine closely. Now he worked himself with Reese clearly in mind—the scent of him, the heat of his body, the rakish grin that he used when others weren't looking, and the endearing tenderness of his voice. He jerked his hips, adding to the pleasure and praying for it to go on as long as possible.

He couldn't hold out forever, though. With a guttural cry, he came, milky whiteness spilling across his stomach. It felt so good, and yet, he knew it could be better. Still, he continued to handle himself until the urgency faded, leaving him feeling limp and spent, but also as though he'd wasted his pleasure on himself. How much better would it have been if Reese had felt his orgasm, had watched his body burst and then settle?

That thought lingered as he lay still for a few minutes, before another, more potent one flooded in to take its place. Reese loved him, wanted him. He'd said as much. And though deep inside, Freddy had suspected the truth for almost as long as they'd known each other, hearing Reese's confession overwhelmed him with emotion. He was loved, not as a son or a brother or a friend, but beloved.

A strange sort of trembling followed as the truth of the new world he'd been hurled into seeped through him. It was too powerful to grasp all at once, so he got up to clean himself off, then crawled into bed properly, still naked. He closed his eyes, but far more troubling thoughts assailed him. He'd fallen off the cliff without being able to stop himself. There was no way he could deny who and what he was now. And there was no way he could continue to deny that he was desperately in love with Reese.

CHAPTER 7

*R*eese was up with the dawn chorus the next morning. Not that he'd slept more than a few, fitful hours during the night. His mind kept turning over the events in the library—the way Freddy had seemed so keen to kiss and touch him, the way his eyes had been hazed with passion as he stroked Reese's cock with fascination and insistence, the way Freddy had been as hard as iron...and the way he'd pulled away and fled when Reese sought to give as much pleasure as he'd taken.

He refused to feel guilty. Not during his restless night, not when he woke up before dawn, and not when he rode into St. Albans to be first in line at the post office when it opened so that he could send an emergency telegram to his solicitor to put a certain, new plan into action. What he and Freddy had shared was beautiful and raw. Even though fear had gotten the best of

Freddy, their time was now, Reese could feel it. He sent off his telegram, instructing his solicitor to do whatever it took, to sell investments, tap into capital, and even to borrow if he had to in order to purchase Silverstone Castle. It was the least he could do for the man he loved.

None of that calmed the restlessness that itched down his back and made his steps faster once he returned to Albany Court. He had to talk to Freddy, had to get to the bottom of what was holding back the man he adored enough to wreck himself. There was a problem, but the promise between them was too great to let it stand in their way. He would find the problem, bring it out into the open, then conquer it. And once that was done, he would show Freddy a whole new world of love and delight.

"You look entirely too excitable for your own good," Henry commented as his and Reese's paths crossed in the front hall.

Reese grinned, his heart feeling as though it were electrified, and changed directions to meet his brother and walk by his side. He slapped Henry on the back as they walked. "I think things are finally starting to look up for me," he said.

Henry laughed. "Finally? Just starting now?" He shook his head and chuckled. "You're a successful marquess with a well-managed estate, heaps of friends who enjoy your company, and the most adorable son in England, and you say things are just starting to look up?"

"I think you know what I mean," Reese said, sending Henry a slightly sheepish grin.

Henry paused a few yards shy of the noisy breakfast room, his brow inching up. "Oh, so there was progress, then?"

"Definitely." Reese nodded, feeling his cheeks heat, unable to keep the joy out of his expression. A moment later, that joy and its accompanying smile faltered. "You don't approve," he said.

Henry grinned and clamped a hand on Reese's upper arm. "Of course, I approve," he said, keeping his voice low. "I want you to be happy and to have love in your life. Just because I don't understand or share your particular passions doesn't mean I don't think you should be fulfilled."

Reese let out a breath, his already agitated emotions welling within him and squeezing his throat. "Thank you, Henry. It means a lot to me. Not many men would see things as you do."

Henry shrugged and walked on, Reese with him. "The world is filled with things I'm not a part of and don't fully comprehend. I'm not like Father, you know. I don't believe everyone in the world should be exactly the same as me and only do things that I would do myself."

"I'm lucky to have you as a brother." He let out a breath, slowing down as they reached the breakfast room door. His heart thumped in anticipation of seeing Freddy and everything that they might not be able to hide bursting out in full view of their perceptive friends.

"Things aren't completely decided yet," he warned Henry. "There are still a few edges that need to be smoothed."

"I've full confidence that you'll smooth them in no time," Henry said, patting his back as they turned the corner into the room.

The breakfast room was a scene of lively activity, which was a bit mind-boggling so early in the morning. The sideboard was loaded with dishes containing every sort of breakfast food known to man, much of which already looked as though it had been picked over and enjoyed. Almost all of Reese's guests were already seated around the breakfast table—which his staff had extended for the house party—eating and talking and, if he wasn't mistaken, playing some sort of wild card game organized by Lenore at the far end. Two pots of coffee and two of tea were on the table, along with a veritable army of dishes containing various stages of breakfast.

"Oh, Reese, there you are," Lenore said from the end of the table, where she had taken up the marchioness's place. Reese doubted she knew the seating protocol of an English country estate, but something about seeing her commanding the place of honor was both amusing and intimidating. "I'm teaching Lady Natalia and Lady Diana to play Cowgirl's Shootout. You must join us."

"Cowgirl's Shootout?" Henry asked with a laugh from the sideboard, where he was piling a plate with food. "I've never heard of it."

"That's because my darling daughter made it up,"

Mr. Garrett said from the middle of the table. "She was always making up card games as a girl, and it seems she hasn't stopped."

"If I make up card games, it's because I come by it naturally," Lenore said with a fond smile for her father. "Papa was a card sharp before he met Mama. In fact, he won Mama in a card game."

A ripple of exclamations and laughter rang from the table. Reese found himself laughing along with the rest of his guests. Laughing as his gaze darted around the table, looking for Freddy. He'd seen within a second of entering the room that Freddy wasn't there, but his heart urged him to search, as though he were hiding behind the curtains or under Lenore's deck of cards.

"Let Reese eat before he joins us," Diana said, picking up a scattering of overturned cards from the table in front of her. "Besides, I think I finally have the gist of the game and I want to improve my skills before inviting anyone new to play." She sent a sharp, sidelong look to John, who was happily lounging in the seat beside her.

"All the practice in the world won't help you beat me, once I master the game myself," John said.

Diana made some sort of reply that had the ladies laughing in shock, but Reese didn't hear it. He couldn't hear or see or feel anything else from the moment Freddy stepped into the room. His heart leapt to his throat as Freddy strode in, paused for a fraction of a second as their eyes met, then moved on toward the sideboard, his face flushing.

Reese cleared his throat and forced himself to keep it together as he, too, walked to the sideboard and took a plate. "Did you sleep well?" he asked, certain his hands were shaking with the overabundance of emotion coursing through him as he stood side-by-side with Freddy, pretending to be calm.

"Not particularly," Freddy said with equal amounts of false calm.

"I'm sorry to hear that." Reese scooped eggs onto his plate, then added ham.

"I had too many things on my mind," Freddy went on, his tone more honest, as he helped himself to a scone, spooning clotted cream onto his plate. His cheeks flared bright red as he stared at the dollop of cream for a moment, then cleared his throat and moved on.

"I had a lot on my mind as well," Reese admitted, lowering his voice. He couldn't form words to follow that statement, though.

"We both have quite a bit to think about," Freddy said, even more seriousness in his words.

"Perhaps some decisions to make?" Reese suggested, inching down the sideboard and loading his plate with things he had no intention of eating just so he could stay by Freddy's side longer.

Freddy pressed his lips together, seemingly focused on the selection of breakfast meats in front of them. Reese could practically hear the gears of his thoughts turning. He could certainly feel the heat pouring off of him. He wanted to say something, to tell Freddy that everything would be all right now, that he would purchase Silverstone Castle and give it to him as a token of love, that Freddy wouldn't have to worry anymore, about his estate or about the two of them. They would take things slowly if he wanted to, but it would be so much better if they jumped in with both feet.

Freddy cleared his throat again to break the silence. "I'm sorry for running away," he said softly, inching closer to Reese.

Behind them, Lenore was explaining her game to everyone, which had sparked loud conversation and masses of laughter. The noise was almost like a wall sealing Reese and Freddy off from the others.

"I had a lot of time to think last night," Freddy went on, his voice low and tight. "And I think—" He paused, peeking sideways at Reese, whose heart was in his throat. "I think that I know what I want," he finished. He followed his words by taking a large, thick sausage from the sideboard and setting it deliberately on his plate.

Reese's cock jumped with excitement—which was damnably inconvenient with the bulk of their friends seated at the breakfast table mere feet behind them. The signal was unmistakable, if crude. And there wasn't a damn thing Reese could do about it at the moment.

"Understood," he said, his voice hoarse. "Perhaps we should skip breakfast to talk about this more."

Before Freddy could answer, Lenore called, "Will you two stop lollygagging over there and join us at the table? You can learn to play while you're eating."

Reese glanced to Freddy, only just realizing that neither of them had so much as peeked at each other during their conversation. If that wasn't suspicious to anyone with half a brain, then he didn't know what was. He straightened his shoulders, doing a far better job of pretending innocence than he'd ever done, grinned at Freddy, then turned to the table.

There were only two seats free, and they were on opposite sides of the table, nowhere near each other. He couldn't very well ask someone to move so that he could sit next to the man who had jerked him off in the library the night before and whose cock he intended to swallow as soon as he had the chance. Instead, he kept his smile in place and slipped into the chair closest to him. In his current state, the faster he hid everything from the waist down under the tablecloth, the better.

"Freddy, you can sit here, next to me." Lenore beckoned for Freddy to come around the table. "You wouldn't mind moving, would you, Lady Natalia?"

"Not at all," Natalia said with a blush, picking up her plate and teacup and moving to the other free seat, which happened to be next to Townsend. Reese smirked, wondering how long Lenore had been plotting that maneuver.

As soon as he'd taken his seat and pulled his chair into the table, Freddy glanced across at Reese. His smile was far too obvious, as far as Reese was concerned, but it was a smile. Reese didn't care if every one of their friends came to the conclusion that he and Freddy had engaged in bizarre sex acts the night before. Progress had been made. All he had to do now was make it through a lively and distracting breakfast. After that, he would get Freddy alone, they would talk about where they wanted things to go, and a new life would begin.

At least, in theory.

"What on earth was that look for?" Diana asked Freddy, her brow creased in confusion, even as she smiled. She glanced between Freddy and Reese. "Are the two of you plotting something?"

"Not at all," Reese said, reaching for the nearest coffee pot. His face was as hot as the coffee he poured.

"That wasn't a look of nothing," Diana pressed on. Her grin grew. "Tell us. What are the two of you up to?"

"They're thick as thieves, those two," Lady Beatrice agreed, her eyes sparkling as she jumped into the conversation. "I'm sure they're up to no good."

"It's probably nothing," John said, outwardly nonchalant, but not looking either Freddy or Reese in the eyes.

"You would say that, but only because you don't have an ounce of feeling in you," Diana snorted.

"I didn't see anything unusual," Lenore said, then rushed on with, "Now, let me explain the duel portion of the game to you."

"They're plotting," Diana pressed on. "You can see it. No two people look at each other like that unless they're conspiring."

"Stop being so nosey," John snapped

"What's gotten into you?" Diana rounded on him.

"I can't wait to find out what they have in store," Lady Beatrice went on with a giggle.

Freddy's smile had vanished entirely and he stared at his breakfast with horror in his eyes and a deep flush painting his cheeks. Reese had a hard time hiding his wince of sympathy. Discretion was a hard lesson to learn sometimes.

"I always think good friends are up to something," Natalia joined the conversation—which was now splintering into several conversations—with a shrug. "Freddy and Reese have always reminded me of...of Rupert and Cece, in an odd way."

She opened her mouth to say more but was cut off by Townsend choking on his coffee and sending a spray of it across his mostly-eaten breakfast. His eyes went wide, and he glanced from Reese to Freddy and back again. "Good Lord," he said. "Are the two of you—"

"I propose that we have a Cowgirl Shootout tournament this morning," Lenore nearly shouted, standing from her place. "We have quite a few decks of cards, after all, and I would be more than happy to tutor everyone who doesn't already know the rules in the finer points of gameplay."

"I think that would be a splendid idea," John said, equally as loud.

"If you're playing, I'm not," Diana huffed.

"Of course, you are," Lenore said. "You have to play. You're an expert, remember?"

"Any expert at one of your card games is a special woman indeed," Mr. Garrett said.

For a surreal moment, Reese thought he was flirting with Diana. Diana must have thought so as well, because her mouth hung open in the middle of whatever tirade she'd been about to throw at John. Across the table, Natalia gaped, then burst into peals of laughter. Henry elbowed Mr. Garrett hard, but Reese caught the grateful look in his eyes.

They'd skated perilously close to the edge—fallen right over it where Townsend was concerned—but thanks to the forbearance of their friends, Freddy and Reese had been saved. Reese continued with his breakfast, second-guessing his earlier thought that he didn't care who thought what about him and Freddy. Townsend clearly hadn't known, but he'd just put two and two together. He was busy staring around at the others now, looking as though he were trying to figure out why no one seemed fussed and whether he should care himself.

But it was Freddy whom Reese truly cared about, and Freddy looked as though he'd come face to face with a wild tiger and barely escaped with his life. His smile was gone and the color had drained from his face. He picked at his breakfast, his brow knit in thought. Reese could only sit where he was, praying all the progress they had made was still intact. Breakfast couldn't be over fast enough. Not only was Reese convinced he would have to teach Freddy everything there was to know about their kind of love, he could see now that he would have to instruct Freddy how to carry on an affair without letting on to the rest of the world how he truly felt.

His chance felt imminent as everyone finished their breakfast and rose from the table. Reese rose as well and was just calculating how he could get to Freddy's side as covertly as possible when a footman dashed into the room with a folded slip of paper on a salver. Reese readied himself to receive whatever news it was, but the footman headed straight for Freddy.

"What's that?" Lenore asked, shifting to Freddy's side and reading over his shoulder as he opened the paper.

Freddy's anxious look vanished into shock as he said, "There's a buyer for Silverstone Castle."

Hot and cold flushed through Reese, and his heart sped up. He walked around the table to look at the telegram. "How wonderful," he said, having a hard time keeping his excitement in check again. "You're saved."

"Yes, I'm saved," Freddy said, sounding nowhere near convinced. "My estate agent and man of business, Mr. Bledsoe, wants me to go to Silverstone at once to deal with the technicalities of the sale." There was an overwhelmed, hollow ring to Freddy's voice, as though he believed it was the beginning of the end of his family's legacy.

Reese couldn't wait to see the look on his face when he learned everything was just as it should be after all. "I'll come with you," he said.

"To Silverstone Castle?" Diana said, blinking. "In the

middle of a house party where you are the host?"

She had a point there, but Reese chose to ignore it. "By the look of things, Freddy needs moral support right now."

"Quite right," Lenore added. Reese couldn't ignore the way she once again seemed to be interceding to get the two of them together. That could only mean one thing—she knew. Which was preposterous, seeing as any woman who had figured out what Reese and Freddy were—or were about to be—to each other would likely perish in outrage. But Lenore smiled at both of them and said, "We can continue on with the party ourselves."

"Or perhaps this would be a good time to relocate the party to London," Mr. Garrett said judiciously.

"We really should be getting back," Diana admitted, glancing to Lady Beatrice and Natalia. "The election is about to end, and even though the May Flowers are focusing on women's suffrage now, we should make our presence known in Westminster."

"We certainly should," Lady Beatrice agreed.

"It seems settled then," John said, glancing pointedly to Reese instead of taking the opportunity to tease Diana, for a change. "You two will go to Silverstone Castle to deal with the sale and I'll escort the ladies back to their London abodes in time for the election results."

"We don't need you to escort us anywhere," Diana said with a sigh.

"Of course, you do," John grinned, following behind

her as she swept out of the room. "You need me in more ways than you can count."

The mass of their friends swept out of the breakfast room. Reese hung behind a bit, enough to have a word with Freddy.

"I really should pack," Freddy said, attempting to rush ahead.

Reese caught his hand before he could get away. When Freddy cringed and reluctantly looked at him, he said, "I know. You're not used to that kind of scrutiny. I am. We don't have to talk about any of this now. There will be plenty of time at Silverstone for all sorts of talk."

Freddy's shoulders relaxed. "That's why you want to accompany me, isn't it?"

Reese's confession about the sale was on the tip of his tongue, but something held him back. He wanted his surprise to come at just the right moment, and that moment wasn't it. So he said, "Yes. We'll have all the time we need to work through this at Silverstone. Alone."

Freddy's smile returned, and he nodded to Reese before striding out of the room.

Reese let out a breath of relief, not sure if he had handled the situation like a master or fumbled his way through it.

CHAPTER 8

*S*ilverstone Castle wasn't far from Albany Court, all things considered. A generation or two ago, it would have taken the better part of a day and a half to get there, but thanks to the miracles of modern transportation, Freddy and Reese crossed through the crumbling front gates and rolled up the weedy drive to the front door by the middle of the afternoon.

"I'm sorry that I've let the place go so much," Freddy blurted as he opened the hired carriage's door and hopped down. "The drive needs new stones and since I've only been able to retain one gardener, too many things have fallen by the wayside."

He spoke hurriedly, stepping away from the carriage as Reese alighted and glancing quickly around to assess who might be watching them. For one, blissful moment that morning, he'd entertained the idea that he might be able to get away with forming some sort of deeper understanding with Reese. But the moment attention had been drawn to the two of them at breakfast, culminating in Dr. Townsend's outburst, Freddy had second-guessed everything.

"It kills me to think of the enterprising young men and women I've had to let go from the household staff in the last few years," he went on, searching in his pockets for money to pay the carriage driver. "Especially after all the work I've put into the estate. Mr. Taylor, the butler, says he understands, but I know I've caused him great inconvenience."

His movements turned jerky and clumsy as he realized he'd left his wallet in his traveling bags because there was nothing in it. He slapped at his pockets, as if a few coins would magically appear, all while his face heated with embarrassment.

"I'm certain Mr. Taylor is a kind and forgiving man," Reese said, utterly at his ease and in command of the situation, as he took out his own wallet and paid the driver without batting an eyelash.

The driver touched the brim of his hat to Reese with a smile before marching around to take down their traveling bags and to hand them off to Freddy's lone footman. Mr. Taylor stood by the front door, ready to greet Freddy and surveying the scene with a smile. Freddy nodded to him as he and Reese started toward the door, but inside, he felt as small as a mouse. He loved Reese desperately, but watching him pay the driver so casually, as if it were a given he would pay for everything, didn't settle right. How far of a leap was it before Reese paid for him?

"Don't worry about it," Reese said, patting Freddy's back as they walked up the steps and crossed into the house ahead of Taylor. "Everything will work out for the best. You'll see."

If only Freddy believed him. Reese's hand lingered on his shoulder, and as much as he liked the touch, he felt as though every set of eyes in the county were watching them. Even the sad portraits of disapproving ancestors on the wall.

"Welcome home, my lord," Taylor greeted them once they were in the front hall. "And Lord Howsden." He bowed to Reese. "It is a pleasure to see you again."

"Thank you, Taylor," Reese said before Freddy could squeeze in his own thanks. "It's always a delight to visit Silverstone."

Taylor nodded to Reese again, then turned his attention to Freddy. "We received your telegram this morning, my lord. Mrs. Ball has prepared your room and one for Lord Howsden as well."

"I hope you haven't put me on some cold and distant hall, Taylor," Reese addressed the butler with a sly grin. "I would hate to make more work for your staff. A room across the hall from Lord Herrington would be much easier on the maids."

The back of Freddy's neck prickled at the request. In

the first place, it was glaringly obvious that Reese wanted a bedroom as close to Freddy's as possible. He couldn't have announced his intentions louder if he'd flat-out told Taylor that he intended to creep across the hall and bugger Freddy senseless that night. Secondly, it wasn't Reese's place to issue the order. Freddy was master of Silverstone Castle. At least, he was for a few more days. According to his agent, he would meet the new owner the next day and that would be that.

Taylor glanced to Freddy. "Is that your wish, my lord?"

It was small comfort that at least Taylor remembered who paid his salary, as meager as it was.

"Yes," Freddy said with as much confidence as he could, which wasn't much. "Lord Howsden is right. It would be easier for Hannah to set and light the fires and make up the rooms if they were across the hall from one another."

"Very good, my lord." Taylor bowed. "Would you care for tea after your journey? I can have Mrs. Ball prepare some for you."

"Actually," Reese cut in before Freddy could answer, "I would quite like a walk around the grounds, if that's all right with you." He glanced expectantly at Freddy.

There was so much to read in Reese's expression that Freddy didn't know where to begin. Did Reese simply want to stretch his legs after traveling or did he want the two of them to be alone so they could talk or more? And was he interrupting and overriding him out of simple enthusiasm or were they already assuming the roles that a relationship of the sort that waited for them would force on them?

"A walk would be lovely," Freddy said, smiling at Reese, then nodding to Taylor. If the worst was about to happen anyhow, he might as well get it over with.

"I shall put Mrs. Ball on notice to have tea ready when you return, my lord." Taylor nodded, then directed the footman to take the bags upstairs.

Freddy turned and headed right back out the door they'd just come in, Reese half a step behind him.

"Is Mrs. Ball your housekeeper or your cook?" Reese asked once they were outside. They took the path that led down the hill and that looped past the tenant farms before heading back toward the house.

"She's both," Freddy admitted gloomily. "I can't afford to pay for more." He paused. "I'm sure she despises me for piling work on her shoulders."

Reese laughed and slapped Freddy's back. "No one could hate you, Freddy. No one at all."

He kept his arm slung around Freddy's shoulders as they walked. Freddy's instinct was to slip his arm around Reese's waist for maximum closeness, but he couldn't bring himself to do it. There was still no telling who was watching, who might judge them.

"Aside from Taylor, Mrs. Ball, Hannah the maid, and that footman—"

"Jerry," Freddy filled in his name.

"Jerry," Reese repeated, "what other staff do you have?"

"That's it," Freddy said with a sigh. "That's all I've been able to manage these last few years."

"I see." Reese gave his shoulder a squeeze. Freddy both loved the comfort and writhed at the implication of dominance, knowing there was more to come. "Well, I wouldn't worry too much," he went on. "I'm certain the new owner will bring the staff numbers up to full strength as soon as he takes possession."

The twinkle of confidence in Reese's eyes was reassuring, but it only highlighted how far Freddy had let every detail of his estate slide.

"It's my father's fault, really," he blurted, desperate to have Reese not think badly of him. "He bankrupted the estate long before I inherited."

"So I've been told," Reese said, his voice gentler. They slowed their steps as they turned a corner, walking through a scenic patch of woods that Freddy's great-grandfather had planted back in the day when such things were fashionable. "Was it gambling or simply bad investments?" Reese asked.

"Both." Freddy rubbed his temples. "He hid all of it from the rest of us. When Henrietta married Richard, he threw a lavish wedding that impressed everyone."

"I remember," Reese said. "Even Lady Genevieve Tavistock was impressed."

"Even her. So you have an idea of just how much money was spent." He paused. "We didn't get the bill until after he died several months later."

Reese winced. "How bad was it?"

"So bad that I didn't tell Henny," Freddy said, sending a wary look Reese's way. "And don't you tell her either. She still doesn't know all the details."

"My lips are sealed."

The thought of Reese's lips spilled warmth through Freddy that he wasn't ready to face, so he went on. "Her wedding was the straw that broke the camel's back, but that camel had been lame for a long time."

"I assume there was nothing to be done once the old bastard died," Reese said.

Freddy winced. "My father wasn't a bastard, just dismal with money."

"I'm sorry. I shouldn't have presumed." Reese pulled his arm away, leaving Freddy feeling as though he'd lost something. "My father was a rank bastard who despised his sons and treated them accordingly, but that doesn't mean everyone's father is."

"Father did his best," Freddy sighed. "He was loving and encouraging to us all, but especially after Mama died, he was reckless and distant." Freddy glanced across the farmland attached to the estate as they came out of the woods. "I wasn't able to hold onto any of this, no matter how hard I tried. And I did try," he finished, his voice dropping to a dismal mumble.

Reese stopped, turning to face him. Freddy glanced up to him, and before he could catch his breath, Reese moved closer, cradling the side of his face with one hand. The compassion in his eyes was enough to undo Freddy.

"You did your best," Reese said. "I know you did. I watched your every attempt. I know how hard you worked for this place."

Freddy's heart felt as though it were about to burst through his ribs. Passion was one thing, but the pure, unadulterated caring that radiated from Reese was intoxicating. If Reese had just wanted him for carnal reasons, he could have resisted. But no, Reese loved him. Deeply.

In spite of the two of them standing out in the open, Freddy expected a kiss. Part of him longed for it, even though it would mean surrendering more of himself. But Reese stayed where he was, studying Freddy with a mysterious grin.

"I tell you," he said, his grin growing, "you truly have no reason to worry. I know, beyond a shadow of a doubt, that everything will work out well in the end."

"I wish I believed that," Freddy sighed.

"Believe it," Reese said. "Believe me."

When he put it like that, Freddy wasn't sure how he could not believe. His heart nearly exploded when Reese cradled his face with both hands and leaned in for the lightest of kisses. The contact was brief and teasing, but it filled Freddy with hope that perhaps Reese was right.

"Now," Reese said, rocking back, clearing his throat,

and letting his arms drop to his sides. "Show me these tenant farms of yours."

Freddy laughed. "Such romantic words for such a tender moment."

"I am positively dripping with romance," Reese laughed with him.

It was easier to continue on with the mood lightened. Even with the sky darkening as rain threatened to move in, Freddy was beginning to think that maybe everything would work out after all. Not just the debacle of his estate, but the dangers of an illicit romance. As they approached one of the farms, he caught himself thinking that just about anything would be worth it if he could kiss Reese again.

"He seems to be having a bit of trouble," Reese said as they came close to the fence that enclosed a cow pasture.

Freddy shook himself out of his silly thoughts and assumed the role of master of the estate, even if it wouldn't be his for long. "Mr. Owens has been farming at Silverstone for as long as I can remember," he told Reese quickly. "His father and his grandfather, and probably even more generations of his family, have been good and loyal tenants for hundreds of years." As they approached the gap in the fence where Mr. Owens worked, he called out, "Having a bit of trouble, Owens?"

The middle-aged man glanced up from his labor and smiled. "My lord." He swiped his hat off with his free hand, holding a hammer tight in the other. "I didn't expect to see you for another month at least."

Mr. Owens's smile was as settling as Reese's kiss, though not nearly as exciting. "This is an unexpected visit," he said, stepping over several long pieces of wood that had been laid out in the grass to shake the man's hand.

"Begging your pardon, my lord." Owens quickly put his hat back on. "You won't want to be shaking hands with me when I'm this much of a mess."

"Nonsense," Freddy said, taking the man's hand anyhow. When he let go, he turned slightly to the side and gestured to Reese. "This is my good friend, Lord Howsden."

"I remember, my lord." Owens shook Reese's hand as well and looked as though he'd been handed a purse of stardust. "You were here at Christmas in eighty-four, I believe."

"It might have been eighty-three," Reese said as though talking to an aristocratic friend. "It was a delightful Christmas." He glanced to Freddy.

A sudden bolt of wariness zipped through Freddy. Was Reese's expression too obvious?

"What seems to be the trouble here?" he asked, hoping to avoid any and all suspicion.

"The fence has been in need of repair for a while, my lord," Owens explained with a more serious frown. "I'm doing my best to get this bit done before the rain sets in."

"And where are your sons?" Freddy asked, reaching for the buttons of his jacket, already planning to help.

"Dan is in school, my lord," Owens answered. "And Ben took that job at Hurlock Heath to earn a bit extra."

"Understood," Freddy said, shrugging out of his jacket. "I can't speak for Lord Howsden, but I'm certainly willing to help you finish up here today."

"I'm game," Reese said, removing his jacket as well. He grinned at Freddy as though they were about to play a particularly jolly game.

"Oh, I couldn't ask you to help, my lords," Owens said, looking equal parts shocked and grateful. "Not in your fine clothes."

"We've got other clothes," Freddy said, draping his jacket over a finished part of the fence.

"And who says we need clothes anyhow?" Reese added with a wink.

Freddy's blood ran hot and cold. He dared a glance at Owens, but the man didn't seem to have a clue that Reese's words were anything more than a silly joke. He'd already moved to pick up a new fence post.

"I can't say I'm not grateful for the help," Owens said. "If one or both of you can pull up the old, rotted fence post, we'll just get this new one in, then lay the rails."

While Owens walked off in one direction, Reese inched closer to Freddy. "Does he know about the sale of the estate?" he whispered.

Freddy shook his head. "I haven't told any of the tenants that the whole place is up for sale, although I'm sure rumors have reached their ears. And it sold so fast I haven't had an opportunity to alert them myself." He unbuttoned his cuffs and rolled up his shirtsleeves, a frown creasing his brow. "I can only pray that the new owner keeps the old tenants on."

"I'm sure he will," Reese said, his mischievous smile back. "I'm certain of it."

He clapped Freddy's back, then strode over to where Owens had the old fence post ready to pull up. Freddy's skin tingled in the wake of Reese's touch. It was astounding in several ways, as though he'd had his epiphany about his feelings for Reese mere hours ago, and now the floodgates were open and he couldn't get enough of what he'd denied himself for so long.

The fence work proved to be exactly the sort of physical challenge Freddy needed to get his mind back where it belonged. He was no weakling, but he hadn't done anything quite as strenuous since leaving the army a year before. Flexing his muscles and using his strength reminded him just how much he enjoyed a little hard labor now and then. He was able to keep up with a farmer like Owens admirably well. He didn't even need Reese's help to wrench old posts from the ground and to toss them aside.

"Good Lord, Freddy. If I'd any idea you were such a crack hand with manual labor, I would have put you to work at Albany Court ages ago," Reese commented about half an hour later, when Freddy was drenched with sweat and had discarded his waistcoat and untucked his shirt. The rain had started as well, plastering the linen shirt to Freddy's torso.

"I credit the army," he said, tossing the latest of the old posts onto the pile they'd been making.

Only then did he catch a glimpse of the way Reese was watching him as if he were a feast just waiting to be devoured. The lust in his eyes was so unmistakable that Freddy instantly darted a look to Owens, praying the man's attention was elsewhere. It was, which was probably why Reese felt no qualms about ogling him. Heat coursed through Freddy that counteracted every drop of cool rain.

He headed back to where Owens was assessing the last of the fence posts, and Reese fell into step with him.

"As soon as we get back to the house," Reese rumbled, as low and dangerous as the thunder they could hear in the distance, "I am going to do things to you that will make you blush and sigh and come so hard you'll black out."

"This should be the last one," Owens said, turning toward them at exactly that moment.

Reese stepped away from Freddy, marching straight to the last post and leaving Freddy with his mouth dropped open in shock, his blood racing, and his cock straining against his trousers.

"We'll be lucky if we can get this one to stand up straight, what with the rain picking up the way it is," Owens went on, oblivious to the undercurrent.

"Oh, I'm certain we'll be able to get it to stand up straight and stiff in no time," Reese said, moving to stand by the post with a sly grin. "Freddy, would you do the honors?"

Owens still didn't seem to have a clue, so Freddy cleared his throat and marched to the last post, gripping it tightly and working with Reese to loosen it from the ground. Try as he did, Freddy couldn't banish the thought that he was working a giant phallus. When it finally came free from the increasingly muddy ground with a sticky pop, his face went bright red as his mind conjured up a world of other meanings.

They finished up the work in a rush, slipping on the muddy ground and doing a poorer job than they had with the other posts. At least the work got done. Freddy was drenched in sweat, rainwater, and mud by the time they finished, though, and Reese didn't look much better.

"Do you need help with anything else?" Freddy asked, shaking Owens's hand as they prepared to leave.

Owens laughed. "I always need help around the farm, my lord, but not today."

"What about tomorrow, then?" Freddy asked, not sure if he was motivated by the desire to help out, to show off his strength to Reese, or to avoid the all the new feelings that had been awakened in him.

Owens tilted his head to the side. "If you're offering, I've a roof that needs repairs, my lord."

"Consider it done," Reese said, stepping forward from where he'd collected his and Freddy's discarded clothes. "We'll be here tomorrow afternoon to help."

"Thank you, my lord," Owens said, looking as though he couldn't believe his luck.

"Yes, thank you," Freddy said as they started back to the house at a brisk walk. "You didn't have to offer help."

"Believe me, I did," he said. Heat and mischief filled his eyes as he went on with, "I've got a lot more help to give you before the day is done, love."

Freddy sucked in a breath, alive with lust and expectation, but with no idea what he was about to walk into.

CHAPTER 9

*R*eese's pulse pounded through what felt like
every cell in his body as he and Freddy
walked back to the house in the driving rain. If he could
have gotten away with running, he would have. It took
every ounce of his self-control to seem casual and in
control when what he really wanted to do was gambol
across the field, shouting in triumph. The moment he had
waited for and wanted for nearly ten years was finally
upon him.

"I hope Owens's fence holds," Freddy called through
the noise of the rain as they reached the front drive. "The
mud isn't ideal for new fences."

Reese glanced sideways at him, taking in Freddy's
pink cheeks and the stalwart, forward direction of his
gaze. If he wanted to pretend they weren't about to do
scandalous things to each other until they were both limp
with satiety, then he could play along.

"We'll go back tomorrow and check on him," he said, picking up his pace as they mounted the stairs and dashed through the front door as Mr. Taylor held it open for them.

The butler must have been keeping an eye out for his master, knowing he would come home a mess. "I took the liberty of having Hannah light fires in both of your rooms, my lord," he addressed Freddy. "And I laid out towels, washbasins, and dry clothes for you."

"Thank you, Mr. Taylor," Reese said, nodding to the butler then smiling at Freddy.

"Yes, thank you Taylor," Freddy said, the barest hint of indignation in his tone.

"Sorry," Reese muttered as they made their way, dripping, up the stairs. "You should have been the one to answer him, not me." Freddy said nothing, which was a bad sign, so Reese rushed on with, "I'm just so used to organizing the staff at Albany Court."

"And I can barely handle the smallest of staffs," Freddy murmured.

Reese wasn't certain the comment was meant for his ears, but the mood needed lightening, and Freddy had handed the comment to him on a silver platter. He swayed closer as they walked and whispered, "You'll be handling a sizeable staff in a matter of minutes."

Freddy jerked to stare at him, eyes wide, just as they reached the door to his room. His cheeks flushed with heat, and expectation had replaced indignation in his eyes. His lips twitched in what might have been a grin, but it was eclipsed by the raw anxiety that radiated from him.

Reese reached for the handle of Freddy's door, opening it and gesturing for Freddy to walk inside. His mind raced, working out a strategy for putting Freddy at ease before lust clouded his thoughts. Instinct told him this would be Freddy's first real experience, so he would have to tread carefully.

"Looks like Hannah has already brought tea up," Freddy said, walking deeper into the room and shedding his jacket. Reese closed and locked the door while he faced the other direction. "There will probably be tea in your room. We can clean up, have a bit of refreshment, then come back—"

Without waiting, Reese marched across the room and swept Freddy into his arms, silencing his nervous talk with a kiss. The contrast of hot and cold as their bodies, complete with wet clothes, melded together, heightened the sensation of closeness as Reese nibbled at Freddy's lips. He wanted all of Freddy, every last bit of him, right away, but he forced himself simply to kiss him at first, lips and tongues entwining.

Freddy moaned deep in his throat as their mouths slanted over each other. His hands moved tentatively to Reese's waist, then the buttons of his coat, then he flattened his palms against Reese's chest, as if he didn't know what to do. It was charming in the extreme and only fired Reese further.

He brushed his hands up Freddy's sides, humming

with desire, and threaded his fingers through Freddy's wet hair. "I love the taste of you," he panted between teasing kisses. "I want to taste all of you, every part."

Freddy shuddered, the sound he made not quite forming into words. He gripped Reese's lapels and tugged him closer, thrusting his tongue along Reese's in a surprising burst of aggression, even though he clearly didn't know what to do next.

Reese knew and then some. He indulged in Freddy's kiss as long as he could before breaking away, panting and shaking, to work loose the buttons of Freddy's soaked waistcoat. The fact that Freddy had put the waistcoat back on and buttoned it in the rain, after manual labor, was endearing in the extreme and so Freddy. Undressing him was a treat that Reese had been waiting for.

Better still, Freddy reached for Reese's buttons with eager, trembling hands as well. The two of them fumbled and laughed their way through rows of buttons and layers of soaked fabric, peeling off their clothes and letting them drop to the floor in soggy piles. Their eagerness was almost silly, but it brought a joy that Reese couldn't remember feeling in his entire life.

At last, he tugged Freddy's shirt from his trousers and pulled it up over his head. The sight of Freddy's broad chest with its dark hair and nipples tight with cold made his head spin with lust. He could barely wait until Freddy pulled his shirt off to circle his arms around Freddy's waist and tug him close. The sensation of his skin against Freddy's was glorious. He stroked his hands across Freddy's back and sides, kissing his cheek, his neck, and his shoulder.

"Is this right?" Freddy panted, his hands seemingly everywhere on Reese's back and sides.

"Yes, darling, it's absolutely right," Reese answered, nipping Freddy's shoulder lightly.

Freddy sucked in a breath, but Reese had only begun treating him. He dropped his hands to Freddy's backside, squeezing him and pressing their hips together. He was painfully hard and desperate to free his eager cock from his trousers, but he couldn't resist moving against Freddy. Freddy was rock hard as well and groaned at the friction Reese's movements caused.

"God, I like that," Freddy gasped, his face pinching with emotion. "I shouldn't, but I do."

A flag went up somewhere in the back of Reese's lust-crazed mind, but he ignored it for the moment. There was so much more to do with Freddy, so much more to explore. He kissed Freddy's shoulder, bringing his hands up to stroke his thumbs over his nipples until they grew even harder than they were. Freddy made a sound of surprise and delight, then reached for Reese's face, directing his head back up so they could kiss once more.

The urgency for more pushed Reese to fumble with the fastenings of Freddy's trousers. He wanted to feast on the sight of Freddy's body, naked and aroused and splayed on the bed, waiting for him. There was only one way to accomplish that. As soon as they were undone, he pushed Freddy's trousers down. His magnificent cock jumped up, standing proud and tall. It was even bigger than Reese imagined it to be, and it was all he could do to resist the need to drop to his knees to draw it into his mouth. The last thing he wanted was for Freddy to pull away from him now the way he had the night before.

Instead, he took a small step back and hissed, "I hate shoes." He bent to grab hold of one of his boots, barely able to keep his balance. "They slow everything down."

Freddy blinked at him, then glanced down at his own, muddy boots. Or perhaps he was looking at his thick, hard cock jutting up from the dark curls between his legs. The sight of him with his cock out and his trousers sagging around his thighs was magical. It took a supreme effort of will for Reese to yank his boots off and toss them aside without reaching for Freddy.

A moment later, Freddy sucked in a breath and inched back to sit on the edge of his bed. He tugged at his boots with almost frantic strength as Reese shucked his trousers and drawers. Freddy's eyes went wide at the sight of Reese's prick, hard and throbbing with need. The lust in his eyes had Reese's heart pounding. He climbed onto the bed, resting on his back with his legs parted, everything on display.

"I'm all yours, darling," he said, passion making him hoarse. "Anything you want."

Freddy's second boot dropped to the floor with a thump as he stared at Reese, heat in his gaze. For a moment, he sat there, frozen as he took in the sight. Reese wriggled slightly with impatience, debating whether grabbing his own cock and pumping would hurry Freddy along or embarrass himself by causing him to come prematurely.

He didn't have to decide. Freddy stood, throwing off his trousers, then climbed onto the bed. Reese's body clenched at the sight of him on his hands and knees moving closer, his erection bobbing stiffly between his legs.

"Come here, darling," Reese murmured, beckoning to him.

Freddy reached his side, still on his hands and knees and trembling slightly. "I...I know how this goes," he said, his voice strangled. "I know what you want, how you want me. And I...I will submit. For you, I'll submit."

A flash of alarm and confusion shot through Reese. It doubled when Freddy sucked in a breath and moved his knees apart, thrusting his hips back as though he were assuming some sort of position. And while the temptation did, in fact, stir inside of Reese to mount Freddy like a bull and bury himself deep inside his arse, not only were they nowhere near prepared for that sort of intercourse, in that moment, it felt obscene.

"Nonsense," he laughed instead, reaching for Freddy and knocking him off-balance enough that his stance faltered. When Freddy fell to the bed beside him, Reese rolled to his side, fitting their bodies together like puzzle pieces.

He made a sound of delight deep in his throat as he wrapped his arms and one leg around Freddy and kissed him. The mating of their mouths was a thousand times better with their naked bodies pressed against each other. Reese reached between them, stroking his hand along Freddy's cock and lower to cup his balls. Freddy moaned in surprise, the tension in his body quickly shifting from fear to expectation.

"You're beautiful," he sighed, rolling farther until he was on top of Freddy. He jerked his hips against Freddy's, rubbing their cocks together, trying hard not to come too soon. "I've never seen anyone so beautiful," he went on, kissing Freddy's lips, then his neck, working his way lower.

"I...." Freddy sucked in a breath as Reese flickered his tongue across his nipple.

"I have so much to teach you," Reese went on when Freddy's single syllable failed to form into words. "So very much."

He shifted down, pushing Freddy's knees apart and resting between his legs. The look of surprise that lit Freddy's eyes as Reese stroked his inner thighs, inching closer and closer to the cleft of his arse, was worth every moment of every year that Reese had had to wait for the moment. It was plain as day that Freddy truly didn't know the first thing about the sort of pleasure two men could find together. He seemed to think there was only one way to engage in intimacy. Schooling him in everything else would be a pleasure.

He bent down to lay kisses on the insides of Freddy's thighs, humming in triumph as Freddy tensed and panted. The scent of his musk was heady, heightening Reese's own pleasure and warning him that he wouldn't be able to hold out forever. He stroked a hand up the opposite thigh he was kissing, then gently closed it around Freddy's white-hot prick. After a cursory stroke, he lifted his head, closing his mouth around Freddy's tip.

Freddy let out a shattered sound, thrusting his hips up and sinking himself deeper in Reese's mouth. It was everything Reese had waited for and more. Freddy filled him, unknowingly daring him to swallow deep. It had been a while since Reese had done anything close to what he and Freddy were doing, but he bore down on Freddy, relaxing his throat to take as much of him in as possible.

"God, Reese," Freddy growled, panting wildly. He gripped fists full of the bedclothes, jerking as Reese worked on him, taking him deeper and deeper.

Reese moaned in ecstasy as Freddy's body grew tenser and tenser, working its way toward orgasm. He couldn't wait for the moment, and yet there were so many more things he wanted to share. Still drawing Freddy in and out of his mouth, he slipped a hand between Freddy's legs, toying with the pucker of his arse.

"Oh," Freddy gasped a moment later, sucking in a breath. "I'm coming, I'm—"

His whole groin tensed, and, like lightning, hot liquid hit the back of Reese's throat. He swallowed reflexively, helping Freddy along as he pulsed with orgasm.

As soon as Freddy's body went limp, Reese came up

for air, then shifted his body over Freddy's. He kissed his way across Freddy's damp chest to his neck, then jerked his cock desperately against Freddy's hip. Freddy surprised him by grabbing hold of his arse, which was exactly what Reese needed to tip him over the edge.

He growled as orgasm roared through him, shooting from his spine to his cock. His seed spilled across Freddy's belly, and it felt as though a part of his soul transferred between the two of them. The power of the pleasure of spilling himself for Freddy was thundering and left him limp with joy and amazement.

He collapsed where he was, on top of Freddy, their bodies limp and twined together. Reese was highly aware of every inch of their skin pressing together, their softened cocks nestled safe between the two of them. If he could have paused that moment and lived in it forever, he would have.

"That wasn't at all what I expected," Freddy whispered as their bodies began to cool.

"No?" Reese asked in a bleary voice.

Somehow, he managed to slide off of Freddy and to pull back the bedcovers so that the two of them could snuggle together beneath them. The sweetness of their arms and legs tangled together, their satisfied bodies embracing as they lay on their sides facing each other, was heaven. Reese slowly stroked Freddy's side, hip and backside, half hoping they would both rebound fast so that they could do it all again.

Freddy stared at him in confusion, brushing Reese's

tousled hair back from his forehead. "Why didn't you fuck me?"

Reese flinched, blinking and nearly laughing. "I did fuck you," he said, "Surprisingly thoroughly, considering how desperately I've wanted you."

Freddy's brow knit in confusion. "No, I mean, why didn't you...." His face flushed a deep red and he glanced down, dark lashes brushing his cheeks. "I thought the way it works is that you fuck me in the arse."

Reese couldn't help but laugh, his heart squeezing with greater tenderness for Freddy than ever. "We'll get there," he said. "I doubt you have any lubricating ointment lying around in your bedside drawers, though."

"What?" Freddy's confusion was greater than ever.

Reese drew him closer, kissing him with all the softness of his satisfied heart. "You can't just go sticking cocks in people's arses without preparation," he said. "Well, you can in a pinch, but it's rough. Trust me, it's a thousand times nicer, incredibly nice indeed, with proper preparation. You'll be begging for it once you've seen how nice it is."

Freddy continued to stare at him as though he'd grown another head.

Reese narrowed his eyes in thought as he studied him. "What did you think this would be like?" he asked, genuinely wanting an answer.

Freddy glanced down sheepishly again, though he continued to stroke Reese's back and nestle against him.

"I...I assumed that because I'm yours now, you would use me in whatever way you see fit."

A thread of worry cut through Reese's joy and satisfaction. "You are mine, Freddy, but I am yours now as well."

Freddy met his eyes, more confused than ever. "Isn't that how it works?" he asked. "One is the master and one is the—" he gulped, "—slave?"

Reese tensed. "What on earth gave you that horrible idea?"

"University, for one," Freddy said. "Don't you remember the way an upperclassman would always choose some poor lad to service him during the year?"

Reese's mouth dropped open in shock while his memory rushed back to those early days, when he and Freddy first met. "You're talking about Robinson, aren't you?"

Freddy nodded.

"Good God, Freddy. Robinson was a devil. He preyed on boys who were weaker than him, forced them to do things they didn't want."

Freddy's throat bobbed as he swallowed. "My bed in the dorm was right next to his door. I don't think he knew I could see and hear the things he did to those boys."

"But those weren't relationships, they were crimes," Reese insisted.

"And in the army," Freddy went on, a desperate edge to his voice, as if he were working to prove a point. "The senior officers quite frequently plucked the weakest men from the ranks to use for their own satisfaction."

"Then it was the same thing as Robinson," Reese insisted.

Freddy shook his head slightly. "Private Benton relished his role, I think. He...." Freddy swallowed again. "The more humiliating the better for him, I suspect."

Reese let out a harsh breath, stroking Freddy's face. "I've never met this Benton fellow, but yes, there are some people who enjoy being punished. I don't understand it, but I know it's there." He paused. "Are those the only examples you have experience of?"

Freddy glanced away, nodding slowly.

"Darling." Reese turned his face forward, stealing a light kiss. "Your mind has been poisoned by bad examples. Our kind of love is as rich and varied as any other kind." His voice softened and he stroked Freddy's side tenderly, holding him close and wanting to show him every gentle kind of love under the sun. "I don't love you because you offer yourself up for me to use your body. I love your cleverness and your strength. I've never known any man who has had to persevere over such difficult obstacles. All I want is to give you pleasure, to make you feel good, better than you've ever felt before. I just want to adore you and make your life as joyful as possible."

Freddy's eyes went glassy, and he blinked as if fighting tears. "I'm not sure I know how to be that way," he whispered.

"Then I'll teach you," Reese promised, kissing him

again. His body was beginning to stir once more, and he could feel Freddy's slowly coming to life again as well.

"No one has ever cared for me like this," Freddy whispered on. "I don't know how to be this way."

"It's easy." Reese brushed his hand to Freddy's backside, teasing his cleft and moving gently against him.

"I like this," Freddy sighed heavily. "God, I like it when you touch me, when you arouse me. I feel like a whole different person when you tease my body alive as you did. And when you swallowed my prick like that—"

Reese surged into him, kissing him hard and thrusting his tongue into Freddy's mouth. The love he felt was so expansive that he couldn't comprehend all of it. He wanted to make Freddy come so many times his cum turned to froth and he couldn't move from exhaustion.

He had just tightened his embrace when there was a knock at the door. Both Reese and Freddy froze stiff.

"My lord," Taylor's voice sounded from the hall. "I hate to interrupt your nap, but you have a visitor."

Reese wondered if the butler was fooled at all or if he knew exactly what he was interrupting.

"A visitor?" Freddy called, his voice tight and high-pitched.

"Yes, my lord. Your agent, Mr. Bledsoe, is here."

CHAPTER 10

Freddy rolled away from Reese and nearly fell out of bed. His body was so warm and sated that it was as though his bones had turned to jelly. All but one "bone", which was doing a good job of stiffening all over again. He forced himself to ignore the awakened pulse of lust blooming within him, though, and stumbled around the bed toward his wardrobe.

"Thank you, Taylor," he called through the door. "Tell Mr. Bledsoe I'll be down in a moment. I was...I was taking a nap after helping Mr. Owens mend a fence and getting caught out in the rain." He cringed as he spoke. Stating what Taylor had just said was suspicious in the worst possible way.

"Very good, my lord," Taylor said. His footsteps walked away from the door.

Freddy let out a breath, sagging against one of his bedposts for a moment. He prayed to God that Taylor wasn't suspicious and didn't realize Reese was in the room with him, that the butler didn't have the slightest clue what he'd actually been doing. Reese had been as silent as a tomb through the whole exchange, which would help the ruse. But Freddy shuddered to think what any of his meager staff would have thought if they'd walked past his bedroom half an hour earlier. He and Reese hadn't exactly kept things quiet.

"That was a close shave," Reese said, relaxing to his back and folding his arms behind his head as it rested on the pillows.

Freddy stared at him, drinking in the erotic sight of his bare chest, showing above the bedcovers. Reese's hair was tousled and his lips red from kissing, and other things. He looked thoroughly debauched and proud of it as he studied Freddy with passion-hazy eyes.

"A little closer than I'd like," Freddy finally managed to say.

He started to push away from the bedpost, but Reese stopped him with, "Wait. Let me just look at you for a moment."

Freddy's face heated as he glanced down at his naked body. He must have looked just as satisfied as Reese did, which made it all the odder to be stared at. His penis was only slightly hard now, but the scrutiny of a lover's gaze was enough to change that.

He sucked in a breath. He supposed Reese was his lover now. To Freddy's surprise, the idea excited him instead of repulsing him. With one dazzlingly hot encounter, Reese had shattered everything Freddy thought he'd known about relations between men like them. If what he had to look forward to was more kissing and touching, stroking and swallowing, more love and tenderness, and not being dominated and treated like a sexual slave, then all of the combined forces of nature and Mr. Bledsoe's business couldn't keep him out of Reese's bed.

"Good God, but you're driving me mad the way you're looking at me right now," Reese purred. He squirmed, slipping one hand under the bedcovers to grab himself. Freddy bit his lip as the bedcovers shook, hiding nothing about what Reese was doing to himself.

Freddy's cock jumped in response, but there was no time for indulgence. "As soon as I get this business with Bledsoe sorted, I want you to continue my lessons on love-making," he said, dragging himself away from the bed with painful reluctance and heading to the wash-basin that Taylor had had set out earlier. "I'm particularly interested in learning how to fit you into my mouth the way you did with me."

"Damn Bledsoe," Reese said, breathless and flushed, still working himself under the covers. "I've spent a decade fantasizing about how hot and wet your mouth would feel while sucking my cock."

A shiver of pure lust shot down Freddy's spine, filling him with astoundingly distracting emotion. "I'm not going to be able to clean up and face the sorry business ahead of me with you jacking off in my bed, Reese," he said. The reminder that Bledsoe wasn't there for a happy purpose cooled Freddy's ardor a bit.

Reese let out a laugh and pulled his busy hand out from under the bedcovers. "You're right," he said, lying there, catching his breath for a moment. The bedcovers tented over him. "I should clean up and head down myself."

"You don't have to," Freddy said, finally able to focus on running a wet washcloth across his still overheated body to wipe away the last remnants of intimacy. "Bledsoe is probably just here to discuss the sale offer and the buyer."

Reese rolled out of bed. Freddy thought passingly that he was suddenly tense, but he dismissed the thought.

"Do you have a robe I could borrow?" Reese asked, walking to the wardrobe.

Freddy swallowed at the sight of his erection bobbing and the strength and movement of his muscles as he opened the wardrobe door. "Whatever you can find in there is yours," he said, forcing himself to look away and avoid temptation. "I really should hurry."

Reese found and put on a robe, then crossed to where Freddy hunched slightly over the washstand. He slipped his arms around Freddy from behind, pressing his hard cock insistently against the cleft of Freddy's backside. In spite of the layer of robe between them, Freddy clenched with a combination of fear and desire.

"I swear," Reese murmured in his ear, kissing the back of his neck, "you'll like it. With everything prepared properly, you'll wonder how you ever could have been anxious about it."

It wasn't that Freddy didn't believe him. A huge part of him wanted to bend over and beg Reese to fuck him hard right then and there, preparation or not. His cock throbbed and his pulse raced so hard it made him dizzy. But there was business to take care of, and even with his newfound desire, there was more to life than fucking.

Reese seemed to sense that. He kissed Freddy's neck one last, lingering time, then backed away. "I'll meet you downstairs as soon as I can," he said.

Freddy turned to him as he crossed the room. "Thank you, Reese," he said, too many emotions jumbled into the simple words.

Reese paused with his hand on the door handle and winked. His grin was cocky and carnal, so much so that Freddy considered telling him not to go and jumping back into bed with him for a wild moment. But any way he looked at it, there wasn't time. Reese popped his head into the hall, then dashed out, shutting the door behind him.

Freddy let out a breath of relief. He loved Reese. He wanted Reese. But it was a thousand times easier to think without him in the room. He finished cleaning up, relieved that his erection calmed with a little cold water and anticipation of what awaited him downstairs. He dressed in the clothes Taylor had laid out, checked and double-checked his appearance in the mirror to make absolutely certain he didn't look like a debauched tart, then headed downstairs.

His heart was lighter than it should have been under the circumstances as he strode into the library, where Mr. Bledsoe stood by one of the bookshelves, perusing the titles.

"Mr. Bledsoe." Freddy made his presence known. "So sorry to have kept you waiting. It's been an...active day and you caught me in the middle of a nap." The words rushed out, feeling as transparent as glass.

Mr. Bledsoe turned away from the shelf and came to greet Freddy with a broad smile. "No, no, my lord. It is entirely my fault. You weren't expecting me until tomorrow. But I simply couldn't wait to rush out here to tell you about the extraordinary offer for Silverstone."

Freddy shook the man's hand, blinking at his words. "Extraordinary offer?" He let go of the man's hand and gestured for him to have a seat on one of the leather-upholstered sofas.

Mr. Bledsoe crossed to the desk to retrieve a small briefcase instead. He opened it and took out a small sheaf of papers. "I've never seen a transaction happen so quickly," he said, animated with excitement. "And I've certainly never seen terms like this."

Freddy's brow knit in confusion and he gave up the idea of sitting himself. Instead, he strode to Bledsoe at the desk. "What sort of terms? We set a steep price for the estate, I know, but we didn't expect anyone to actually meet that offer, did we?"

"That's the extraordinary thing," Bledsoe went on, his hands shaking slightly as he held up the papers. "The buyer *has* put forward the price we asked. Not only that, I've received word that the bank draft is ready to be deposited already."

Freddy gaped at the man. "An offer has been made matching our asking price *and* the money is ready to be transferred?"

"Yes." A tight laugh escaped from Bledsoe. "But the offer is even more extraordinary than that, my lord. The buyer has no wish to evict you from the property."

"I beg your pardon?" Freddy blinked and shook his head.

"You heard me correctly, my lord. The buyer wishes to purchase the estate for the full asking price, but he has requested that you continue to occupy and administrate it."

None of it made sense. Freddy shifted his weight from one leg to the other, tilting his head and studying Bledsoe as if he'd heard wrong. "The new owner is forking over a mountain of money to...to what? To claim ownership while I continue to live here?"

"Consider it a gift."

Freddy snapped straight at the sound of Reese's voice from the library doorway. Reese stood framed perfectly in the space, dressed casually and with this wet hair combed back. He wore a grin of utter triumph and undisguised affection. Although, taken together, the emotions struck Freddy as a look of possession.

"Ah, there's the new owner now," Bledsoe said, still brimming with exuberance. "I had no idea that you and Lord Howsden knew each other."

"We know each other, all right," Reese said, making it sound dirty, as he strode into the room. "I only regret that I didn't have a chance to let Lord Herrington know about my little gift before you let the cat out of the bag, Mr. Bledsoe."

Prickles raced down Freddy's back. Of course, Reese had bloody well had time to tell Freddy about what he'd done before Bledsoe showed up. They'd been in each other's company almost constantly for days.

"When did you do this?" he asked Reese, his voice tight.

"Bright and early this morning," Reese said, still full of smile and swagger as he came to sit on the edge of the desk. He looked as though he owned the place...which, of course, he did.

"I told you, everything moved extraordinarily fast," Bledsoe said, apparently unaware of the thick emotion now swirling in the air.

Freddy stared at Reese, his heart sinking farther and farther as the sting of betrayal filled him. Reese's pleased grin faltered, then faded as well.

At last, Freddy cleared his throat and caught sight of Taylor waiting in the doorway. "Taylor, could you show Mr. Bledsoe to a room? He's traveled a long way in bad weather, and I'm certain he could use a hot fire and some warm tea."

"Yes, my lord." Taylor bowed slightly and stepped forward as if to guide Bledsoe.

"I could use a bit of a nibble," Bledsoe said sheepishly. "But if you wish to tackle signatures and paperwork first...."

"No, I insist you rest," Freddy said, trying and failing not to snap. "I would like to speak to Lord Howsden for a moment in private as well."

"Ah, I see." Bledsoe nodded and headed toward where Taylor waited. "I understand completely."

"Thank you, Mr. Bledsoe," Freddy called as the man left with Taylor.

As soon as they were gone, he rounded on Reese, the full force of his hurt welling up within him.

"I thought you would be pleased," Reese spoke before Freddy could, standing straight and eyeing him anxiously.

"Pleased?" Freddy gaped. He was exhausted, his nerves had been taxed in a thousand different ways since morning, and his heart didn't know whether to break or harden.

"Yes?" Reese asked, assuming a softer stance now that they were alone.

"Pleased that you have just purchased me, lock, stock, and barrel?"

"I've purchased your estate," Reese corrected him. "Or at least I will once all the paperwork is sighed. And I want you to have it."

"But I won't have it," Freddy said, trying not to shout

and shaking with the effort. "I'm selling it because I cannot afford the expense, because in spite of spending every ounce of my effort and time for the past year and a half, I couldn't save it. If you've purchased it, it will, of necessity, continue to run on your money."

"It will run on the profits, once we work on improvements," Reese insisted.

"Your improvements," Freddy said, shaking with frustration. "You clearly intend to take a firm hand in the running of this estate that you say you are gifting to me."

"But I want you to stay here," Reese said. He stepped closer, brushing his hand along the side of Freddy's hot face. "I want us to stay here together. This can be our place."

"And that is your price?" Freddy continued to argue. "You front the money so that, to all the world, it appears as though I haven't been an utter failure and lost my family's estate, and all so that you can keep me here?" He pushed Reese's hand away from his face.

Reese's face pinched in uncertainty. "Yes?" he said. He shook his head slightly.

"Keep me like a mistress?" Freddy's eyes widened.

"No, not like that. Like a friend." Reese huffed out a breath. "Tell people I've invested in the property, if you'd like. Not a soul in the world would question my staying here from time to time if I own a stake in the land."

"You would own all of the land," Freddy said. "You would own me."

"Would that be so very bad?" Reese asked, reaching

for Freddy once more and running his finger down the row of buttons on Freddy's waistcoat. "It's a fair bargain, if you ask me. You get to keep your family's estate and save face and I—"

"Get to fuck me whenever you want?" Freddy seethed. "Is that how I'm to pay you back for rescuing me?"

"Well, I wouldn't say no if you wanted to show me a little gratitude from time to time."

Freddy's mouth dropped open and his head spun. If Reese was joking, he'd picked a piss-poor time for it. Freddy had no idea if he was serious or teasing him. The fire of lust still smoldered in Reese's eyes, but with it burned the same sort of superior fire Freddy had seen in the eyes of the most dictatorial officers he'd served under.

"Fine," Freddy seethed. He glared at Reese for a moment before dropping to his knees in front of him. "I was a fool to think you wanted anything else from me," he said, fumbling with the fastenings of Reese's trousers.

Reese's eyes went wide and he jerked his hips away, batting Freddy's hands aside. "What are you doing?" he hissed. "We're not behind closed doors."

"Why should we hide our bargain, as you call it, from the servants?" Freddy said, his voice taking on a wild pitch. He reached for Reese's trousers again. "You purchased me to service you, did you not? Purchased me for the price of my family's estate and heritage. You told me in no uncertain terms that you wanted to teach me.

Fine. You win. Why don't you just stick your cock down my throat now?"

"Freddy, stop," Reese snapped, hitting his hands away harder. "Pull yourself together."

Hurt continued to pulse through Freddy, like shards of glass in his veins. He stood, breathing heavily as he glared at Reese. "You orchestrated this whole thing, didn't you?"

"I am purchasing Silverstone Castle to save you from ruin, if that's what you mean," Reese answered, clearly agitated but trying to hold his own.

"Because you didn't think I could handle my own affairs."

"Freddy, you were selling," Reese said, his voice harder. "You were reduced to selling your family's hereditary estate."

"Yes," Freddy fired back. "Which was my decision and my responsibility. You've completely robbed me of choice, and without once consulting me on the matter. Just like a master treats his slave."

"That wasn't my intention at all."

"And you seduced your way into my bed this afternoon as a way to sample the merchandise," Freddy growled.

"I love you," Reese roared, then checked the doorway to make certain they weren't being overheard. He lowered his voice as he went on with, "I have for ages. I'm not going to apologize for wanting you as well, or for having you at last."

Freddy winced at the way he said it, knowing full well Reese didn't see what was wrong with his words.

"I'm buying Silverstone for you, but it is not in any way connected to or contingent upon you spreading your arse cheeks on a regular basis so I can use you for my own pleasure," Reese went on in a tight whisper.

Freddy's eyes went wide. "Isn't it? Did you not promise me, less than an hour ago, as you jerked your cock against me, that I would enjoy it? Wasn't that just another way of saying I should take you to the hilt and be grateful for it?"

"No," Reese shouted. "Not in the least."

Freddy let out a bitter laugh and started to turn away. Reese caught him, forcing him back and gripping the side of his face. He stole a searing kiss that made Freddy's insides scream with need and betrayal. He clamped his arms around Reese's waist, squeezing his backside, loving and hating what they were doing in equal measure. If any of the servants happened by, all of their secrets would be out.

Sense slammed into him, and Freddy yanked back. He and Reese separated with gasping, panting breaths.

"I love you," Reese growled, frustration rippling off of him. "You cannot stop me from purchasing Silverstone and saving you from financial ruin."

"You didn't bother to ask if this is what I wanted," Freddy fired back at him. "You've bought my pride along with these hallowed walls, and I will never get it back."

"I love you, you ungrateful bitch," Reese insisted, tipping into anger.

Every one of Freddy's nerves frazzled. He'd never once, in all his life, been called by any sort of feminine pejorative, though he knew it was common to men like him. Coming from Reese, it felt like a fist in his gut. Not only had Reese taken his pride, he'd robbed him of his masculinity too. He might as well resign himself to a life as Reese's fuck toy, like Benton had been to Col. Wallace in South Africa.

"I'm sorry, I didn't mean it," Reese rushed to say, his anger pinching into regret. "You've thrown me for a loop is all. I thought you would be pleased."

"What am I going to tell my sister?" Freddy seethed. "How do you think I'm ever supposed to look Henny in the eyes again, once she finds out you've swooped in, like a deus ex machina, to buy the estate? What conclusions do you think she is going to draw when she sees you staying here with me, the two of us alone, secluded?"

"Henrietta knows which way the wind blows," Reese answered, fidgeting.

"Yes," Freddy said, jaw tight. "She does. How do you think she'll view this bargain of yours? How do you think John will view it, or Harrison, or, God help us, Townsend?"

"I'm buying the estate to help you," Reese insisted again.

"And in the process, proving to everyone who cares to look that I'm not man enough to save what belongs to my family on my own, that I have to be bailed out by my scandalous, male lover."

"No one will see it that way," Reese said, staring hard at Freddy. "No one will know about us at all if we just—"

"What astounds me the most in all of this is how you believe I'll fall into bed with you again at the snap of your fingers," Freddy interrupted him.

"Won't you?" Reese asked, pulling himself to his full height, face pink with emotion. "You wanted it so badly you were nearly weeping for it. And I still see that lust in your eyes."

"Maybe so," Freddy growled. "But unlike you, I am an expert at restraint. And I respect myself, even if you don't respect me."

He was finished with the conversation, finished with being made to feel like a serf who should show gratitude for his master running rough-shod over him. He narrowed his eyes at Reese for a brief moment, then turned to storm out of the room.

"Freddy, wait," Reese called after him.

Freddy paused at the door and turned to him, hissing, "I'll be locking my door tonight. So unless you want to embarrass yourself and display to the entire household just what kind of a man their new owner is, save yourself the trouble and stay in your own bed."

"Freddy," Reese appealed one more time.

Freddy turned away, marching on, too wounded to stay and face the argument for a second longer.

CHAPTER 11

*I*t was already late when Freddy walked out of the library, leaving Reese feeling as though the puppy he'd adored for ages had bit clean through his hand while feeding it. The sting of betrayal turned his stomach and left him in a foul mood. He spent a few minutes pacing the library, barely restraining himself from pulling every book from the shelf and throwing them across the room. He had come close to bankrupting himself to save Freddy's ungrateful hide and that was the thanks he received?

Still brimming with fury, he marched to the desk and snatched up the papers Bledsoe had brought with him. A quick scan proved that they were the sale documents for Silverstone Castle. He found pen and ink and signed his name to every spot that needed his signature, then threw the pen at the closest window with all his might. It clattered off the glass, fell, and immediately bled a dark black splotch onto the carpet.

It was only once he stormed up to his room, sparing a glare at Freddy's closed and presumably locked door, that the irritating voice of his conscience cut through the hurt of what felt like rejection. He should have talked to Freddy about the sale first. He should have explained things more clearly. He shouldn't have taken for granted that Freddy would see things the way he did. And, if he were completely honest, he shouldn't have bedded Freddy before settling the whole thing.

Taylor, or some other member of Silverstone's staff, had anticipated Reese's needs in nearly miraculous style, and there was a full supper waiting in his room, which he discovered after slamming his door and hoping Freddy heard it. That tiny act of kindness and consideration sapped the last of Reese's anger. He crossed to the table and flopped into the chair, reaching for the silver dome that covered a still-warm dish of shepherd's pie and beans cooked with butter and garlic. Tears instantly sprang to his eyes and he let out a sob before he could stop himself. Freddy must have told Mrs. Ball that shepherd's pie and anything cooked in butter and garlic were his favorites. There was no chance such a simple dish would be served to a man of his status otherwise. That simple act of tender consideration filled him with misery as it highlighted everything he had potentially just thrown away.

But no, one fight, their first fight, wasn't the end of things. He set the cover aside and dove into the meal with determination, even though his stomach was tight and every bite tasted like ash. Freddy would see the wisdom and the benefits of his act of devotion, his bargain, as he had so callously called it, once he had a chance to think on it. Silverstone Castle had been saved, whether Freddy agreed with the method by which it had been saved or not, and once they calmed down, everything would be as it should.

Reese repeated that mantra to himself as he finished his supper and set the tray out in the hall so that he wouldn't be disturbed by servants that night. He insisted he was right as he undressed and crawled into bed naked. He told himself that Freddy was merely overwhelmed by the rush of changes that he'd experienced that day. It didn't bode well that, in spite of being stark naked in a bed mere yards away from Freddy, in Freddy's house, that he hardly felt a whisper of desire and remained as limp as a dead fish. He blamed it on the activity of the afternoon and told himself not to worry about it, then tossed and turned through a fitful night of second-guessing and frustration.

He was bleary and aching the next morning when he dragged himself out of bed, washed and dressed, and headed downstairs for breakfast, determined to stand his ground. His determination faltered for a moment when he strode into the room to find Freddy and Bledsoe already there, Freddy sitting at the head of the table with Bledsoe on his right. Reese's heart instantly ached at the pale and wan cast to Freddy's face, then ached harder when Freddy glanced dolefully up at him as he put down the pen he'd been holding.

The pieces didn't quite connect in Reese's mind until Bledsoe glanced Reese's way with a smile, rising from his chair.

"What brilliant timing, my lord," he said, gathering up the papers that had rested on the table between him and Freddy. "Lord Herrington has just signed the contract, as I see you must have done last night. All that's needed now is to take the document back to London and complete the sale."

The raw feeling that ripped through Reese's chest was as far from the victory he thought he'd feel at Freddy going along with his plan and selling. He cleared his throat and pushed the tangle of emotions away before it could weaken his resolve and dent his certainty that he was doing the right thing.

"Thank you, Mr. Bledsoe," he managed to grind out as Freddy's agent met him just inside the doorway, shaking his hand vigorously.

"I suppose this means I work for you now, my lord, as the estate agent," Bledsoe went on in a jovial tone, his smile brightening. "Although I assume, based on the conditions of the contract and what Lord Herrington was just telling me, that, in future, the estate will be administrated more as a business partnership than a sole proprietorship."

Reese glanced to Freddy, barely raising one eyebrow, before focusing on Bledsoe. "Yes, that is correct," he said.

He couldn't bear to see the smoldering anger and disappointment hanging over Freddy, or the obsequious joy in Bledsoe's expression, so he turned to the sideboard and fixed himself a plate. Not that he had any more appetite than he had the night before.

"Now that money is no barrier," Bledsoe went on, returning to the table, "I have quite a few ideas for improvements and modernization that will surely increase the estate's profits. Cottages for one. I think it would be wise to convert at least one of the old farms that is no longer productive to rent-producing cottages. You could even set up some sort of factory on the land and house its workers in such cottages."

Reese made a sound as though he were listening and interested—neither of which were true—without checking to see if Bledsoe was talking to him or Freddy. He had a sinking suspicion that he was the one being addressed.

His theory seemed to be proven true when he turned toward the table with a full plate only to find Freddy getting up from his spot at the head of the table.

"Are you going somewhere?" he asked, trying his damnedest to sound casual.

Freddy picked up his plate with one hand and his coffee cup with the other, scooting to the side, moving a few places down the table, and setting them at a new place. "Just vacating the head of the table to the new master," he said.

Reese winced at the way he emphasized "master". He

wasn't about to play Freddy's sour games, though, and instead of taking the vacated seat, he set his breakfast at a place across the table from Freddy and sat without looking at him.

As he reached for the coffee pot, Bledsoe went on with, "Mr. Taylor will be delighted to be able to bring the staff of the place up to full strength. And I know Mrs. Ball will be more than happy to hire a cook so that she can focus on housekeeper duties."

"Yes," Freddy agreed in a sharp voice. "Management of this household has been a disgrace for these past few years."

Bledsoe's mouth flapped open for a second, then his face went red, as though he realized the insult to Freddy that he'd inadvertently hurled. "Yes, well, you did an admirable job with what your father left you, my lord. Quite admirable. Most men would not have been able to hold on as long as you have. Admirable indeed." His clumsy words faded as no one reacted.

The table fell silent. Reese poured every last ounce of his effort into choking down food he had no appetite for as though he were a starving man offered a feast. It didn't help the state of his stomach that he couldn't resist glancing across to Freddy every few seconds, hoping and praying that the man he loved would see fit to end his temper tantrum and recognize the offer of love and support for what it was.

No such concession was to be had. Breakfast continued in increasingly awkward silence until Freddy took a last gulp of his coffee, stood, and said, "I'm heading back down to Owens's farm to help with those other repairs he mentioned."

"I'll come with you," Reese said, standing so fast that his chair scraped noisily and nearly toppled.

"It really isn't necessary," Freddy said in a frosty voice. "I'm sure you'd prefer to meet with Mr. Taylor and Mrs. Ball to discuss the increase of the staff and all the ways you wish to command the place be run, now that you are master."

"No," Reese said with what he thought was heroic patience. "I would rather go down to the farm and help Owens *with you*."

Freddy stood stock still for a moment, his eyes locked with Reese's. The battle of wills was horrifically uncomfortable to Reese. It was not at all what their relationship was normally like or what it was supposed to be. But he refused to be cowed.

At last, Freddy grumbled, "Suit yourself," and turned sharply to march out of the room.

Reese started to follow, but Bledsoe stopped him with, "Is it something I've said or done?"

Reese laughed humorlessly. "Not to worry, Mr. Bledsoe. I'm the villain in this farce. I committed the sin of saving my friend from ruin without consulting him first."

"Ah," Bledsoe said with a judicious nod.

Reese had the uncomfortable feeling that he did understand, at least partially. He doubted Bledsoe knew the depth of his and Freddy's relationship, but friends quarreled whether they'd seen each other naked or not.

Freddy was halfway down the front stairs outside of the house by the time Reese caught up with him. The rain had blown itself out during the night, and the sun was out, drying everything with its warm glow. A balmy breeze set the grass of Silverstone's lawn waving, and birds chattered merrily as they flitted about, snatching up worms that come out in the wet. All of nature seemed overjoyed in a complete contrast to the smoldering frustration that buzzed around Reese and Freddy as they marched down toward Owens's farm.

"You signed the document," Reese said when he couldn't stand the silence anymore.

"I had no choice," Freddy growled.

"You could have rejected my offer."

Freddy let out a bitter laugh. "No, I couldn't. There weren't exactly a line of amorous benefactors waiting to purchase the place."

"You could have waited until someone else came along," Reese insisted.

"No." He shook his head, glancing ruefully at Reese. "I waited too long as it was. My father's creditors would have swooped in by the end of the month."

His words were too gloomy and genuine to be hyperbole. That did nothing to take the sting out of Freddy's resentment, though.

"Then stop acting like I've bent you over a barrel and taken what I wanted by force," Reese hissed.

"Oh, I'm sure that bit will come later," Freddy seethed, walking faster so that he got ahead of Reese.

"Just because you're inexperienced does not mean that you should be equating this sale to sex," Reese called after him, confident that no one was close enough to hear.

Freddy paused and whipped back to him. "And you are, no doubt, deeply experienced," he said with a faint sneer. "Which is just one more thing for you to lord over me." He turned and marched on.

Reese's mouth dropped open, but he couldn't think of a blasted thing to say. Had Freddy just insulted him for having other lovers in the past? They'd never once discussed their pasts, not even touched on the subject in passing, so Reese didn't have the first clue whether Freddy was jealous on top of everything else.

He shook his head and walked on, catching up to Freddy's side but staying silent. The only thing he could grasp anymore was that Freddy was bitterly angry and it was his fault. Beyond that, he was fumbling in the dark with no idea how to make it better.

"My lords," Owens greeted them inside a cobblestone courtyard between the various buildings that made up the center of his farm. "I didn't think you'd actually come back."

"Of course, we came back," Freddy said, a brittle edge to his voice. He cleared his throat, put on a smile, then went on in a much more jovial tone with, "I made a promise, and I always keep my promises."

"As do I," Reese added. If Freddy could pretend that

nothing at all was wrong, so could he. "What sort of work do you have for us today?"

Owens regarded the two of them as though he'd been given an extra slice of Christmas pudding. "It's all roofs today, my lord," he said, gesturing to the ancient stone barn on one side of the courtyard. "The tiles had needed replacing for quite some time, but the rain we've had this month has really done it in."

"What do you need us to do?" Freddy asked, unbuttoning his jacket and moving to drape it over a stone wall.

"First, we need to pry up the old tiles," Owens said. "Then we need to assess the condition of the foundation under the roof. If everything is in good shape there, we finish by fitting new tiles in place."

"I'm yours to command," Reese said, following Freddy's lead and removing his jacket, ready to work.

He *was* ready to work. Though manual labor had never been something he'd found himself in need of doing, it proved to be the very best of distractions when the alternative was throttling one's lover to within an inch of his life for being a stubborn prick. Better still, the complexity and intensity of the tasks Owens needed done meant that he and Freddy barely needed to look at each other, let alone speak.

Since Freddy was the physically stronger of the two of them, he took the lead in pulling up old roof tiles and tossing them down to where Reese could cart them off to be reused or discarded. It was mind-numbing labor, but he didn't mind. Since the roof was in relatively good condition, within a few hours the tiles had all been removed and the new ones were ready to be nailed into place.

"I can do that," Reese said, eager to prove that he was good at something besides sucking cock and ruining lives.

"I'm sure you can, my lord," Owens replied, still in a good mood. "I'll just show you how it's done."

Owens climbed up the ladder to the barn's roof, gesturing for Reese to follow him up while Freddy held the ladder. As Reese climbed, he risked a glance at Freddy. Exhaustion had taken over from anger in Freddy's expression. The fact that he looked at Reese at all—even if it was with a dull, defeated look—was a step in the right direction. Fights happened, but they could be sorted.

"Now," Owens said once they were both sitting on the precarious roof by the section that had been cleared for new tiles. "Each of these has holes drilled for the nails." He held up a clay tile. "You see how the old ones are over there. The aim is to fit them as close and tight as possible so that the rain won't seep through to the pitch."

"I'm glad we didn't have to replace the pitch," Reese said with a smirk, reaching past Owens for a hammer that sat on the old section of the roof.

"That's a task for another—" Owens started to say.

He didn't have a chance to finish. Reese's foot slipped on a loose tile, and with it, he lost all purchase on the slanted surface. His other foot gave out from under him, and before he knew what was happening, he was tumbling head over arse off the roof. He landed with a hard thump that took the breath out of him and a blow to the head that knocked him senseless on the cobblestones below.

Every inch of his body flared with pain, especially his head. His vision blackened, and for a brief moment, he thought he would be sick. Even as he lay there, writhing in pain, though, he knew it could have been worse.

"Reese, Reese!" The frantic sound of Freddy's voice seemed distant and hollow for a moment before slowly forming crisper sounds. "My God, Reese, are you all right?"

He still hadn't fully regained his bearings when he felt himself lifted and pressed against something warm. A few blinks later, he realized Freddy had dropped to his knees and pulled him into his arms.

"Are you all right?" Freddy asked. "Did you hit your head? Is anything broken?"

"Just my pride," Reese managed to groan. He realized a moment too late that that might not have been the best choice of words, considering the way Freddy had accused him of robbing him of his pride the day before. "I don't think anything is broken," he said to cover the mistake.

"I'll run for the doctor, my lord," Owens said, scrambling down the ladder. "If he hit his head, it could be bad."

"I don't think I hit it as hard as I could have," Reese insisted, raising a hand to test his head. No blood came away when he did. The more he thought about it, the more convinced he was that he'd hit it against something other than the cobblestones. In fact, as he tried to sit up in Freddy's arms and look around, it appeared as though he'd had the good sense to fall into a patch of old hay that might have been a stack not too long ago.

Owens was already gone, though. Reese caught the sight of his retreating back as he struggled to sit up on his own power.

"Don't try to move too much," Freddy said, manhandling him to sit with his back against the barn. "You might not have hit it hard and there might not be any blood, but heads are something that should not be played around with."

"I'm all right," he insisted, although, in truth, pain still throbbed through him. Bruises could be as bad as breaks sometimes.

"The way you fell," Freddy went on, panting as though he'd run to Reese's rescue. "It was terrifying."

"It was terrifying from my perspective as well, thank you very much," Reese said with a weak laugh.

"I don't know what I would have done—" Freddy started, but clamped his mouth shut over his words.

Reese studied him for a moment, taking hope from the fact that Freddy was fussing over him so much when he had been dripping with resentment just minutes before. "Come here," Reese said, gesturing for Freddy to move in closer.

As soon as Freddy scooted a few inches so that he nearly covered Reese's body with his own, Reese reached for him, closing his hands on either side of Freddy's face, and drawing him in to steal a kiss.

Whether Freddy was startled by the kiss or whether he needed it as badly as Reese did, for one blissful moment, he gave in, kissing Reese in return. Their mouths melded together, tongues brushing as they tasted and drew comfort from each other. It was exactly the healing balm Reese needed.

As soon as that thought began to settle in Reese's bones, Freddy pulled back sharply, sucking in a breath.

"Don't ever do that again," he said in a thin, tight voice, brushing his lips with the back of his hand.

"What, kiss you?" Reese asked, feeling calmer than he had all day.

"It wasn't fair," Freddy went on. "I don't want you."

"Yes, you do," Reese laughed softly, then winced as he rested back against the barn. "You may be furious at me, but you still want me."

"Bastard," he hissed, standing and stepping away.

"Where are you going?" Reese called after him.

"To find the doctor," Freddy said, storming off.

"Isn't that what Owens is doing?"

"I'll speed him along," Freddy growled.

Reese let him go, blowing out a breath and wincing. As much as he wanted to call Freddy back, there was no point. Freddy's anger was only skin deep. At least, he hoped it was. Though he still had the feeling it would be no easy task getting past everything that was broken between them.

CHAPTER 12

*A*s soon as the village doctor checked Reese over and declared that nothing was broken, Reese was not concussed, and that he'd been damn lucky to avoid any serious injury, Freddy's heart stopped racing and the slight trembling that he hadn't been able to stop since watching Reese tumble to the cobblestones subsided.

"I can prescribe laudanum, if you need something for the pain, my lord," the doctor said after Reese thanked him, "but rest is the best cure for a tumble like that."

Freddy blanched slightly at the other meaning of the word "tumble" and took a step back.

"Rest sounds perfect," Reese told the doctor with a smile, though it was clear he was still in a bit of pain. He turned to Owens. "I'm sorry that I won't be able to help you with the rest of the roof."

"Not at all, my lord," Owens said, nodding deferen-

157

tially. "You're more than welcome to rest in the farm-house if you'd like. My wife would be happy to tend to you."

"Thank her for me," Reese said, moving to thump Owens's shoulder, "but I think it would be best if I returned to the big house." He glanced meaningfully at Freddy.

"I can help you finish the roof," Freddy immediately told Owens.

"Oh, I couldn't ask you to do that, my lord," Owens protested. "I'll find someone in the village to help."

"It wouldn't be any trouble at all," Freddy pressed on.

"No, no. You should see to your friend."

"Yes, I would agree that Lord Howsden needs obser-vation," the doctor agreed. "Blows to the head can be deceptive sometimes. He'll need someone to watch him to make certain there is no serious injury. If anything changes, send for me at once."

Freddy let out a long breath and rubbed a hand over his face. It seemed that no matter what he did, he wouldn't be able to extract himself from Reese. At least, not for the moment.

"All right," he said quietly, glancing at Reese and attempting to hide his maelstrom of emotions. "Do you need to be carried back to the house?" he asked in a wry voice, falling back on peevishness to hide his more serious feelings.

"Don't tempt me," Reese said with a wry laugh.

Reese thanked Owens and the doctor again, insisting

that he would pay the doctor generously for his time—something that made Freddy feel even worse as he should have been the one to make the offer—and started out of the farmyard and up to the house. Freddy walked by his side in silence, dreading any sort of conversation they might get into.

Reese said nothing, though. He didn't complain either, although Freddy could see that he was clearly in pain and that the long walk was more of a struggle than he likely would have admitted. He developed a slight limp as they grew closer to the house and he kept testing his right shoulder with a wince.

It was only as they neared the gravel drive that looped past the front door that Freddy scolded himself for spending so much of the walk looking at Reese, noting his body, and speculating how he must be feeling. He snapped his eyes forward at once when it hit him. Damn Reese for being so much of a temptation. He should have been repulsed by him after the way he'd so completely undermined him. He shouldn't have cared one whit whether the high-handed bastard was in pain or not. He deserved to feel as much pain as Freddy felt in his soul. But that must have been the nature of the bargain they'd entered into. Reese had him by the balls in every way imaginable, and now he cared how the arse felt, even though he was still angry enough to give Reese another telling off if given half a chance.

"Good heavens, has something happened, my lord?" Taylor greeted them in the front hall, glancing rapidly

159

back and forth between Reese and Freddy, as though he wasn't certain from whom he took his orders anymore.

"Lord Howsden fell off a barn roof at the Owens farm," Freddy said, surprised that he managed to get the first word in.

"The doctor says I'm fine," Reese added as Taylor opened his mouth in shock, his eyes going wide with concern. "I just need rest." He paused. "And perhaps an aspirin tablet or two would not be remiss."

"Certainly, my lord," Taylor bowed to him and started back, like he would turn and run to fetch the moon for Reese if he asked for it. "I'll have Mrs. Ball prepare tea for you as well."

"Thank you, Taylor."

Reese had barely finished speaking and Freddy had already started to walk away—though he had no idea where he would go—when Bledsoe stepped into the front hall from the library, a bright grin on his face.

"Ah, there you are, gentlemen," he said, coming forward. He was dressed for travel, with his coat draped over his arm and his traveling bag in hand. "I'm glad I waited to depart until you returned."

"You're leaving already?" Freddy asked, striding forward to meet him. He may have had his plans swiped out from under him and his control of things with it, but he could still act as though he were the master of the house. For a few more days, at least.

"The papers are signed," Bledsoe said, "and there's nothing more I can do to advance the sale from Silverstone Castle. I need to return to London at once to begin the proper transfer of titles and funds."

"Thank you for your help, Mr. Bledsoe," Reese said, walking up behind Freddy and reaching to shake Bledsoe's hand.

Freddy's back went stiff at the sensation of Reese standing by his side, more command in his little finger than Freddy had in his entire body.

"The pleasure is all mine, my lord." Bledsoe took his hand with a smile. "I would expect the two of you are eager to return to London post haste as well, what with the election results soon to be announced."

"I don't know," Reese said with his usual charm. "I wouldn't mind idling away some time at Silverstone while Lord Herrington shows me the ropes of how the place is run." He sent a sideways glance to Freddy with just a hint of pleading.

Freddy cleared his throat. "I expect we'll be headed to London ourselves tomorrow," he said in a gruff voice. "If you will excuse me, gentlemen."

He bowed to both Bledsoe and Reese, then turned to march off, heading upstairs to his room. It wasn't the most gracious move he'd ever made, but he needed to be alone. He needed to think. He needed undisturbed silence to comprehend the tangle his life had become.

To his great surprise, Reese didn't try to follow him. More than that, he managed to make it to his room, wash up, change his clothes, and even take a short, restless nap, and Reese didn't once knock on his door or try to wheedle him into relenting from his coldness. Instead of bringing Freddy peace, his isolation only magnified his thoughts in his head.

He'd kissed Reese next to the barn, careless of who might have popped around a corner to see them. Anyone could have—

No, that wasn't why the kiss needled its way under his skin, like a thousand burrs he couldn't reach to brush away. He'd kissed Reese because he'd had to. His soul would have been shattered if anything had happened to him. The relief he felt when the doctor pronounced that Reese was relatively sound in body had been so palpable that he'd been tempted to kiss him again. And what did that make him? It had been so easy to keep his feelings for Reese in their place before they'd come to Silverstone Castle, before he'd broken the barriers between them and gone to bed with him. Reese was absolutely right when he said he still wanted him, but that only proved that Reese held all the cards now, that he had complete power in the situation.

A knock at the door shook him out of his restless thoughts and he sat up abruptly on the bed, heart racing.

"Who is it?" he called, both dreading and longing for it to be Reese.

"Hannah, my lord," the maid's voice came through the door. "Mrs. Ball sent me up with supper, since she didn't think you'd want to take it down in the dining room."

Freddy muttered curses to himself as he jumped off

the bed, glancing to the clock on his mantel as he rushed to the door. He'd slept for longer than he'd thought.

"Thank you, Hannah." He did an admirable job of pretending nothing at all was wrong as he let the maid in and took the tray from her, walking it to the small table in the corner of his room by himself.

"Mr. Taylor told me to say that Mr. Bledsoe made it off to London without a problem earlier," Hannah added.

"Give him my thanks as well," Freddy replied, hoping she didn't think he was being rude by hurrying her out of the room and shutting the door behind her.

Once she was gone, he turned to lean his back against the door and let out a breath. Damn the disappointment that coursed through him. He was a man. He shouldn't sulk just because the lover whom he was currently infuriated with hadn't been the one to bring him his supper.

"I'm going mad," he grumbled to himself as he crossed to his table and sat hard in the chair. Everything that had happened at Silverstone in the past two days was completely barmy.

That thought stayed with him as he removed the cover from his supper and took up his fork and knife, but it, and every other thought, were dashed from his brain when his door opened less than a minute later and Reese strode in, carrying his own supper tray on one arm, without even knocking.

"I beg your pardon," Freddy snapped at him, sitting straight, jaw clenched.

"You're not getting it," Reese said, closing and locking the door behind him.

Freddy swallowed hard and took in the sight of him. He'd changed out of his dusty clothes and now wore a robe. Freddy thanked God that the cuffs of pajamas poked out from the bottom and the sleeves and that Reese hadn't barged into his room naked. Reese carried his tray to the table, cleared a space as best he could with one hand, and set his tray down, all while Freddy gawped at him.

"What the devil are you doing?" Freddy asked, clenching his fork in his hand.

"Having supper with you," Reese explained without looking up at him as he sat in the chair across from Freddy's. He removed the cover from his own plates.

"Without knocking?"

"Without knocking," Reese confirmed. He set the silver domes that had covered both of their plates on the floor, clearing the space between them, then started eating.

Freddy stared at him, at the broad line of his shoulders and the grace in his arms, at his damp, tousled hair and the strong lines of his face, and at the way his mouth moved as he ate. Everything about him appeared utterly casual, but Freddy could also see the tension in the way Reese sat. By all accounts, Reese was still in some degree of pain. And Freddy could feel the way he was holding his breath, as though praying his arrogant move would work.

And dammit, but it was working. Freddy's heart thumped faster and his prick refused to be still. It was all he could do to pretend he was as much at ease as Reese was pretending and to eat food that he barely had the spare attention to notice.

"Are you feeling better?" he asked, taking a bite of roast.

"Yes," Reese said. "The doctor was right about his rest cure. And aspirin works wonders."

Freddy grunted in reply, trying to focus on eating.

"And you?" Reese asked. Anyone observing them from the outside would see only two friends devouring a meal together after a trying day.

"I'm fine," Freddy snapped. "I wasn't the one who fell."

"Weren't you?"

Freddy clenched his jaw and glanced up. He let a few beats pass before sighing and saying, "If you have something to say, just say it."

Without hesitating, Reese said, "I've loved you since university. Almost from the first moment I met you. You were—you are—the most handsome man I've ever met."

Freddy laughed without humor as he continued to chew. "Just another pretty face," he grumbled to himself after swallowing and reached for the wine Mrs. Ball had so cleverly sent up with the food.

"No," Reese insisted, his patience seeming to wear thin. "More than just a pretty face."

"What, a pretty arse too?" Freddy took a gulp of his

wine.

Reese huffed a breath and put his knife and fork down. "Stop being deliberately irritating, Freddy. It's not like you at all."

"Who knows what I'm like, now that I've got your dog collar tight around my neck?"

"Stop it." Reese raised his voice. A deep frown etched his brow. "I'm sorry I bought Silverstone without consulting you. But as I am trying to tell you, I've loved you for more than a decade. I love you for your strength and your kindness. I've admired the way you've fought with everything you have to save what belongs to your family, in spite of the mess your father made of it. I love you because of that. You are a thousand times stronger than I will ever be."

Freddy ached to find some sort of snappy reply, but nothing came to mind. Reese was right, that sort of behavior wasn't him, much though he wished it were at that moment. The result was that he had absolutely nothing to say and no way to defend himself.

"I thought that by stepping in to help, I could finally express my love in a way that would truly matter," Reese went on.

Freddy's heart was in serious danger of softening, but he wasn't ready to let go of the frustration and helplessness raging through him yet.

He shifted in his chair, putting his wine glass down and staring hard at Reese. "You've loved me since university," he said, stating fact.

"Yes," Reese answered.

"But you've had other lovers since then." His intent was to aim low in his attack, but his heart squeezed in pain at the very thought.

Reese sighed and let his shoulders drop. "Yes, I have," he answered quietly.

"In spite of loving me." Freddy stared hard at him.

Reese met his stare and held it. "I was convinced for too long that my love would always be unrequited."

A frown pinched Freddy's brow. Had Reese not known what he was? Didn't all men like them automatically know each other on sight?

Instead of asking that, he said, "So you warmed your bed with other men until you figured it out?"

"Yes," Reese answered, still staring hard at him.

"Without being in love with any of them."

"Not the way I love you."

Freddy pursed his lips, trying to hold onto the illusion that he was merely angry and not desperately curious to know how love and lust worked. It was embarrassing that he'd been so much of an innocent about things for so long.

He blinked as an uncomfortable thought came to him. "Sebastian, as in Lord Gregory," he said, chest squeezing. "Were the two of you lovers?"

Reese's steadiness faltered. "Yes," he answered, glancing down for a moment.

"Was that why he was at Albany Court before I

arrived?" Freddy's voice was suddenly loud, even to his own ears. "For a tumble?"

"No." Reese met his eyes again. "What was between Sebastian and I was years ago."

"So, what was between the two of you?" Freddy's heart thumped faster.

Reese sighed and sat back, shaking his head. "Pleasure, Freddy. That was what was between the two of us. Fun. We knew what each other liked and enjoyed giving it. That's what people do, men and women. And don't go turning all red on me, like some prudish mama."

"I am not—" Reese clamped his mouth shut. His face was as hot as a furnace, and he had to admit that Reese had shocked his sensibilities.

"Sex is fun, Freddy, no matter who you're with. As long as everyone is willing and eager, it's a fine way to spend an evening. Better than a night at the opera." A grin tugged at the corner of his mouth. "But love is a different thing entirely, and sex with someone you love...."

Freddy swallowed, irritated to find himself leaning forward, eager to hear how Reese would end the sentence. "What?" he asked at last, when no answer came. "What is sex with someone you love?"

Reese crossed his arms. "I've only had it once, so I hardly consider myself an expert." His gaze bored relentlessly into Freddy's.

The answer threw Freddy off balance. He refused to look away from the challenge in Reese's eyes, but his mind was a complete blank. As desperate as he was for a biting reply, his thoughts were nothing but a buzz while his heart pounded madly in his ears.

In the end, he couldn't think of anything to do but to finish his supper, though he still barely had a clue what he was eating. Reese followed suit, and within seconds, the only sounds in the room were the clinks of silver cutlery against china plates.

Gradually, as the silence lengthened, the stark tension between them began to mellow to something new and unfamiliar, something that hung in the air like a whisper. Freddy's shoulders unbunched, and he realized that Mrs. Ball had actually outdone herself in preparing the meal. The fire in his grate was just the thing to take the slight chill out of the air as the sky darkened. Slowly, Freddy's limbs grew heavier, and it became harder to keep his eyes fully open. The past two days had been taxing in the extreme, and there could only be more to come.

At last, he bent sideways to fetch the cover for his tray and clapped it over the remains of his supper. He stood and stepped away from the table.

"We'll have to head to London tomorrow," he said as Reese reached for the cover of his own tray. "Sale aside, you know Diana and the rest of the May Flowers will want us to support them in everything surrounding the election. And you still have guests."

"You're right," Reese said with a sigh, standing and picking up his tray. "I'm sure Henry is doing an admirable job of entertaining Mr. Garrett and the incomparable Lenore—" he sent a knowing grin Freddy's way, and Freddy found himself returning the grin for Lenore's sake, "—but I should be there."

Freddy unlocked the door, opened it to peek out into the hall, and when he saw the passage was empty, he stepped back, holding it open for Reese. As Reese walked into the hall with his tray, Freddy returned to the table to fetch his own tray. Who knew what Taylor would think of him leaving his tray in the hall, as if Silverstone were a hotel, but once he shut his door for the night, he didn't want anyone to disturb him for any reason.

Which was why it came as a complete shock that, after leaving his tray in front of his own door, Reese marched straight back into Freddy's room.

"What are you doing?" Freddy asked, his heart racing all over again.

Before he answered, Reese plucked Freddy's tray from his hands and set it in the hall. He then shut Freddy's door, turned the lock, then undid the tie of his robe. "What does it look like I'm doing?" he answered at last. "I'm going to bed." He shrugged out of his robe and moved to toss it over the back of the chair he'd used at the table, then walked to the bed.

Freddy gaped at him as he tossed a few, decorative pillows aside and pulled back the bedcovers. "I have no intention of letting you fuck me tonight," he said at last, even though the thought of everything they'd done the day before suddenly loomed large in his mind.

"Freddy," Reese said in a weary voice as he climbed into bed and arranged a stack of pillows behind him. "I fell off a roof today. I ache in more places than I can name. I'm in no shape for carnal gymnastics this evening."

Freddy scowled at the disappointment that pulsed through him. "Then what are you doing?" he asked.

"Dammit, man, you are too full of questions tonight," Reese snapped, reaching for the bedcovers and snuggling down. When Freddy did nothing but stand there and stare at him, he went on with, "I don't want to fuck you tonight, but my day has not gone at all as I thought it would, I'm physically and mentally exhausted, I'm in pain, and I would very much like to sleep with you. Sleep."

Freddy's mouth dropped open, but no words came out. He shifted his weight, studying the sight of Reese against the pillows of his bed. It was somehow even more intimate than the way he'd splayed his naked body across the coverlet the day before.

"Are you coming or not?" Reese asked, his eyes closed.

"I—" Every nerve in Freddy's body prickled. Delicious flickers of arousal swirled in him in spite of the fact that he knew it was not the time. Something about Reese looked vulnerable, actually vulnerable, as he pretended to be asleep. It was even more irresistible than the fieriest kiss.

Freddy said nothing, but he shrugged out of his jacket

and went to work removing the rest of his clothes. Part of him wondered what it would be like to climb into bed naked and to surprise Reese, but a deeper part of him wanted to experience the ordinary. He took his clothes to the wardrobe and put on his pajamas instead. He even brushed his teeth before creeping uncertainly to the bed and climbing in on the opposite side from Reese.

"Not like that," Reese said in a groggy voice as Freddy started to settle in on his side. "Turn toward me."

Freddy hesitated, wondering if Reese had changed his mind about sex, then shifted to his side facing Reese. Reese wriggled backward until Freddy couldn't help but close his arms around him as their bodies fit together.

"There," Reese said, letting out a satisfied sigh and adjusting the bedcovers over the two of them and the pillow under his head. "That's better."

He didn't make a single comment about the erection that Freddy couldn't avoid poking him in the back. He just snuggled deeper into bed and let out a long, satisfied breath.

It took Freddy several more minutes to slowly adjust himself so that the situation was comfortable. Once he found exactly the right position, it dawned on him that nothing had ever been more comfortable in his life. He was warm, cozy, and, in spite of the sting of betrayal that still pulsed within him, content. The last thing he remembered thinking was that there was no way he would possibly be able to fall asleep entwined with Reese the way he was, but sleep took him anyhow.

CHAPTER 13

*R*eese's body still ached and his head throbbed just a bit from his fall as the train he and Freddy had taken to London rolled into St. Pancras Station the following morning. But balanced against the fact that he'd had the best night's sleep he'd managed in years with Freddy's arms around him, it was a burden he could bear.

Slightly less bearable was the way Freddy barely spoke to him from the time he shook him awake before dawn and ordered him back across the hall to his own room to avoid suspicion from the servants, to the moment they took their seats on the train. Freddy had been quiet at breakfast, frowned more than smiled as they packed up and traveled to the Bedford train station, and was nearly silent on the entire train journey to London.

"You're more than welcome to stay at Howsden House," Reese finally burst, eager for Freddy to stay with

173

him, as the train slowed. "There's plenty of room. The marchioness's chamber has been vacant for all these years now, and even though it adjoins my dressing room, I don't think anyone would bat an eyelash if—"

"Henrietta and Fergus have returned from Ireland for the election," Freddy cut him off, standing to fetch his bag from the rack above them as the train lurched to a stop. "I'm eager to catch up with them."

Reese let out a tight breath and watched Freddy, disappointment squeezing his heart. Freddy had been so distant with him during the journey that anyone would think they were riding in a crowded third-class car instead of a private, first-class one.

Reese stood, reaching for his bag, but as soon as he moved it to the seat, he rested a hand on Freddy's shoulder. "I don't want us to part like this."

"Like what?" Freddy blinked at him, doing a poor job of keeping his expression neutral.

"We know where we've been and we know where we're going," he said, cryptic, but hopefully clear enough for Freddy to catch his meaning.

"Do we know?" Freddy asked, scooting toward the compartment door.

"Yes," Reese said without hesitation, meeting and holding Freddy's eyes.

"And what if I don't want to go there?" Freddy did an unfortunately good job of holding his own.

"You do, darling," Reese said, keeping his voice low. He brushed the side of Freddy's face with his fingers, darting a sidelong glance to the compartment window to make certain the disembarking passengers rushing past weren't spying on them. "I could feel it in the way you held me last night and I can feel it now."

For one moment, tension radiated off of Freddy and his jaw was hard. Then he blew out a breath and his shoulders sank. "I'm too tired to face this right now, Reese. I just want to go home to my sister. And I still can't shake the feeling that my...*company* is part of the bargain for Silverstone's salvation. I'm just not ready for it."

Reese opened his mouth and swayed forward, but before he could do or say anything, Freddy turned the handle on their compartment door and stepped down onto the platform.

Reese followed, but there wasn't a damned thing he could do from the moment his feet hit the ground.

"There you two are," Lenore said as she marched down the platform to greet them both with hugs and kisses to the cheek that made half the passengers rushing around the station raise their eyebrows in shock. "Home at last. Or at least back with your friends at last."

"Lenore, what are you doing here?" Reese laughed as he stood back to survey her in a brand-new gown of the latest style, a dazzling hat laden with ostrich feathers covering her dark hair. "How did they let you onto the platform without a ticket?"

"I told the porter I was coming to meet friends," she said, hooking one arm through Reese's and one through

Freddy's to walk between them back to the heart of the station. "And I refused to take no for an answer."

Reese saw just what that meant as they passed the porter taking tickets at the end of the platform. The man glared at Lenore, then sent censorious looks to Reese and Freddy that warned them to keep their woman in check. Heaven only knew what thoughts hid behind the man's look.

"So, how was the journey?" Lenore asked, sending a mischievous look between Reese and Freddy, as though juicy gossip was to be had.

Freddy immediately answered, "Reese bought Silverstone Castle right out from under me without so much as a by your leave," without a smile.

Lenore smiled as she steered them toward Henry, Ellie, and Mr. Garrett, who stood near a newsstand by the station's exit discussing something with serious faces. "I thought he might do that."

Freddy nearly missed a step as he whipped to stare at Lenore. "You did?"

Lenore hummed in assent and nodded. "Reese and I had a little conversation to that effect in York. Right before we happened upon the fair. Perhaps I could take credit for inspiring him with the idea?" Her smile widened.

Freddy's frown darkened into a scowl and he released Lenore's arm. "Excuse me," he said in a tense voice. "I need to hire a hack to take me to Henrietta's house."

Without a further goodbye, he marched off at a

clipped pace, dodging people to leave the train station as fast as possible.

Lenore let out a surprised breath, her smile fading. "It would appear that things did not go according to plan."

"Oh, they went according to plan, all right," Reese said, unable to keep the frustration out of his voice. "If the plan was to enrage Freddy by destroying his pride and robbing him of the ability to deal with his problems on his own, as he puts it." He couldn't possibly explain the sexual aspect of the whole muddle to a woman, so the pride angle would have to do.

And yet, Lenore studied him with a shrewdness in her eyes that gave Reese the uncomfortable feeling she knew the whole story.

"And how did the two of you get along while you were alone together?" she asked pointedly, deepening Reese's suspicion that she knew all.

She couldn't have been more than twenty, she was a dollar princess from a ranch in America's wild west, she had the subtlety of a clarion blast, and yet, Reese was suddenly consumed by an urge to make her his confidant in all things.

"Mixed results," he said, darting glances from side to side to be sure no one was listening. Henry, Ellie, and Mr. Garrett noticed him and stopped their discussion to come his way. "I thought we were getting somewhere, we did get somewhere, but the sale dashed all that to pieces."

He held his breath. If Lenore truly did know which

way the wind was blowing, his words would be informative. If she was innocent, they would just confuse her. He risked a peek at her and was alarmed to find sympathy in her eyes.

He didn't have a chance to pursue the matter, though.

"Welcome home, brother," Henry said, meeting him and Lenore near the exit and proceeding out to the street with them, Ellie on his arm and Mr. Garrett striding at his side.

"Welcome home, Reese." Ellie stepped away from Henry long enough to kiss Reese's cheek before returning to Henry's side.

Henry grinned. "It seems far too right and natural for us to be welcoming you home when we're in London, even though we haven't lived here for ages."

"I can assure you, I am beyond grateful to have you here at the moment," Reese said, his smile as casual as he could make it.

It was clear Henry knew there was something else afoot, though. They walked down the street a bit to where the Howsden family carriage was parked, piling easily inside. Reese searched for Freddy, but he must have found a cab and departed already. Conversation on the way to Howsden House was mostly about the sale in technical terms. Henry only asked once how Freddy took the whole thing, and when Reese's answer was short, he didn't pursue the matter.

At least until the two of them were alone in Reese's

private study a few hours later, after Reese was settled and had given Harry the hugs and kisses he deserved before sending him back up to the nursery with Henry and Ellie's children.

"I saw the way Freddy broke away from you as you came off the platform," Henry said as he helped himself to a brandy and poured one for Reese as well. He handed the tumbler to Reese with a look that demanded the rest of the story.

Reese took the glass and rubbed his free hand over his face, his muscles still aching, before downing a large gulp of burning liquid. "I thought he would be pleased," he said with a sigh, then finished the glass. So what if he ended up sloshed before supper? It might be a relief.

"I take it he wasn't?" Henry raised one eyebrow, moving to the sofa and gesturing for Reese to sit.

"He found the gesture emasculating," Reese said, unsure whether he wanted to rehash every aspect of his misstep. He flopped on to the sofa and studied Henry for a moment. He couldn't blame it on the alcohol that he'd just swallowed, but he charged ahead anyhow with, "I probably shouldn't have slept with him before telling him about the purchase."

Henry's eyebrows flew up and he choked on his sip of brandy. "Was that...did you...had you ever...."

Reese shook his head. "That was the first time. It might be the last time too." He refused to believe that, though. Not after the way Freddy had been so tender with him the night before. And he'd been sporting a cock-stand as hard as an oak when he'd first climbed into bed. The problem between them wasn't physical at all.

He reached for the newspaper Henry had brought from the train station as a desperate means of distraction, but Henry kept talking as he leafed through it.

"So you've made progress, then?" he asked.

"One step forward, two steps back," Reese sighed, glancing past news about the election and the Empire's financial situation and only barely seeing it.

"But you did take a step forward," Henry pressed on. "Toward what I know full well you've wanted for ages now."

"Wanted, had, and lost," Reese said. He had no idea whether his brother was merely humoring him while secretly condemning him or whether Henry genuinely wanted him to be happy, no matter how perverse that happiness was.

"You can get him back again," Henry went on after a small pause. Reese dropped the edge of the newspaper to raise an eyebrow at him. Henry shrugged and continued with, "I've watched the two of you interact. He cares for you. And you were telling me how much you cared about him years ago." He shrugged again, sat back in his seat, and raised his glass to his lips. "Ellie and I fight sometimes. And then we make up. The making up is the best part." He grinned before downing his brandy.

Longing squeezed Reese's chest. Fantasies of him and Freddy making up flashed powerfully through his mind, making him far hotter than he wanted to be around his brother. He cleared his throat and focused on the newspaper instead.

"I can only hope and pray that Freddy will extract his head from his arse and realize that buying Silverstone Castle was the best thing that either of us—"

He stopped dead, his words freezing on his tongue and his heart dropping to his stomach. The words jumped out from the page of the newspaper like a slap to his face. "Earl of Gregory Exposed as Sodomite."

Reese swallowed hard, his back going straight. He raced through the article, his eyes going wide.

"Information of a reliable sort has been given to this paper as to the disgusting and perverse proclivities of one Sebastian Stone, Earl of Gregory. Tales of debauchery and wickedness of the most evil kind have been brought to light, including photographic evidence that has made this reporter retch at its explicitness. Charges of Gross Indecency will most certainly be brought against Lord Gregory, and this paper expects that an entire cesspool will be revealed as the matter is investigated. Readers of this paper are advised to strike Lord Gregory from their list of acquaintances with all due haste."

"Shit," Reese hissed, his hands beginning to shake. It was exactly what Sebastian had fretted about when he'd come to Albany Court to ask his advice about a strange encounter he'd had with a man threatening blackmail. Sebastian had been terrified, but Reese had advised him not to take the matter seriously and certainly not to give in to the blackmailer's demands. "Shit, shit, shit."

"What is it?" Henry asked, leaning forward.

Reese slapped the paper shut, throwing it aside. He sprang up from the sofa and crossed to pour himself another, large brandy.

"Reese, you're worrying me." Henry got up to follow him.

Reese downed a gulp of brandy and spent a moment coughing before answering. "A friend of mine was just dragged out into the sunlight," he said, unsure how to even begin to explain the implications. "It will ruin him."

Henry reached for Reese's arm. "Will it affect you?" He knew exactly the question he was asking.

Reese drew in a breath and held it, thinking. At last, he blew out the breath. "I don't know. I've been careful. But then, we're all careful. One could argue that every man Sebastian has ever befriended, or even talked to, could be in danger right now, whether they're like us or not. The press is horrific, and public opinion is not exactly in our favor."

"What can you do to protect yourself?" Henry asked.

Reese winced. The obvious answer was to not have anything to do with Sebastian and to keep a low profile until the whole thing blew over, but he hated it.

"I don't know," he answered instead, taking another swig of brandy. "I might not have to do anything. This could just be a tempest in a teapot. We can only wait and see."

Henry thumped his back, leaving his hand there for a moment. "I'll do whatever I can to support you," he said.

Between the alcohol, the mess with Freddy, and his concern for Sebastian, Reese was near tears in an instant. "Thank you," he said, putting down his glass so he could hug his brother. "I may need to take advantage of that support soon."

"HENRIETTA, YOU HAVE NO IDEA HOW HAPPY I AM TO see you," Freddy said, not caring that his voice was too thick with emotion to be manly. He didn't care if Fergus or Dr. Townsend—who had moved in to Tavistock House and was currently pushing Fergus to try out a pair of special crutches he'd built—were in the room either. He ran into his sister's arms and hugged her for all he was worth. "It's been a terrible last few days."

As soon as the words were spoken, he wondered if they were a lie. They hadn't been all terrible. They'd been downright wonderful before they fell apart. And he still couldn't shake the oddly peaceful feeling of rightness sleeping in the same bed with Reese the night before had given him, in spite of his anger. But none of that outweighed the vise of humiliation and heartbreak he felt trapped in.

"I missed you too," Henrietta said, hugging him back with all the sisterly affection he needed and more. "I take it something happened," she whispered in his ear as they embraced so that neither Fergus nor Townsend could hear.

"Too much to recount," he whispered back. "And I

wouldn't want to shock your sensibilities by repeating it all."

He tried to move away, but Henrietta continued to cling to him, her arms suddenly as strong as iron. "Did he make you do something you didn't want to do?" she asked.

Yes, frankly, he had. He'd made him sign away his heritage and his pride. But that was clearly not what Henrietta was thinking.

"No," he whispered. She let him go, but he stuck fast by her side, turning his back and hers on Fergus and Townsend so they still couldn't hear. "Quite the contrary. He helped me to do something I think I might have wanted to do for a long time."

"Oh?" Her face lit with surprise and perhaps even delight.

"And then he purchased Silverstone Castle as payment," he finished.

Henrietta stared at him, mouth open in shock, blinking rapidly. Color flooded her face and she shook her head. "He bought Silverstone because you...." She pressed her mouth closed instead of finishing the sentence, fury lighting her eyes. "Like you are a common whore?"

Her words stung, which shocked Freddy. "No, I don't think it was like that precisely," he rushed to say. Though hadn't he spent hours railing at Reese with exactly the same argument? Hearing it come from someone else changed everything, though. And if he were honest, he didn't want to think about what he and Reese had done as prostitution. "He thinks he's done me a favor by saving the place."

"And requiring...favors in return?" Henrietta's anger only seemed to be growing.

Freddy winced and rubbed a hand over his face. "It wasn't like that."

"Then what was it like?" Henrietta asked, crossing her arms.

"The two of you seem awfully angry for a brother and sister reunited," Fergus called from across the room.

Freddy's blood ran cold—as if Fergus's words meant he could see right through to everything that was actually going on—and he and Henrietta both snapped to face him. Freddy's brow shot up. Instead of lounging in his chair, Fergus stood. He was slightly hunched, as his arms were fastened into the odd crutches Townsend had made for him, but the poles of the crutches were long enough that Fergus could stand upright on his own power.

"Look at you," Henrietta said in wonder, abandoning Freddy to go to Fergus. She paused in front of him, clapping her hands over her heart and taking in the sight.

"Don't rejoice and throw a party yet," Fergus said with a rakish grin, his one eye twinkling. "All I can do is stand here."

"But once you learn the swing maneuver I showed you, you should be able to propel yourself across any room with ease," Townsend said, an almost childlike delight in his eyes.

"I'm not going to bloody well swing myself around a room like a monkey," Fergus replied in a particularly salty Irish accent.

"I think you will find your mobility in tight places greatly improved by this innovation," Townsend insisted. "We gave it quite a few trial runs at Campbell House, and even Lady Natalia mastered the necessary motions with ease."

Freddy's first instinct was to murmur, "I just bet Lady Natalia mastered the necessary motions," but as soon as he realized it was Reese he imagined making the ribald joke to, his heart sank. He would have given anything for the old ease and camaraderie he and Reese had enjoyed to be back again. It just didn't seem possible that they would ever be able to be so at ease with each other now.

"All right, damn you," Fergus grumbled. He screwed up his face in concentration, then moved the crutches forward, balancing momentarily on his useless legs. When he shifted his weight to the crutches, he was able to drag his body forward. "There," he said. "I've taken a step. Are you happy?"

"Immensely," Henrietta said, kissing his cheek. "And if you keep working at it, perhaps you'll be able to make your way up stairs on your own instead of needing someone to carry you."

Fergus sent her a look that could have melted all the candles in the room. They obviously had some sort of heated, inside joke about stairs. But the more his sister and Fergus flirted with each other, the heavier Freddy's heart grew. Dammit, but he wanted to have that sort of easiness with Reese. He wanted to be able to flirt with him and make suggestive jokes. He wanted to steal kisses and touches when no one was looking. He wanted to punch Reese in his gorgeous face as well, but that didn't cool the ardor that he'd discovered at Silverstone.

"So what were the two of you whispering about like conspirators?" Fergus asked, taking a few more awkward steps toward Freddy.

"Good, excellent," Townsend said, oblivious to anything but his patient.

"Silverstone Castle has been sold," Henrietta announced, glancing to Freddy for approval.

"It has?" Fergus smiled from Henrietta to Freddy. "That's a relief."

"Reese bought it," Freddy said, jaw clenched. "Without consulting me about whether he should first."

"Ah," Fergus said. Freddy was grateful that the single syllable contained the sympathy of understanding. "Still, at least a friend will own it now instead of some stranger."

"He wants me to continue living there and managing it. With his help," he added as a fresh wave of humiliation washed over him. In all the fuss of fractured romance, he'd completely forgotten that offer to help restore Silverstone's fortunes with correct management. It would be just another area where Reese would dominate him and crush his authority in the eyes of those who had known him since he was a boy.

"I see," Fergus said, coming closer to Freddy still, Henrietta walking at his side and looking like she would catch him if he fell. Fergus shot a glance to Townsend before lowering his voice a note and saying, "I definitely see."

Freddy and Henrietta also glanced at Townsend, who was blissfully ignorant of the fact that he was preventing a much more intimate conversation. The man's concentration was elsewhere. He rushed forward, dropping to a crouch and studying the crutches. "I think I could adjust the height a bit to make it more comfortable."

Fergus exchanged a glance with Freddy. "What are you going to do about the situation?" he asked, his brow arching above his eyepatch.

Freddy shrugged. "I have no choice but to let the sale go through. It's already gone through. Or, at least, the papers have all been signed. As for the rest of it...." He sighed and rubbed his face. "I'm in his debt."

He couldn't say more, not with Townsend tinkering about between the three of them. The way he'd grasped the truth of the situation at the breakfast table a few days ago didn't give Freddy confidence he would be as understanding as the rest of his friends. Fergus and Henrietta had at least a glimmer of understanding.

"I'm furious with him for...imposing on you like that," Henrietta said at last, darting a glance to Townsend. "It's unconscionable."

"It wasn't entirely like that," Freddy said, aching to be

able to talk more freely and dreading the possibility at the same time.

"Reese isn't the tyrannical sort," Fergus said slowly, choosing his words carefully. "And I know he...considers you to be his *very best friend*." He had to settle for a telling look instead of blabbing outright that Reese loved him.

"That hasn't changed." Freddy spoke delicately, anxious they'd said too much already. "And I still consider him to be my *very best friend*. I just don't like being backed into a corner."

Henrietta and Fergus exchanged wide-eyed looks.

Freddy puffed out a breath and quickly said, "That one wasn't a euphemism."

They relaxed as though relieved.

"There." Townsend stood, his oblivious grin still in place. "I've got a few ideas for improvements, but really, all it will take is practice to be dancing about in no time." He smiled at Henrietta and Freddy as well as Fergus.

An awkward crackle hung in the air between them. There was so much more Freddy wanted to say, but not with Townsend around.

"Perhaps you could give those crutches a try at the May Flowers rally tomorrow," Henrietta suggested. She glanced to Freddy. "It will be just the thing to get outside in the fresh air, around good company, and to make all your troubles seem lighter."

Freddy smiled at his sister, wanting to hug her again. "Maybe that would be just the thing."

"Perhaps your friends will be there so that you can discuss matters further with them," Henrietta added.

Freddy smirked at her. So that was her plan. Get him back together with Reese to sort things out. "Maybe."

"I'll be damned if I'll swing around in public without proper training on these things," Fergus said with a laugh. "I'll stick to the chair in public for now."

"But it would be such good practice," Townsend said.

"Later," Fergus snapped. "Now, help me figure out how to get out to the hall and up the stairs."

While Townsend spotted Fergus as he made his way out of the parlor and into the hall, Henrietta moved closer to Freddy, resting a hand on his arm.

"We'll sort this out," she said, full of just the sort of love Freddy needed to see. "And Silverstone Castle is in good hands."

"It is," Freddy admitted, sliding his arm around her. "I'm just not entirely certain whose hands it's in."

CHAPTER 14

"Friends, we are only days away from the announcement of the results of this election," Lady Diana spoke in a loud, clear voice, addressing the crowd that had come to the May Flowers's rally in St. James's Park. She went on in a grave voice. "We have all seen the newspaper reports and early projections of a Conservative Party win, therefore, now more than ever, it is vital that we band together to support the cause of the rights of women, specifically our right to vote."

Her words were followed by some cheers but just as many grumbling jeers from the men that had gathered in the park to watch what they must have seen as an amusing spectacle. Freddy glared at every one of the sneering, condescending men, convinced that women like Lady Diana and his sister would do a far better job than any man of not only voting, but running the country.

"A woman's right to suffrage is fundamental," Lady

Diana went on. "Just as the right of every working-class man to vote is fundamental."

"Hear, hear," Freddy called, adding his voice to those supporting the May Flowers.

One of the dismissive men standing nearby glanced to him, sniffing and curling his lip in disgust. The gesture was no doubt because of his support for Lady Diana, but Freddy instantly felt it as disgust over everything he now knew he was. He snapped his eyes forward to the dais where the May Flowers stood, his heart beating faster and sweat breaking out on his back. There was no possible way the man—or anyone else—could know who he was on the inside or what he'd done with Reese at Silverstone...could he? Was there some sort of mark on his forehead now, like Cain after being banished from Paradise, that told the world who he was? Was he standing in a certain effeminate way? He cleared his throat and snapped his back military straight.

"I don't know how I let you convince me to bring these things out in public." Fergus's grumble as he used Townsend's crutches to push himself out of his chair was just the distraction Freddy needed to remember there was more to the world than his fears.

"Do you need help?" he asked, against his better judgement, knowing how Fergus was, crossing to Fergus's side.

Henrietta stood on Fergus's other side, looking just as guilty for offering help to a proud man but just as determined to do so. Even Ricky looked as though he would catch Fergus if he fell, though to be fair, Ricky had his eye on Fergus's chair, as though he wanted to wheel himself around in it for fun.

"No, I do not need anyone's help," Fergus growled as he pushed himself to stand.

"See how easy that is?" Townsend was the only one of them who dove in to help without asking first. He adjusted Fergus's grip on the crutches and pushed his back straighter, correcting his posture.

"Will you stop your fussing, man?" Fergus snapped, doing everything Townsend gestured for him to do. "Half of St. James's Park is watching us, and I'd rather they watch the speeches."

He was right. Freddy glanced around, finding a dozen curious onlookers studying Fergus and whispering to themselves as they did. Fergus ignored them, but Freddy bristled at the idea of so many eyes on him. How did Reese and others like him do it? How could they casually stroll about in society with the sort of secret they carried without feeling like everyone knew? His predicament had been so much easier when he'd been able to deny the truth to himself.

"I would now like to call upon a very special guest speaker," Lady Diana said from the dais. "A woman of intelligence and standing from America. A woman who, in her home state of Wyoming, has been able to vote for her entire adult life. She will speak about the example of her home state and how beneficial the vote has been to women. Please allow me to introduce you to Miss Lenore Garrett."

Freddy's attention shifted back to the dais and his heart lifted a bit as Lenore marched up to the podium amidst anemic clapping, instantly taking charge with a smile and a saucy tilt of her chin.

"Ladies and gentlemen," she began with more confidence than Freddy could ever imagine having, "it is a great pleasure for me to speak to you today, and about something near and dear to my heart. And yes, it is true. At home in Wyoming, I, and every other woman, enjoy the full right to vote in elections that shape our communities. Unlike the ladies of so historical and important a place as Britain, I have a voice in my own destiny. And I am here today to tell you what that is like."

Freddy smiled in spite of himself. Leave it to Lenore to be a sheep marching into a den of wolves and ordering them all into line.

A moment later, his smile faded and his chest squeezed. If Lenore was there speaking, then Reese had to be in the crowd somewhere. He scanned the audience as covertly as he could, catching the eye of the dismissive man as he did. He forced himself to ignore the man's scornful look and to keep searching, but even scanning the crowd for Reese felt far too obvious now.

All of his own apprehensions vanished as soon as he spotted Reese standing with Henry, Ellie, and their children, and Mr. Garrett and Harry at the far side of the crowd. They'd parted so abruptly and under such uncomfortable circumstances the day before. He still didn't have the first clue what he wanted from Reese or what he wanted from himself. Well, he knew, he just wasn't certain he wanted to know. The bargain Reese had made for the salvation of Silverstone Castle still rankled him. But one look at Reese's pale, drawn face, the tension in his shoulders, and the way he seemed to have shrunk an inch and pulled into himself set Freddy's heart racing. Something was wrong.

"Ricky," he said as casually as he could, which wasn't very. "I see Harry over on the other side of the crowd. Shall we go say hello to him?"

"Yes!" Ricky leapt up from Fergus's chair, where he'd made himself at home. "Yes, please. Mama, can I go see Harry?"

Henrietta smiled at Ricky, then looked knowingly at Freddy. "Certainly, darling," she said, arching one brow at Freddy.

Freddy acknowledged her teasing expression with a flat look, then took Ricky's hand and proceeded around the edge of the crowd to him.

"And I can assure you," Lenore spoke on as they wove and dodged their way through the increasingly agitated crowd, "the participation of women in the political life of Wyoming has only added to the vibrancy and richness of our Western culture."

Freddy wished he could give Lenore more of his attention. When he glanced her way as he and Ricky circled the crowd, she spotted them and smiled briefly before roaring on. A few bystanders near him glanced to see whom she had acknowledged, which only added to Freddy's dread at being singled out.

His nerves were raw by the time he reached Reese's group at the other end of the crowd.

"Hiya, Harry." Ricky rushed forward to his mate, banishing all awkwardness at their approach. "Wanna play?"

"Can we, Papa?" Harry asked, twisting to Reese.

"Of course you can," Reese said. "But stay within sight."

The boys rushed off at a speed only young boys could manage, taking the oldest of Henry and Ellie's children with them, and making a bee-line for the pond and its waterfowl. Freddy smiled as he watched them go, but the smile was all an act. As soon as he turned back to Reese, his smile vanished and the world seemed to squeeze in to include only the two of them.

"Is something wrong?" he asked, inching closer to Reese and extending a hand. He caught himself a moment later, pulling back and clearing his throat. "Forgive me. Good morning, Henry, Lady Howsden, Mr. Garrett."

Ellie laughed. "I will never get used to being addressed as 'Lady Howsden'. Back home, I'm just Mrs. Howsden." She stepped forward to greet Freddy with a surprising kiss on the cheek, as though they were family.

Mr. Garrett shook his hand in a more usual greeting, but even though he shook hands as well, Henry looked far graver than the others. "I was hoping you'd show up," he said, darting a quick glance to Reese.

Something was definitely wrong. But how could it be? They'd parted ways less than twenty-four hours before. That wasn't nearly enough time for the world to get wind of the scandal of their attachment and to ruin lives.

"It's nothing," Reese said with a shrug, stepping forward to shake Freddy's hand. His grip was as tight as iron, too tight. He shot a glance at Ellie and Mr. Garrett before letting Freddy's hand go and pretending to be fascinated by what Lenore was saying.

Freddy's heart pounded so hard against his ribs it made his head swim. He shifted to stand easily by Reese's side, smiling at Lenore the way he knew he should. "She's quite the public speaker," he said, glancing to Mr. Garrett.

"Lenore has never been shy in a crowd," Mr. Garrett said.

"Why, in America already, there are groups of women forming to fight against the injustice of disenfranchisement," Lenore was saying, pounding a fist on the podium as she did. The crowd was completely under her spell. "Those groups are forming here in England as well."

Freddy inched closer to Reese. "What's wrong? You weren't like this when we parted yesterday."

Reese sucked in a breath and leaned toward him. "I've had some disturbing news," he whispered.

Both of them kept their eyes on Lenore, pretending to comment on what she was saying.

"Is it anything I can help with?" Freddy asked.

Reese glanced sideways at him. "I'm surprise you would ask after the way you stormed off yesterday."

Freddy let out a tense breath. "Just because I'm furious with you doesn't mean you aren't my friend. And if you're in some sort of a bind...." He let the sentence go as the audience burst into applause.

Lenore took a bow as though she'd completed a performance as Lady Macbeth, then walked to the side of the dais and descended. She held her head high as she made her way through the crowd, pausing here and there to accept congratulations from some of the ladies in the crowd. Lady Diana took to the podium to announce the next speaker, but Freddy pitied whoever would have to speak after Lenore.

As soon as Lenore reached them, accepted her father's kiss on the cheek for a job well done, then moved to stand with Reese and Freddy, she said, "Thank God you're here, Freddy. Maybe you can get Reese to tell me what's had him so jumpy this morning."

Freddy blinked at her bluntness.

Reese lost another shade of color from his cheeks. "Lenore, please. I told you nothing is the matter," he said without his usual restraint.

"And I said that I don't believe that for a moment." She glanced to Freddy, as though he could do something about it.

It was the oddest moment Freddy could have imagined. Reese, who was usually so calm and in command of things, was as anxious as Freddy had ever seen him. Lenore stood with her arms crossed, as if demanding he make things right. The fact that she was looking to him for leadership, him and not Reese, felt as though they'd stepped through Alice's looking glass.

Freddy stood taller and glanced around for a quieter area. He spotted Ricky, Harry, and little Edgar by the edge of the pond throwing stones into the water. "I think it would be wise for us to make certain the boys aren't throwing their stones at the ducks," he said with a significant look for both of his friends.

"Yes." Lenore caught on immediately. "Papa, we're going to check on the boys," she told Mr. Garrett before sweeping in between Freddy and Reese and catching both of their arms to whisk them off.

"Best of luck with that," Henry called after them with a wry grin.

They made it well away from the crowd and managed to look as though they really were there to mind the children before Lenore came right out with, "Now, Reese, tell us what has you in such a tizzy."

Reese's mouth dropped open and he floundered for a moment before saying, "It really isn't anything you need to concern yourself with."

Freddy agreed. Lenore had done them the favor of maneuvering them into a position where they could talk more freely, but now he wanted to face the situation with

Reese privately. He had no idea how to get rid of her, though. "Perhaps you could wrangle the boys and keep them from falling in the water?" he suggested.

"I can't help you work through your problems if you don't tell me what they are," Lenore said, looking like a particularly fierce governess.

"Lenore, as much as I appreciate your concern—" Reese began.

"This is about that article in The Mail, about your friend, Lord Gregory, isn't it?" she cut him off.

Reese's jaw dropped open in surprise, but not denial. Freddy's gut clenched with a fit of jealousy so strong that it embarrassed him. Reese had said that whole thing was in the past, which was the cause of the embarrassment, but that didn't calm Freddy's jealousy at all.

Once the initial rush of emotion passed, Freddy sucked in a breath and frowned. More pieces fit together in his mind, and he didn't like the picture they were forming. "What article about Lord Gregory?"

Reese studied Lenore for a long moment, then turned a serious frown on Freddy. "Sebastian's business has been dragged out into public," he said in a barely audible voice. "He was exposed in the paper yesterday."

Freddy's gut clenched. He didn't need any further explanation. Panic pressed down on him. "And...and what about it?" he stammered, not knowing what else to say. He thought of the dismissive man, the way it suddenly felt as though everyone around him knew the truth.

"I don't know," Reese admitted with a painful shrug. "You know he came up to Albany Court last week because he was afraid someone was nosing around in his business."

"I met him," Lenore said. "He was a charming gentleman."

The full story fell into place at once in Freddy's mind. "That's why he was so anxious at the train station when I first reached St. Albans. He knew this was coming." He paused. "Where is he now?"

"I don't know," Reese said. "He was—" His words dried up and he clamped his mouth shut, suddenly straightening.

A moment later, Freddy saw why. A portly, middle-aged man in a bowler hat was striding toward them, some sort of large envelope in his hand. Freddy instantly snapped straight as well, and Lenore followed suit. The three of them must have looked like conspirators plotting as they huddled together, judging by the smug look on the man's face.

"Lord Howsden?" the man asked, marching straight up to Reese, as bold as brass.

"Yes?" Reese assumed the most imperious manner Freddy had ever seen from him.

The man either didn't care or didn't have the time to follow normal standards of deference toward the aristocracy. He handed Reese his envelope, his grin growing even more smug.

"What's this?" Reese asked, taking it gingerly.

The man merely chuckled and took a step back. "There's information in there about how to contact me."

Freddy's heart raced, even though the man barely acknowledged him as he took a large step back, then turned and strode off, as though on his way to tea with the queen. There was something decidedly sinister about him, something that set Freddy's teeth on edge.

"What's in the envelope?" Lenore asked as the three of them shifted back into their huddle.

Reese shrugged and shook his head, working the fastening of the envelope open and reaching inside.

He drew out three, large photographs and a piece of paper. At the barest glimpse of the first photograph, Freddy gasped so hard he thought his lungs would implode. It was a photograph of Reese and Sebastian in an extraordinarily compromised position. More than compromised, the photograph was pornographic. As were the other two, though Freddy only caught the barest glimpse of them before Lenore wrenched them out of Reese's hands.

"Good Lord," she exclaimed, her eyes going wide. "These leave nothing at all to the imagination. I mean, I've heard of how it's done, but I've never actually seen a visual demonstration." The barest hint of a grin tugged at her lips as she studied the top photograph.

"You shouldn't be seeing these," Reese hissed, tearing the photographs out of her hand and doing a clumsy job of shoving them back into the envelope. The piece of paper slipped loose and fluttered to the muddy ground beside the pond. Reese fumbled the photographs as he bent to retrieve the paper.

Freddy silently took the photographs and the envelope from him so that Reese could pick up the paper. He couldn't help but take a long, devastating look at the images as Reese read the paper with shaking hands. There was no mistaking what Reese and Sebastian were doing. The angle was a bit odd and the lighting was dim. Their figures were slightly blurred, but it was clear whoever had taken the pictures had been in possession of the very latest in photographic technology. But far beyond the danger the photographs represented, Freddy's whole body ached to see vivid proof of Reese entwined with another man, obviously enjoying himself.

"Twenty thousand pounds," Reese choked, yanking Freddy back into the present. "Good God. The man wants twenty thousand pounds to destroy the photographs."

"We can destroy the photographs," Freddy hissed, shoving the damning images back into the envelope. "We'll take them home and throw them in the fire at once."

"He has the negatives," Lenore said gravely. She stood shoulder to shoulder with Reese, reading the letter that shook in his hands.

"The what?" Freddy shook his head in confusion.

Lenore pursed her lips in thought, then said, "It's a new kind of photography, invented just two years ago. The new cameras use a kind of...of film instead of a glass plate with chemicals. It means you can photograph things faster, transport the camera more quickly, and, unfortunately, make copies of photographs more easily."

Freddy was tempted to know how she knew so much about photography—or everything else, seemingly—but Reese was still shaking and losing more color by the moment.

"I don't have twenty thousand pounds," he said in a hollow voice.

"Of course, you do," Freddy said. "You're as rich as Croesus."

Reese glanced mournfully at him and shook his head. "I drew on every last farthing I had to purchase Silverstone Castle, every shred of ready money in my account and I cashed in a few investments as well."

"You what?" Freddy's fury at the whole sale made a temporary return. It was one thing to buy up his estate and his pride, but to bankrupt himself in order to do it?

"You aren't paying any bribe, whether you have the money or not," Lenore insisted, taking the paper from Reese's hands and the envelope from Freddy. "Never give in to blackmail."

"That's what I advised Sebastian," Reese said in a sickly voice. "Now look what's happened to him."

"Lenore is right," Freddy said in spite of the dread that filled him at the thought of Reese being exposed in public as Sebastian apparently had. "I am all for our sort bending over backwards to conceal who we are, but not by giving in to blackmail. Twenty-thousand pounds is outrageous."

"If you give in once, they'll only know they can attack you again," Lenore agreed with a nod, making his point better than he'd been able to.

"Besides, nothing has happened to Lord Gregory yet, as far as I know," Freddy added. "Call on him to find out if the article has harmed him in any way before you act," he said, in spite of the fact that the last thing he wanted was for Reese to be anywhere near the man he'd done the things depicted in the photographs with. The mad thought struck him that if Reese was going to do those things with anyone in the future, it would be him. The world really had turned upside down.

Reese shook his head in spite of what Freddy and Lenore were saying and stood straighter, tugging on the bottom of his jacket to straighten it. "I have to give in," he said, stony-faced. "I have Harry to think about." He glanced several yards to the side to where Harry and Ricky were now racing each other along the banks of the pond with Edgar trying in vain to keep up. "If I'm ruined, he's ruined too, and his poor life has only just begun."

"I doubt you'll be as ruined as you think," Lenore said.

Reese turned to her with a sad look. "What those photographs show is illegal," he whispered. "I could go to prison for that."

Lenore swallowed. "That's terribly wrong. Why, back home, Mr. Gunn and Mr. Kopanari have run the hotel together for years. Everyone knows that they're more or less married, but that's their business and not any of ours."

Freddy stared at her, stunned. Reese did the same. Her statement was so cool, so casual. No wonder she seemed to accept the undercurrents between him and Reese. She'd lived with her own example of their sort for who knew how long. But then, enough of their friends had known about Reese for ages, and none of them had breathed a word about it or run to the authorities to report him. Freddy supposed it was entirely possible that there were people, like Lenore and her entire hometown, apparently, who knew the truth and ignored it.

Unfortunately, the man in the bowler hat wasn't one of those people.

"Talk to Lord Gregory," he said, daring to rest a hand on Reese's arm. "Find out how things are with him before you do anything."

Reese nodded, but before they could say more, they were interrupted by Henry, Ellie, and Mr. Garrett approaching. The May Flowers' speeches had ended and the crowd was dispersing.

"Have you sorted everything out?" Henry asked with an oblivious smile that Freddy envied.

"Yes, we have," Reese said, doing a terrible job of pretending ease. He took the envelope from Freddy and stuffed the whole, awkward bundle inside his jacket. "We were just thinking that tea at Howsden House would be an excellent idea right about now."

"That sounds lovely," Mr. Garrett said.

"We'll invite Lord and Lady O'Shea as well," Reese went on. "That'll give Harry and Ricky a chance to cause even more trouble together."

"I'm sure Edgar would appreciate that," Ellie laughed, smiling warmly at Henry.

Freddy envied the unquestionable ease of their relationship. He was jealous of how open and affectionate they could be with each other, even though, from what he understood, Ellie had been a wildly unsuitable bride. No matter what sins existed in her past, at least it wasn't illegal for her and Henry to be together.

"We will get this sorted out," Lenore declared, taking both Reese's and Freddy's arms as they headed away from the pond. "I refuse to let the two best friends I've made in England so far suffer for such a silly reason."

"Thank you," Reese said, though he was still clearly miserable.

Freddy watched him until Reese glanced his way, then he smiled. The sting of betrayal still hung over him, but stronger than that was the love he had for Reese. And anyone who attacked Reese attacked him.

CHAPTER 15

*N*othing surprised Reese more than Freddy's offer to accompany him on his call to Sebastian the next day.

"You don't have to do this," he said as the two of them walked side by side through Mayfair. "I understand how uncomfortable this must make you."

"No more uncomfortable than I already am," Freddy said, staring straight forward. "I'm only uncomfortable with the circumstances. Why now? You say those photographs of you and Lord Gregory were taken years ago. So why would the blackmailer wait to act on them until now?"

"I don't know," Reese grumbled, as tense as a bowstring. "It must be part of some master plan. Blackmailing one of us is bad, but blackmailing several of us in turn could create a genuine panic within our community.

Maybe that panic will make people pay him more and pay faster."

"Well, I, for one, refuse to be intimidated."

Reese studied him as they continued in silence. Something had changed with Freddy in the last twenty-four hours. He strode with his back straight and his eyes bright, as though he were on a patrol through the Transvaal. The way his shoulders were squared and his stride was deliberate reminded Reese that Freddy was a soldier at heart. Seeing him so confident drove Reese wild with lust, but those feelings had to be pushed aside to face the matter at hand.

"There's no way to know if Sebastian even wants company right now." Reese picked up the conversation to fill the silence. "If things are bad for him, I'm certain his father and brother will be there for him. His father is the Duke of Reith, and unlike my own father, he loves Sebastian unconditionally."

He was rambling. It wasn't like him at all, and it was embarrassing.

"He's your friend," Freddy said, nodding to a woman Reese vaguely knew as they passed her. "He'll want to see you."

"If he does, we won't stay long," Reese continued. "Didn't Bledsoe want us in his office to finalize the sale by noon?"

Freddy darted a flat, sideways look at him, the lines of his face hardening. He wasn't just a soldier, he was an officer ready to mete out punishment. Another inconvenient wave of desire swept through Reese. It scattered quickly, though. Reese couldn't tell if Freddy was still furious with him over the sale. For a change, Freddy's expression betrayed nothing.

"I'm certain Sebastian will be pleased to see you as well," he blabbered on as they reached the corner to turn onto Sebastian's street. "He's always spoken very highly of you. And, whether you know it or not, you're a calming presence, so—"

His words died on his lips and both he and Freddy froze as they turned the corner. Ahead of them, halfway down the street, A sleek, black police wagon was parked outside of Sebastian's front door. Sebastian himself stood at the top of the steps, his hands fastened behind his back, a police officer on either side. Lord Reith and Sebastian's brother, Lord Marshall Hengrove, stood as close to Sebastian as the officers would allow as they escorted him ignominiously down the steps and toward the wagon. They, too, were grave-faced, but where Sebastian had lost all of his color and all sign of hope, Lord Reith and Lord Hengrove radiated fury. But none of them spoke, as if they knew all arguments were pointless.

As they reached the pavement, Sebastian glanced in Reese's direction. His eyes widened in recognition for a split-second before panic overtook him. Sebastian jerked his head to the side and mouthed the word "go", urging Reese and Freddy not to be seen. A moment later, the officers manhandled Sebastian into the wagon, shoving and snarling in spite of Sebastian's lofty status. Men like them had no status once they were discovered.

"Come on," Reese muttered, pushing Freddy's arm to propel him back the way they'd come. Freddy might have been the soldier, but Reese knew when to retreat.

It wasn't until they were halfway down the street they'd just walked, moving so fast that they overtook the woman Freddy had greeted minutes before, that Freddy hissed, "They arrested him?"

"Of course, they arrested him," Reese answered with equal parts anger and fear. "He broke the law."

"In private," Freddy said, irritation plain on his face. "He didn't hurt anyone."

"None of us do," Reese sighed. "But the law is the law."

"It's unjust," Freddy growled.

"And how many people do you think would stand up and say that?" Reese asked.

Freddy didn't answer. He kept his lips pressed tightly shut and his shoulders bunched as they slowed their pace and paused to hail a cab at an intersection of a larger road. Once they were safe and secure inside, on their way to The City for their meeting with Bledsoe, Reese blew out a breath and rubbed his hands over his face.

"That's it for me, then," he said, his heart sick. "If they've arrested Sebastian, they'll come for me next. My face was as visible in those photographs as his was."

Freddy's expression pinched, but then it evened out and he shook his head. "There must be more photographs, ones with Sebastian and some other bloke. Otherwise the man in the bowler hat would have come for you when he first approached Sebastian last week."

Freddy could have been right, but it didn't make Reese feel at all better.

They fell into silence again as the cab carried them into the bustling business district of London. It was not lost on Reese that to reach The City, the beating heart of the vast metropolis's financial district, it was necessary to pass through Westminster, where the high court and the law had its center. He wanted to shrink away from the windows as they passed the very building where Sebastian was bound to be charged with gross indecency, unless his father's influence could save him, but Freddy maintained his composure, so Reese was determined to as well.

Everything seemed blissfully normal when they reached the stately building where Bledsoe had his London office.

"Mr. Bledsoe will be with you shortly, gentleman," a young clerk greeted them with the utmost respect, escorting them through the halls to a handsomely appointed office with a stunning view of St. Paul's Cathedral. "Would you like tea? Something stronger perhaps?"

"Tea would be fine," Freddy answered with a kind smile. Even in the midst of disaster, Freddy remained kind.

"Right away, my lord." The clerk bowed and smiled

as he backed out of the room adding to Reese's growing sense of the surreal.

As soon as the two of them were alone, Freddy walked to the window, glancing out at St. Paul's and the cityscape as it stretched off to the horizon. Reese paced the room, wondering how long Bledsoe would be and worrying about Sebastian, about whether he was the next one to be arrested, and about whether Freddy was still upset with him. The clerk returned with surprising speed, setting out a simple tea service for them.

"Mr. Bledsoe sends his apologies," he said as he backed toward the door, like a page in a royal court, once more. "He asked me to tell you that he will be here with the last of the papers within half an hour."

"Thank you." Reese nodded to the man, and as soon as he was gone, crossed to the table to pour a much-needed cup of tea. "Would you like one?" he asked Freddy, hating how formal and stilted he sounded.

Freddy turned away from the window, his deeply thoughtful expression softening. "Yes, I think so."

Reese nodded and poured a cup for him as well, adding cream and sugar in the way he knew Freddy liked. When that was done, he carried the tea to the window.

"I don't like this," he said, letting out an impatient breath as Freddy took his cup.

Their hands brushed as he did, and if Reese wasn't mistaken, Freddy lingered where he didn't have to.

"What don't you like?" he asked in a tired voice before taking a sip.

"This," Reese said, shrugging his shoulders and gesturing with one hand as if to include everything in the world. "I don't like what's happening to Sebastian, but I like what's happening to the two of us even less."

Freddy took a long gulp of tea, then set his half-full cup on the wide windowsill. He turned to Reese, crossing his arms, his expression hard. "What's happening to us?"

Reese shifted to stare out at St. Paul's for a moment, searching for just the right words. "Things should be easy between us," he said at last. "Like they always have been. We're still friends, the best of friends, in spite of everything else."

"We are." Freddy's voice and posture softened more. "But even you must admit that 'everything else' is quite a bit at the moment."

"I know," Reese said, letting out a breath. He set his teacup aside, even though he hadn't taken even a sip. "If I could go back to the way things were before and, perhaps, proceed differently, I would."

Freddy's brow went up and his posture went stiff again. "Are you saying that you regret buying Silverstone Castle now?"

"No, no, not at all." Reese pinched his face and turned to lean against the windowsill. "I don't care how much you hate me for it, I still think buying Silverstone is the best investment I've made in a long time."

"Even though it's bankrupted you?" Freddy asked, slowly sinking to sit on the windowsill beside him.

"It hasn't bankrupted me," Reese insisted in a strong voice, then sighed, his shoulders drooping. "Even if it has set me back a bit."

Freddy made a noise that would have been scoffing, but there was something sympathetic in it, something that hinted they were in the soup together.

Reese inched his hand along the windowsill until it touched Freddy's. Freddy didn't jerk his hand away. That simple fact had Reese's heart pounding in no time.

"I swear to you, Freddy. I swear on everything I hold sacred and then some. I did not purchase Silverstone as a bargaining chip to get you into my bed and to keep you there," he insisted. "I didn't even think that the gesture could be interpreted that way until you called me out for it."

"You never do think of things that way," Freddy said, his jaw tense, shaking his head. "You only think that you are all-powerful and that whatever you want, you can make happen."

"I do not." Reese frowned at him. Freddy stared flatly back, and Reese let out a breath, deflating a bit. "Well, if I do, it's only good things that I want to make happen. I am not a predator, like those army officers you mentioned."

It was Freddy's turn to let his tension go with an exhale. "No, you're not. And I would be lying if I said I didn't enjoy every second of making love with you, or if I said I never wanted to do it again."

Reese's pounding heart squeezed so suddenly that his head swam for a moment. He met Freddy's eyes, searching for the love he was desperate to find there. He didn't have to search long.

"I am willing to concede that your offer to buy Silverstone was an expression of love and not a bid for power," Freddy said, tension leaving him at the admission. "I'm still not entirely happy with it and I still think you were horribly high-handed in the way you went about it."

"I was," Reese admitted, hope fluttering in his gut.

"But I would be a fool if I wasn't grateful." Freddy sighed. "I can learn to live with it, I suppose. Provided you truly do allow me to be a full partner in the running of my own estate, that is."

"Of course." Reese closed his hand tightly over Freddy's. "God, Freddy, do you have any idea how much I love you? I would buy Silverstone Castle twice over and sell Albany Court if I had to if it made you happy."

"Don't you dare sell Albany Court," Freddy warned him, humor lighting his eyes, his cheeks going pink. "Your house feels as much like a home to me as Silverstone does."

Emotion sang through Reese, stinging at his eyes and closing his throat. "You have no idea how happy it makes me to hear you say that."

"As happy as it makes me to say it." Freddy leaned closer to him. "I have to admit that I love you for your high-handed ways, but part of me also enjoys seeing you made vulnerable. The last day has been a revelation in that way. It has put us on more equal footing."

"I could live under the shadow of a thousand black-mail threats if it brings us closer together," he said, twisting to face Freddy more fully and raising a hand to cradle his cheek. "But we could never be on equal terms." When Freddy's expression pinched in confusion that threatened to sink into anger, Reese rushed on with, "You are a thousand times better than me, Frederick Herrington, and you always will be."

Before Freddy could answer or refute him, Reese pulled him close, slanting his mouth over his. He kissed Freddy with all the passion that had been bottled up in his soul for a decade and with all the newfound admiration for the man Freddy was. The kiss was heaven itself, especially when Freddy returned it with full force, caressing the side of Reese's face and threading his fingers up into his hair. Freddy was as hungry for him as Reese had always been, and the promise of everything that could blossom between them thundered through Reese. His body was instantly alive and pulsing, and if they had been anywhere other than a public business office, he would have pressed Freddy up against the nearest wall and had his way with him.

His thoughts reminded him of where he was, and he broke away from Freddy, panting and hot.

"We've no idea when Bledsoe will be here," Freddy said, as if he, too, knew the risk they'd just taken.

"We can't have him finding us like this," Reese

agreed, a wry twist to his lips. He stood and retrieved his teacup, all too aware that his trousers weren't lying as flat as they should have.

Freddy was in a bit of a state too, and it was all either of them could do to walk off their rush of ardor, sipping tea and doing their best to avoid looking directly at each other as they paced the room. Every time they caught sight of each other they burst into laughter, though, which made Reese's heart light and his body rebellious.

They only just managed to pull themselves together by the time Bledsoe finally made his appearance.

"I'm terribly sorry for the delay," the man said as he whisked into the room. "I was drawn into a confrontation between a colleague of mine and his client. The man was being totally unreasonable, and I was called upon to explain several things about estate management and sales. I never would have given them my time, but the colleague in question is courting my sister and—I'm terribly sorry, my lords. You don't need to hear any of this."

"It's quite all right, Bledsoe," Freddy laughed, his mood as different from when they'd entered the room as day was to night. "We're ready to complete the sale if you have everything in order."

"I do, my lord, I do."

With a few, final strokes of the pen, ownership of Silverstone Castle was transferred to Reese and an agreement dividing management of the estate between him and

Freddy as a business venture was signed. It boggled Reese's mind that signing something so simple and so technical could be like signing a marriage license. But there was no getting around the fact that the deed of sale and management agreement were legal documents that would bind his and Freddy's lives together until death did they part.

"I rather feel as though we should have a wedding breakfast after that," he murmured to Freddy as the two of them made their way out through the halls of the office.

Freddy stared at him in surprise, blushing up a storm. "That wasn't what that was," he whispered, darting a glance around to make certain no one was listening to them. "I should think that sort of a ceremony would be far more meaningful."

"You want a meaningful ceremony?" Reese asked, heart thrumming like it never had before as they crossed through the front hallway, buzzing with people going about their business. "I could arrange for something like that."

"Reese, you aren't asking...." Freddy left his sentence hanging with a look as though he could barely comprehend the conversation they were having.

Reese shrugged and nodded to the attendant who held the door for him. "Why not? It all amounts to the same thing, doesn't it? Happily ever after? Or, if you'd like, we could skip straight to the consummation."

Freddy turned an even deeper shade of red as they

stepped out into the bustling street. "When?" he asked, half choking.

"Now, if you'd like," Reese said, risking a saucy look as they started down the street. "I have everything we'll need at home, and—"

He was stopped as a man stepped right into their path. The man wearing a bowler hat.

"Excuse me, gentlemen," he said with the same obsequious grin he'd worn in St. James's Park. "I'd just like to let you know that I have my camera set up on the third floor of the building right across the way there." He pivoted to point to the building beside the one they'd just come out of. "You might also like to know that I've been able to capture some interesting sights through my camera's lens."

Reese's heart dropped to his stomach. Bledsoe's office was on the side of the building the man in the bowler hat was gesturing toward. The window where he and Freddy had sat, where they had kissed, was wide and clear. They'd been so taken with the view of St. Paul's and each other that they hadn't noticed what might have been right across the alley from them.

"I thought you might also want to know that you have until five in the evening on Friday before I take the photographs I already have and the new ones I just took to *The Mail* for publication."

"You bastard," Freddy hissed, starting threateningly toward the man. "You won't get away with this." Reese had to grab his arm to hold him back.

"And how is your friend, Lord Gregory, faring this fine day?" the man asked, unintimidated and grinning like a tiger.

"You won't ruin us," Reese said, trying to be strong but knowing ruin was only inches away.

"My instructions remain the same as what's in the letter I gave you already," the man said. "Though it'll be twenty-five now to keep quiet. Good day, gents."

Without waiting for further answer, he turned and marched off into the milling crowd, disappearing around the corner of the building.

Reese felt as though he'd fallen off the roof all over again, only this time, he'd taken Freddy with him. "I'll find the money somehow," he said in a hoarse voice.

"You'll do no such thing," Freddy growled, marching on and gesturing for Reese to follow.

"But you saw what happened to Sebastian," Reese hissed, catching up.

"Even so," Freddy said, steely with determination. "That's not going to happen to us."

CHAPTER 16

*A*nger of a sort that was entirely new to him flooded through Freddy as he and Reese made their way back to Howsden House. He knew what it was like to be angry at his father for running their family's fortune into the ground. He was certainly familiar with the stinging frustration of Reese running rough-shod over him where Silverstone was concerned. And he knew the hundred different sorts of petty anger that life threw at everyone. But he had never known the boiling, determined, righteous sort of anger that the man in the bowler hat inspired in him, and he had never felt so called to action when it came to thwarting the source of his anger.

"There has to be a way out of this," Reese fretted as they stepped down from the hired cab that had brought them home. "If we could just discover the man's identity, I'm certain there's a way we could turn the tables on him."

Freddy kept silent as they marched to the door and walked through as one of the footmen opened it for them. His mind was spinning as fast as Reese's, but with a more focused purpose.

"He didn't speak with a working-class accent," Reese went on as they shed their coats and hats, handing them off to the footman, "but he didn't have a posh accent either. He's probably middle-class somehow, especially if he has the most modern photographic equipment. Unless someone with money is financing his damnable endeavors."

Freddy hummed, but didn't say more as they marched down the hall to Reese's library. In his mind, it didn't matter who the man was or where he got the backing to do what he was doing. The blackguard's aim was obviously to expose men like them for money using illicit photographs. They couldn't assume the man's targets were only homosexuals either. Who knew what photographs he'd taken in the past and who had paid his ransom to have them destroyed?

"I should go to my solicitor to see if there is any way to free up twenty-five thousand pounds, just to be safe," Reese babbled on, breaking into swift, tight pacing once they reached the library. "I'm not saying I'll pay the man," he added, holding up a hand to Freddy, his face lined with tension, "but it would make me feel more secure to have it available."

"Do you have it available?" Freddy asked. "After Silverstone? Without having to sell an asset that you would do better to keep?" He started toward the window so he could continue to mull over the problem but changed his mind and marched to the fireplace instead. It would be a long time before he would be comfortable sitting in a window again.

Reese blew out a breath and rubbed a hand over his face. "No, I don't. Not really."

Freddy leaned his elbow against the mantel, sending Reese a flat, sideways look. There was no point in reminding him how foolish he'd been to risk so much on Silverstone Castle.

In spite of everything, a tiny grin tugged at the corner of his mouth. So Reese wasn't the infallible god Freddy had always assumed he was after all. As long as he'd known him, Reese had been the brightest and best of all his friends. He'd seemed to handle his affairs masterfully, to always be confident in all things, and to be the most admired and adored person Freddy knew. It was endearing, in a way, to see his clay feet. And arousing, God help him.

Reese stopped short in the middle of his pacing, inspiration lighting his wan features. "We'll contact Jack Craig," he said, changing his path and striding up to Freddy. "Jack will have contacts that can track down the man in the bowler hat, learn his identity. If we ask Jack, he can put a stop to this."

"We're not asking Jack for help." Freddy shook his head and pushed away from the mantel.

Reese frowned. "Why not? He's our best resource in the Metropolitan Police. Why not appeal to him?"

"Does he know?" Freddy asked, knowing he didn't need to explain further. "How many other people would he need to tell in order to get the help we need? He cannot possibly have time to handle an entire investigation like this by himself. How many other people would find out about us, and how many of those people could be trusted not to breathe a word? Can men like us depend on the law when the law is against us?"

Reese let out a heavy breath, his shoulders dropping. "We're doomed, then." He walked away, shaking his head.

"We're not doomed," Freddy said, following him. "Far from it."

Reese stopped whatever pacing he'd been about to launch into, turning to Freddy instead. "How do you figure?" His expression flickered between hope and doubt.

"An unknown man has threatened you, and now me, with ruin if we don't pay him an exorbitant amount of money to keep quiet. He has damning photographic evidence that he is threatening to take to the press," he said, reviewing the facts. "We can either pay his ransom, which we will *not* do," he emphasized, "or we can discover his identity, learn where he keeps his evidence, and destroy it before he uses it."

"But how?" Reese sighed. "We don't have the first clue who he is. There is nothing remarkable about his appearance. Were we to describe him to Jack, for example," he added, holding up his hands to show he wasn't suggesting they rely on Jack, "the description would fit hundreds of men in London. How can we stop a man intent on destruction when he holds all the power?"

"But does he?" Freddy asked, pacing himself as the nebulous ideas that had been forming in his head for the past hour took shape. "We're assuming that, if he did send what he has to the press, everyone who read the resulting article would believe it."

Reese laughed indignantly and threw up his hands. "Did you not see the photographs he has of me? There is nothing to doubt."

Freddy turned to him. "Any newspaper that printed those photographs would be closed down and its owners jailed at once."

Reese lowered his arms and blinked.

"Yes, the journalists who saw them would know the truth, but unless they stood in Piccadilly Circus, showing the photographs to every passerby, they would have no way to disseminate the proof. And I believe that the law frowns on pornography just as sharply as homosexuality."

Reese seemed to think about that for a moment, but shook his head. "Society does not need proof to condemn, especially when enough suspicion exists already."

"Are people suspicious of you?" Freddy asked, cocking his head to one side.

Reese grimaced, then ran a hand over his face as he marched to the table of decanters to pour himself a drink.

"I don't know," he said in a quiet voice. "I've done my utmost to stay out of the limelight and to avoid any scandal."

"And you've been married and have a son," Freddy added, moving to join him. He could use a drink himself to cut through the Gordian knot of the situation.

"Plenty of men like us are married with children," Reese said, sending Freddy a doleful look.

"And how many of them have been carted off by the police like Lord Gregory?" Freddy asked.

Reese swallowed his drink and put the tumbler down. "None," he answered quietly. "At least, not that I know of. It's the rash, overt, single ones who tend to slip up the most."

"Precisely," Freddy said with a nod. "And you are the least rash person I know."

He followed his statement by raising a hand to cradle Reese's hot face. It was a bold move, all things considered, and one he wasn't entirely comfortable with. But it had to be done. He had to let Reese know that he was not alone and that he was loved, in spite of the danger.

For a split second, Reese seemed about to lose his composure. He pulled himself together and rested his hand over Freddy's, meeting his eyes with a longing so deep it took Freddy's breath away.

"Everyone likes you, Reese," Freddy went on, his voice hoarse. "If this bastard does take the photographs to the press, you will have staunch defenders, and I'm certain the rumors would be quashed in no time."

"Not without trouble," Reese admitted, his voice rough as well. He lowered his hand, taking Freddy's with it and holding his hand between them. "And you do not have the protection of a past marriage and a child, like I do. I refuse to put you at risk in this situation."

"He doesn't have to be at risk."

Freddy's blood ran cold and he nearly jumped out of his skin at Lenore's statement. He and Reese both jerked to the doorway, only to find her standing there, leaning against the doorframe. The somber expression on her face hinted that she'd been listening to their conversation for far longer than Freddy was comfortable with. As soon as they saw her, she straightened and walked toward them.

"How much did you hear?" Reese asked, blushing fiercely.

"Enough," Lenore answered. "And Freddy is right. You're one of the most gracious and likable people I've ever met, Reese. Even if every newspaper in London ran with a front-page headline about your proclivities, I wager that the majority of people would choose not to read the paper that day and the whole thing would blow over."

"But Sebastian," Reese insisted, turning to Freddy. "You saw what happened."

"Lord Gregory is a nice chap," Freddy said, fighting the guilt that the truth raised in him, "but he has never been as open or congenial as you. And again, he has never been married and does not have a child."

Reese blew out an impatient breath through his nose. "All right. Let's assume for a moment that I would be able to survive the storm of controversy, should the truth be published." He turned to Freddy. "I will not put you in danger."

"Oh, he won't be in danger," Lenore said, her smile as mischievous as ever.

"I'm afraid he would," Reese said.

"Absolutely not." She slipped closer to Freddy's side, hooking her arm through his. "No one would dare to accuse Freddy of gross indecency, or whatever your silly laws call it, with his glamorous, intelligent, vivacious fiancée at his side."

Her words hit Freddy like a fist in the stomach, sending a shower of prickles down his back and making his hands and feet numb. At least, at first. He turned his head to study her, taking in her cunning expression and the spark in her eyes. Slowly, the initial shock of her suggestion began to wane.

But as quickly as he entertained the idea, he pushed it away.

"I couldn't do that to you, Lenore," he said. "I couldn't trap you in a white marriage. That is to say, there might have been a time when I could have done what was necessary, but now...." He glanced sheepishly to Reese. The idea of giving himself, body and soul, to anyone, for any reason at all, was abhorrent to him, now that he knew where his heart wanted to be.

To his surprise, Lenore laughed. "Dear me, you really aren't skilled at subterfuge over here, are you?"

"I beg your pardon?" Reese asked, a spark of curiosity in his eyes.

Lenore let out a breath and made an off-hand gesture before launching into, "It's simple really. Freddy and I will become engaged. It would be ideal for me in any case because Papa is heading home in a matter of days, but I'm desperate to stay. I've made so many friends here, and Diana has asked me to join the May Flowers."

"Congratulations," Freddy said out of habit, though he was reeling from the way the conversation had flown so far off course.

"Papa would have to let me stay if I were engaged. And if it so happened that, in a few years' time, we should decide to amicably split because I have fallen in love with someone else, well, these things happen." She shrugged and let out a dramatic sigh, the sparkle in her eyes as bright as ever.

Freddy couldn't help but laugh. "So you'd use me as a way to stay in England to hunt for an actual husband?"

"If you wouldn't mind," she said, resting a friendly hand on his arm.

Freddy's laughter grew. "No, I don't think I'd mind at all."

"But, of course, it would be inappropriate for us to live under the same roof, unchaperoned, while engaged," she went on. "So I would have to prevail upon the hospitality of my father's widowed friend, Lord Howsden, for a home until the wedding could take place." She let go of Freddy's arm and shifted to take hold of Reese's. "And that, of course, would mean that my charming fiancé would frequently stay at Albany Court or Howsden House in order to be close to me."

"Or we could all stay at Silverstone Castle," Reese suggested, his grin finally growing as well. "Which is, of course, an investment property that Freddy and I are administrating together, as a business, now."

"Oh." Lenore's expression lit with excitement. "How absolutely perfect. Especially as an infusion of cash from a dollar princess would be just the thing that your business enterprise needs to be a raging success."

For the second time in the conversation, Freddy felt as though the wind had been knocked out of him. Not in the form of a punch to the gut, though. This time he was bowled over by the brilliance of Lenore's plan and her generosity. No one would question his desire to marry a wealthy American heiress. He liked Lenore enough to pretend to worship the ground she walked on in public. No one would bat an eye at her involvement in the business of Silverstone, and, by extension, no one would question her closeness to Reese. Or, if they did, it would only help thwart rumors about Reese's sexual preferences. In fact, they could cause one kind of scandal to squelch another.

"An engagement party," Freddy blurted as the plan began to form in his mind. "We need to have an engagement party. As quickly as possible."

"Are you certain about this?" Reese asked, clearly intending the question to cover the entire situation.

"Yes," Freddy answered. "The man in the bowler hat won't be able to resist showing his face at the announcement of the engagement of one of his targets, you know he won't."

"He won't," Reese agreed, stroking his chin in thought. "And if he does show his face, we can track him once he leaves. We could have him followed home to where he keeps his evidence, and we could destroy it."

Freddy hadn't thought that far ahead, but it did seem like an option. "Perhaps we should involve Jack in some way."

"I've heard so many exciting things about Lord Jack," Lenore said, hugging Reese's arm. "I am simply desperate to meet him. And his wife."

"Yes, well, Bianca has just given birth, so she might not be up for society," Freddy said. "But I believe the rest of the plan is a solid one."

"It's the best we have to go on," Reese said with a sigh.

"I think it's an excellent plan," Lenore said, letting go of Reese's arm. "And now, if you will excuse me, I need to go tell Papa to cancel my passage back to America and to set up a lavish bank account for my new life in England." She giggled, lifted to her toes to kiss Freddy's cheek, then marched from the room with her head held high and a spring in her steps.

Freddy watched her go with a smile, thanking God

for unconventional American women and their wild ways. "I told you we wouldn't have to give in to blackmail," he said triumphantly, turning back to Reese.

Reese laughed and shook his head. "We're going to have our hands full keeping Lenore out of trouble. We won't have time to worry about ourselves."

"I think that's partly her aim," Freddy said, striding to the doorway and glancing out into the hall. His heart was racing after their inadvertent strategy session, and Lenore had raised just enough daring in him that he wanted to do something about it.

"What are you looking for?" Reese asked, walking up behind him and looking into the hall as well.

"I'm, um...." His face flushed as his gaze slipped sideways to Reese. They were in close proximity, but he couldn't do anything more than blush and brush his fingers against Reese's.

Reese drew in a quick breath, color splashing over his cheeks as well. He twined his fingers with Freddy's. "I know just what you're looking for," he said in a low, mischievous voice.

He glanced up and down the hall once more, and when it proved completely empty, he took Freddy's hand and rushed out of the library. Freddy expected them to head for the stairs, but Reese led him the other way, down the corridor and all the way to the back of the house. Freddy couldn't remember the last time he'd been down that hall. It had a closed up look about it, as though it wasn't used with any regularity. Indeed, the tiny parlor

Reese took him too had the faded look of a room that was only occasionally cleaned by the servants and almost never used. Its fireplace was cold, but a cheery ray of afternoon sun poured in through its single window—which was, mercifully, covered by a lace curtain—landing on a plump chaise longue.

"This was Edith's reading room," Reese said before swinging Freddy into his arms and bringing his mouth crashing down over his.

Freddy met the sensual gesture without a shred of hesitation. He'd been aching to have Reese in his arms since their moment of tenderness in Bledsoe's office. Immediately, he circled his arms around Reese and kissed him back with unfettered passion. He still had no idea what he was doing, but it felt right to caress Reese's lips with his own and to slide his tongue against Reese's in a passionate dance.

He wanted more than that, though, and fumbled with Reese's clothes to undo as many buttons as he could get his hands on. Reese jumped to do the same, and within seconds, they were kissing and fumbling and laughing like schoolboys as they loosened each other's clothes. It was wildly silly and delicious all at once, and Freddy couldn't get enough of it.

He managed to pop the last button on Reese's waist-coat, which went clattering into a corner, and tug his shirt out of his trousers so that he could smooth his hands across the hot flesh of Reese's torso just as Reese unbuttoned his trousers and slipped his hand beneath Freddy's drawers. Freddy gasped at the friction of Reese stroking him, groaning as he went as hard as iron.

"I love your cock," Reese panted against Freddy's lips, stroking and kissing his way to Freddy's jaw. "It feels like a canon primed to go off at any moment."

"It might," Freddy choked out, genuinely afraid he might come before he was ready.

"We can't have that." Reese pulled his hand away, stroking his way up Freddy's abdomen and loosening his shirt as he went. He pushed gently, sending Freddy stumbling backward.

As Freddy's calves hit the edge of the chaise, he clasped Reese's face, drawing his mouth back to his own and kissing him with so much passion that Reese stopped what he was doing just to moan in pleasure. Freddy couldn't get enough of the taste of him and the heat of his mouth. All he wanted was to be that close to Reese forever.

A moment later, as Reese tugged and pushed at his jacket, waistcoat, and shirt, peeling them off to expose Freddy's chest, he changed his mind. He broke their kiss and set to work mindlessly undressing Reese as well. He was desperate to see Reese naked and aroused, as he'd been on his bed just days before. He wanted to feast on every inch of Reese and have Reese do the same to him.

The need was so overpowering that he lost track of how they were undressing themselves, only that they were. Before he knew it, they fell across the chaise, naked. Freddy was surprised the elegant piece of furniture didn't crack under the weight of their fall. That surprise was nothing compared to the dazzling pleasure of Reese's body tangling with his, though. It amazed him that something as awkward and clumsy as grasping desperately at each other while grinding their hips together could be so glorious.

In spite of his inexperience, everything he did managed to feel good. Deep sounds of pleasure caught in his throat as he kissed Reese, threading his fingers through Reese's hair with one hand while caressing every inch of his back and arse that he could with the other. Reese was just as needy, playing with Freddy's tongue while thrusting his iron-hard prick against Freddy's. His hand worked magic as well, rubbing one of Freddy's nipples to a hard point. It was almost laughable that Freddy had assumed sex between men was nothing but a cock shoved up an arse when the truth was a thousand times better.

"This is so good," he panted, breaking away from Reese's lips to test the taste of his neck and his shoulder. "I didn't know it could be this good."

"This is just the beginning," Reese growled in return, pushing Freddy to his back against the chaise.

Reese captured his mouth in a long, hot kiss, then broke away to trail kisses down his neck and shoulder to his chest. Freddy's head spun with lust as Reese swirled his tongue around one of his nipples. He had a hard time catching his breath when Reese nudged his knees apart so that his legs fell over either side of the chaise, leaving him desperately exposed. He nearly lost his mind entirely when Reese reached his hand between his legs, caressing his balls for a moment before brushing across his perineum to tease the pucker of his arse. The simple gesture made him feel vulnerable and open, and with that came the shock of wanting to give everything to Reese.

"Fuck me," he whispered, tilting his hips. "I'm ready. I want it."

Reese groaned and dropped his head to rest against Freddy's chest. He shifted his hand to cradle Freddy's aching prick. "Goddammit, Freddy," he panted. "From here on out, I am hiding a jar of lubrication in every room in this house." He glanced up, gaze warm with desire. "But I refuse to let your first time be that uncomfortable."

"Isn't there...can't you do...something?" Freddy asked desperately. The way Reese stroked him had him close to the edge already.

"If you were more used to it we could improvise," Reese started, then shook his head. "I want your first time to be glorious and good, not stressful. For now, you'll have to settle for this."

He grinned impishly up at Freddy before sliding his body down until he was able to hold Freddy's prick upright and close his mouth around the tip. Freddy sucked in a breath then growled with pleasure as Reese teased and licked him, using his tongue and lips to create magic. The intensity of the pleasure was so strong that Freddy gripped the top of the chaise behind him, muscles flexing, and thrust up. Reese groaned, closing his eyes and looking as though nothing had ever given him more pleasure, as he bore down on him. The ray of sunlight that bathed the chaise warmed his skin and fully lit everything Reese was doing to him, which only made Freddy moan and jerk harder. It occurred to him with a carnal flash that he was fucking Reese's mouth just moments before he came with a startling force. White-hot pleasure shot from his spine through his cock, and he cried out in joy at the release.

Reese's answering sound of pleasure was muffled as he swallowed, the sensation drawing even more pleasure from Freddy. As soon as Reese rocked back, panting, Freddy drew on the last of his strength to wrestle Reese onto the chaise, pressing him to his back and closing a hand around his erection.

"My turn," he said, shifting to a level where he could do what he'd only ever dreamed of doing in his most dangerous fantasies.

"Only if you want to," Reese gasped. "I'm not sure there's time—"

Whatever else he planned to say was cut off as Freddy took a deep breath and closed his mouth around the head of Reese's penis. Reese flinched and let out the most delicious sound Freddy had ever heard. Freddy's heart pounded in his chest, in spite of the glow of completion that still surrounded him. Having Reese in his mouth was an entirely new sensation, a new taste. He was bigger than he'd expected and filled his mouth more fully.

Freddy didn't know what to do, but he dared himself to take more of Reese in, to stroke his tongue across the flared base of his tip. He sucked gently, not knowing if that was right either.

"God," Reese panted, grabbing fistfuls of Freddy's hair. "Freddy."

Freddy pulled back hesitantly, then tried to take in more of Reese. He closed his hand around Reese's base for support. It was all so new, so exciting, but also baffling.

"I can't," Reese gasped at last. "I'm so close, but...." He pushed Freddy's head back until his cock slipped out of Freddy's mouth. "Just...hand."

Freddy nodded briefly and moved his hand up and down Reese's shaft. All it took was a few, swift jerks, and Reese erupted with a shudder. He groaned with the release, and Freddy could barely catch his breath as he milked pearly cum from Reese's flushed body. There was something immensely satisfying about causing the man he loved so much pleasure and in watching the tension drain from Reese's sated body. The sight of him spilled across the chaise, panting and loose, cum damp on his abdomen, was so erotic that lust began to stir in Freddy all over again. Enough to make him wonder if his life with Reese would be a never-ending cycle of lust, release, and lust again.

"Come here," Reese panted at last, reaching for him.

Freddy went willingly into his arms, heedless of the dampness that spread across his belly as they tangled together again. His body was still hot and damp with sweat, but he wanted as much contact with Reese as they could manage.

"I love you," Reese panted, kissing him in exhaustion.

"And I love you too," Freddy admitted, his heart brimming to fullness.

"And I damn well am going to fuck you in the arse one day soon," Reese added with a laugh.

It was ridiculous, but Freddy laughed with him. How anyone could think what they had shared, what they were sharing, and what they wanted to share as soon as possible was sinful or criminal was obscene. He'd never felt so much love or so much closeness with another human being in his life. Joining their bodies was only a manifestation of the union of their souls, which grew stronger with each trial they faced. Anyone who tried to come between them or condemn their love as dirty would have him to deal with, and they would pay.

CHAPTER 17

*O*nce Lenore got an idea into her head, she moved fast. Or so Reese discovered within minutes of giving up the delicious moment of intimacy he'd discovered with Freddy, cleaning up as best he could, dressing, and setting Edith's reading room back to rights. He'd only barely had time to direct Freddy to a water-closet to finish cleaning up and to dash up to his bedroom for a discreet scrub when Lenore was causing a scene again.

"But are you certain you want to give up everything to move to England at the drop of a hat, sweetheart?" Mr. Garrett was in the middle of asking her by the time Reese returned to the drawing room, where tea was being served.

"Of course, Papa," Lenore said in a soothing voice, squeezing one of her father's hands in both of hers. "I love Haskell and it will always be my home, but the marriage pool isn't very large."

"There's always Denver," Mr. Garrett argued, more sad than angry, judging by his expression.

"Denver is far away from Haskell too, Papa," Lenore said with a laugh. "If I'm going to marry someone away from home, it might as well be an earl with a castle here in England." She glanced across the room to Freddy, who was watching the scene silently, face red, hair disheveled. All in all, Freddy looked thoroughly debauched, which made Reese's heart pound in his chest. "Besides," Lenore went on, letting go of her father's hand to sweep across the room to Freddy. She took his arm, leaning closer to him. "I'm ever so fond of Freddy."

Mr. Garrett sighed and rubbed a hand over his weathered face. "All right, sweetheart. If that's what you want. Your mother is going to flay me alive when I come home without you, though."

"I'll say," Ellie commented quietly from the corner.

Reese almost hadn't noticed her or Henry as they sat on one of the sofas, sipping tea. Henry wore a slightly puzzled look, and the moment Reese caught his eye, he arched an eyebrow questioningly. Reese crossed to the tea set, ostensibly to pour himself a cup, but as soon as he was close enough to Henry, he murmured, "I'll explain later."

He did explain later, long after supper, after Freddy had gone home to Henrietta and Fergus's house, and after the ladies had gone up to bed. He explained the black-mail and Sebastian's arrest. He explained Freddy's determination not to give in to villains and Lenore's plan to keep them both as free from suspicion as possible. Once everything was explained, surprisingly, Henry agreed with Lenore.

"But two days isn't time for you to plan and execute an entire engagement ball," he said, as energized as Lenore had been when coming up with the plan. "Not with that blackmailer holding the Sword of Damocles over your heads. You need to make the engagement public immediately, yesterday if possible."

"But how?" Reese asked, cradling the brandy he was certain he would need to help him sleep that night after the excitement of the day. "Balls don't happen spontaneously."

"They don't," Henry agreed. "But they're always happening. Do we know anyone hosting one tomorrow night?"

As it turned out, they did. And it wasn't just any ball. Lord Malcolm Campbell and Lady Katya were hosting a ball to celebrate the finalization of the election results. Although, as it turned out, with the landslide Conservative Party victory, the ball had more of a feeling of a party before the end of the world when Reese, Freddy, and Lenore arrived with everyone else the next evening.

"It's a travesty," Lady Katya fretted, as frustrated as Reese had ever seen her. "It's an absolute disgrace."

"Well, Mama," Natalia said with a circumspection beyond her years as she greeted guests by her mother's side. "Isn't that the way of politics? One party holds power for a time, they are the champions and beacons of hope for a few years, then they fall, only to allow the other party to rise and take up the torch of hope for a while? It switches back and forth every few years without fail."

"You are quite right, Lady Natalia," Dr. Townsend said with a broad smile, pushing past Reese, Freddy, and Lenore in the receiving line to stand in front of Natalia, smile bright with interest. "Would you care to dance?"

"I would love to." Natalia took his hand and let him lead her away from her parents and into the ballroom.

"I don't suppose we should point out to them that there is no music playing as of yet," Lord Malcolm growled.

Lady Katya hummed, scowling after her daughter. "The election results have me so frustrated that I can't even tell if I should stand between those two or let them carry on."

Reese sent a sidelong glance to Freddy, wondering if they'd stepped into the middle of something that they would be better to stay out of. Freddy returned his look with a lift of one eyebrow and a twitch of his lips.

"I'm sorry, forgive me," Lady Katya said, turning back to Reese with a huff. "Good evening, Lord Howsden. It is a pleasure, as always, to see you."

"And you, Lord Herrington," Lord Malcolm continued with the standard greeting, though, as usual, he looked like it was more of a nuisance than a pleasure.

"Lady Campbell," Freddy addressed Katya as formally as possible. He darted a glance to Lenore, who hung on his arm, looking as though she'd won a prize at a county fair. "I was wondering if you might allow me to upstage your ball this evening by announcing my engagement to Miss Garrett."

In an instant, it was as though a footman had dropped an entire tray of glasses right next to them. Lady Katya and Lord Malcolm both started, glancing from Freddy to Lenore at first, and then straight to Reese.

"This is unexpected," Lady Katya said, the question carrying at least a dozen other questions within it.

There was absolutely no point whatsoever in hiding anything from Lady Katya and Lord Malcolm.

"It is a matter of some delicacy and even greater necessity," Reese explained in a rush. "As I was explaining to my good friend, Lord Gregory, just the other day, necessity is the mother of invention, and one catches more rats with honey than with vinegar."

On the surface, he was speaking barmy nonsense. But thankfully, understanding lit in Katya and Malcolm's eyes at once.

"Yes, necessity," Lady Katya said. She turned to Freddy and Lenore. "Of course. I will initiate the announcement myself."

They moved on, walking into the increasingly crowded ballroom as more guests arrived.

"Do you think the man in the bowler hat is here?" Lenore asked as they took up a spot near a trio of potted palms that gave them a full view of the room.

"There's no way to tell," Freddy sighed, shifting anxiously, as if he knew a spotlight were on him.

"He must be," Reese said. "He found us in St. James's Park and he somehow knew we would be at Bledsoe's office. I would wager he's been following us in order to catch us out."

"And even if he isn't here," Lenore added, "once the announcement is made and he gets wind of it, he'll act."

Reese agreed with her. He peeked at Freddy, wishing the two of them could conduct their lives in peace, without the scrutiny of the crowd or the threat of disaster hanging over them. Even if they did catch the man in the bowler hat, would there be others? Was it even possible for the two of them to build some sort of happy, peaceful life together?

"Look there," Lenore whispered a few minutes later, as Lady Katya entered the ballroom and marched straight through the chattering crowd to where the orchestra was tuning their instruments on a raised platform. "I think our moment has come."

She was right. Lady Katya stepped up onto the platform and turned to greet her guests. "Ladies and gentlemen, I am so glad to welcome you to our home tonight," she began in her surprisingly powerful voice. "As you may imagine, I am in no mood for long speeches tonight." Several people grumbled and huffed in agreement. "But we do have something to celebrate, even if it isn't the election results. It is my great pleasure to announce the engagement of some good friends of our family, Lord Frederick Herrington and Miss Lenore Garrett, of Haskell, Wyoming." She extended a hand toward Freddy and Lenore.

Gasps of surprise and delight rang through the room, followed by applause as Freddy and Lenore smiled and waved and acknowledged the well-wishes. Reese took a step back, blending into the palms somewhat. A twist of jealousy gnawed at his gut, even though he knew it was illogical. He knew Freddy loved him. He'd had vivid proof of that in Edith's study as they'd enjoyed each other, body and soul. Their lives and hearts were entwined forever now, but they would never be able to acknowledge it publicly, not like Freddy and Lenore were doing for their sham engagement. True love would never receive the outpouring of happiness that it deserved. It was a bitter pill to swallow, knowing that if he and Freddy stood up before the same crowd of friends and acquaintances and professed their love for each other, they would be arrested and jailed.

"To express our delight at this excellent engagement," Lady Katya went on, drawing attention back to herself, "I would invite Lord Herrington and his lovely bride-to-be to open the dancing tonight."

She gestured to the orchestra, who trilled their way

into the opening notes of a waltz. Freddy made a gallant show of bowing to Lenore and offering his hand. Lenore, in true American style and with a theatricality worthy of the West End, took Freddy's hand, giggling and pink-faced, and leapt forward, stealing a bold kiss with everyone watching. A few people gasped in horror, but most of the company sighed romantically as they walked, hand in hand, out to the center of the dance floor. Reese smiled and applauded with everyone else, but the injustice of it all grated at his nerves. At least Lenore was doing a brilliant job of perpetuating the ruse.

The waltz began. Freddy and Lenore managed to somehow look utterly besotted with each other as they swept around the dance floor. Freddy was devastatingly handsome in a suit that fit his muscular form to perfection. Reese entertained a quick fantasy of peeling Freddy out of that suit while he begged to be fucked, like he had the day before. The last thing he needed during a ball where the blackmailer might make a move was an erection, though, so he moved away from the potted palms, searching for a drink.

He'd made it halfway around the ballroom and was striding toward a footman holding a tray of champagne flutes when a sinister voice murmured behind him, "They make an attractive couple."

Reese's nerves instantly bristled, both with fury and with the excitement of the trap they'd set working. He spun to the side to see the man in the bowler hat—without the hat, of course—standing against the wall. His hands were clasped in front of him and he wore a benign smile, all of which contributed to his nondescript look.

Reese changed direction to confront him. "You won't bring him down," he growled, failing to hide his disgust.

The man chuckled. "You think a fake engagement can protect him?" He snorted.

"All you have is a photograph of the two of us taken through a window," Reese said, darting a glance around to be certain no one was listening in. "I'd wager its quality isn't nearly up to par. And I would also wager that our positions relative to each other could be explained away."

The man shrugged. "Perhaps. But I know your type. You're perverted, you are. You can't keep your dicks out of each other. You're no better than vermin. It'll only be a matter of time before I catch the two of you at your evil deeds. And when I do, I'll make you pay for it."

Rage seethed through Reese, but with it was a deadly sort of satisfaction. It appeared he was right about the man following him and Freddy. And if he was busy following them, trying to snap grotesque photographs, he wasn't taking those photographs to the press. It was enough to make Reese wonder if the man was in it to expose what he saw as evil or because he had a deeper fascination with it.

"We aren't paying your ransom," he told the man just as the orchestra finished the final notes of the waltz. A great many more couples had joined Freddy and Lenore on the dance floor, and the milling swirl of them all returning to the edges of the room to find new partners or drinks or to resume conversations provided a grand distraction. "You aren't getting a cent from me."

Out of the corner of his eye, Reese noticed Freddy and Lenore searching for him.

"Oh, I'll get more than a cent," the man said. "I'll get my pound of flesh as well."

Reese glared at him. "Who are you anyhow?"

The man said nothing. Freddy and Lenore spotted him and cut through the crowd, making their way over to Reese. Reese glanced their way, raising his hand to acknowledge them. When he turned back, the man was gone.

Reese swore under his breath, taking a step back and searching for the bastard. He caught sight of the man's back retreating swiftly through the crowd, heading toward the ballroom door. He started after him, but paused, turning back to Freddy and Lenore.

They took a painfully long time to reach him as every other person they passed stopped them to offer congratulations. Reese glanced to the door again, debating whether to leave them behind to chase after the man himself. If they could follow him, see where he went after leaving Marlowe House, discover where he lived, perhaps they could not only stop him from going to the press, they could destroy his stash of blackmail photographs, or even his photography equipment.

"Was that him?" Lenore asked once they finally reached Reese.

"Yes," Reese said.

"What did he have to say?" Freddy asked.

"What you would expect him to say," Reese growled. He took Freddy's hand, heedless of anyone who might be watching, and started toward the door. "We have to find him and follow him."

reddy glanced from Reese's frustrated scowl ahead of him to Lenore and her curious, excited expression behind him as they dodged their way through the crowd at the edges of the ballroom and made their way into the hall. His blood pumped hard and fast at the touch of Reese's hand, both because it was a glorious comfort and because it would give them away in a heartbeat if anyone noticed it. He reached back for Lenore's hand to balance the scene, and was subsequently disappointed when Reese let his hand go. It seemed like an all too apt metaphor for the situation they all found themselves in.

"Do you have any idea where the man went from here?" he asked once the three of them were in the hall and away from most of the other guests.

Reese glanced up and down the long hallway, his frown growing. "No," he admitted at last with a huff. "I wanted to wait for the two of you before chasing after him."

"Which means we've lost valuable time," Lenore said. Her brow knit in thought as she, too, searched up and down the hall.

"We've no choice but to look for him," Freddy said after only a few seconds of contemplation. "I doubt he will have stayed in the house."

"But did he leave out the front door?" Reese asked, gesturing for them to head up the hall toward the entryway. "Would he be that bold?"

"He's been that bold in the past," Lenore said.

Freddy agreed with her logic, but as they reached the front door of Marlowe House, he doubted the man in the bowler hat would have been able to slip out unnoticed. Lady Katya's butler, Stewart, dressed in a livery as elaborate as any of the dress uniforms the officers of Freddy's military days had worn, stood guard, greeting the late-arriving guests and directing two footmen to take coats and hats.

"Mr. Stewart, have you seen a man of—" Freddy began his description, but realized almost at once that describing the man in the bowler hat would be impossible.

"Have you seen a man who doesn't look as though he belongs here," Reese finished for him.

Stewart regarded both of them and Lenore with the barest hint of surprise on his stoic face. "No, my lord. Only Lord and Lady Campbell's guests have been admitted this evening. There have been a few hangers-on without invitations who have been politely turned away, of course, as there always are," he went on, "but I can assure you, no one who should not be here will get past me."

Freddy exchanged a look with Reese. It seemed cruel to inform the man that someone had, in fact, slipped past him, but at least they now knew the man in the bowler hat hadn't come through the front door.

"Thank you, Mr. Stewart," Freddy said before he, Reese, and Lenore headed back down the hall toward the ballroom.

"How many other ways are there to get in and out of a grand house like this?" Lenore asked as they paused at the intersection of the main hall and a smaller, side corridor.

"Who knows?" Reese shrugged. "The front door and the servants' hall are the main ways that I can think of."

"Then we should check the servants' hall," Lenore said, leading them off down the side corridor. She paused a few steps later, turned to them, and asked, "Um, is this the way to the servants' hall?"

Freddy couldn't help but grin. He still wasn't entirely comfortable with engaging himself to Lenore as a ruse, but he had to admit he liked her determination and her boldness.

"It must be," Reese said with the same laughter in his voice, starting after her. "I just saw a maid rush by at the end of the hall."

They continued on, Lenore in the lead. Freddy darted a quick grin in Reese's direction. Reese smiled right back, amusement glittering in his eyes. The expression was so striking that Freddy nearly missed a step. There they were, in the middle of a dire operation taking place during a ball where they had launched the biggest deception he'd ever been a part of in his life, and all he wanted to do was draw Reese into one of the side parlors they passed, throw him up against the wall, and kiss him silly.

Oddly enough, as the thought struck him, he caught exactly the sort of sound he imagined he and Reese would make while locked in an embrace coming from one of the rooms. Lenore must have caught it too, because as soon as she walked past an open doorway and turned her head to glance inside, she gasped and leapt back, nearly bowling into Freddy and Reese as she did.

"What is it?" Freddy whispered, grasping Reese's hand and Lenore's waist to steady both of them.

Lenore whipped her head silently toward him, raising a finger to her lips, her eyes bright with mischief.

"Forgive me," a man's voice said from inside the room. "I shouldn't have taken that liberty."

Freddy's brow shot up. The voice belonged to Linus Townsend.

"I've been waiting for you to take that liberty for so long now," a woman's voice answered. It was Natalia Marlowe, of course. "Kiss me again."

"I want to," Townsend said, his voice rough with

desire, "but I'm afraid if I do it will lead to more. And you remember what your mother said."

"Blast Mama," Natalia answered breathlessly. "I'm tired of being the only one in the family who doesn't know things. I want to know, and I want you to teach me."

"Oh, my darling," Townsend replied, a little too enthusiastically.

His statement was followed by the rustle of fabric and Natalia's long, deep sigh of pleasure. Freddy's eyes went even wider, and he glanced desperately to Reese. Reese, damn him, looked as though he was about to burst into laughter. So much so that he clapped a hand over his mouth to keep it inside. Lenore seemed caught between joining in with their laughter and trying to crane her neck into the doorway just enough to spy on the romantic scene without being caught doing it.

When Natalia let out a long, amorous, "Oh, yes," Freddy knew it was time to act.

"We have to move on," he whispered. "For their sake and for ours."

"Right," Reese said in return, clearing his throat. "Let's just walk past as though nothing is out of the ordinary."

The three of them nodded to each other, then swayed into motion, passing by the doorway as fast as they could. Freddy couldn't bring himself to glance into the room for fear of what he might see. As soon as they'd walked on,

Natalia let out a startled squeal, there was a thump, and then came a flurry of movement.

"Hurry," Freddy murmured, laughing and pushing them on to the corner at the end of the hall. "I don't want them seeing us any more than they want to be seen."

They reached the corner and hurried on, through a second doorway and down a plain set of stairs that lead to the vast, downstairs area. Freddy was tempted to stop and have a good laugh about what they'd just interrupted. Reese was still trying to contain his laughter. It was Lenore who kept them focused on their mission, though.

"Have you seen a man who shouldn't be here dashing about?" she asked one of the harried-looking maids as soon as they reached the foot of the stairs. "Anyone who might have gone out the kitchen door?"

"No, ma'am," the maid said, curtsying and looking desperate to continue with her work. "Begging your pardon, my lords," she said to Freddy and Reese. "You might ask Cook."

"Yes, we should." Freddy cleared his throat, forcing himself to concentrate.

They headed on through the chaos of activity that was downstairs, making their way past startled maids and footmen to the kitchen. But Lady Katya's cook hadn't noticed a thing.

"If someone who shouldn't be here had tried to wedge their way in when we are this busy," she said with a look that was downright mutinous as she continued directing her army of kitchen maids, "I would have noticed and shooed them out at once."

"Point taken, ma'am," Freddy told her with an apologetic smile and a nod. He gestured for Reese and Lenore to hurry out of the kitchen.

"Just because they're busy doesn't mean the man didn't come this way," Reese said, his scowl returning.

"True," Lenore said as they hurried back up the servants' stairs. "But something tells me he didn't leave this way."

"Dammit, we must find him," Freddy growled, then sent an apologetic look to Lenore as they stepped back into the corridor upstairs. "Sorry. I shouldn't use such language."

Lenore laughed loudly. "I've heard a thousand times worse in Haskell, I can assure you."

The amusing, frustrating interlude had done nothing to advance their search for the blackmailer. By the time they reached the front hall once more, the only thing they'd managed to do was waste time.

"The longer this takes, the greater the chance that the bastard will get away," Reese huffed in frustration, pausing to rub a hand over his face.

"Then the two of you will have to go out there and find him," Lenore said.

Freddy glanced to Reese with an expression that said she was right. To Lenore he said, "You wouldn't mind me abandoning you at our engagement ball?"

Lenore made an impatient noise. "The interesting

part has already come and gone. The rest is just me being congratulated by people I don't know for the rest of the evening. Which will be delightful, of course," she added with a wide smile. "Men are always more interested in a woman that someone else has already laid claim to. This is my chance to size up the stock in London's corral." She flickered her eyebrows.

Freddy laughed in spite of himself. It was a bloody shame that he wasn't inclined to appreciate Lenore as a mate. The man who ended up with her would have his hands full, but he would never be bored. He surged forward to kiss her cheek in thanks. "We owe you," he said.

"You're already paying me back a thousand times over," she said before winking once more, then spinning, ball gown flaring, to hurry back to the ballroom.

"Our coats?" Freddy asked Stewart, who had watched the entire scene with an implacable expression.

"Second door on the right, my lord." Stewart nodded down the hall.

It wasn't until they were halfway to the parlor where the coats were being kept that Freddy noticed Reese's tight expression. Once they turned the corner into the parlor and Freddy was certain they were alone, he asked, "Is something wrong?"

Reese's lips twitched and he glanced sideways at Freddy as they set about searching the rows of portable coatracks where the guests' coats were hung. They spotted their things deep into the room.

"Are you certain you don't actually want to marry Lenore?" Reese asked in a thin voice as they pulled their coats from their hangers.

Freddy threw his coat over his shoulders, letting out a breath as he slipped his arms into the sleeves. For some reason, Reese's show of jealousy warmed him from the inside out. He leaned closer to Reese to whisper, "Do you not recall the position you had me in just yesterday and what I asked you to do to me?"

Reese's face flushed a deep, alluring red as he pushed his arms into his sleeves. "That doesn't mean as much as you think, you know." For a moment, Freddy assumed Reese was saying he didn't care for him and was offended, until Reese rushed on with, "There are plenty of men who enjoy the company of both sexes. If you haven't had much experience, how do you know that isn't you?"

Relief spilled through Freddy, bringing laughter in its wake. "Even if it were true," he said, shaking his head, "I've made my choice. I know who I want to be with."

He started back toward the parlor door, but Reese grabbed his arm to stop him.

"Are you certain?" Reese asked.

Freddy rocked back a step to stand eye-to-eye with Reese. "Yes," he said, resting a hand on Reese's hot cheek. "Of course I'm certain. I've never been more certain of anything in my life."

Joy and anxiety mixed together in Reese's expression. "Because if we aren't able to catch this blackmailer and silence him, this might not be the end of danger for either of us."

"We will catch him," Freddy said, amazed that he was so certain.

Reese pulled Freddy's hand away from his face, twining their fingers together and standing closer to him. "I was a lovesick, optimistic fool to think the two of us could just be together, as bold as you please. Just because our friends, or at least some of them, have known and accepted how we feel doesn't mean the world at large will be as forgiving."

Freddy laughed, squeezing Reese's hand tighter. "You were the one who risked everything to buy my failing estate, Reese. You mercilessly lured me into your bed."

"It was your bed," Reese countered him, arching one eyebrow. "And I was extraordinarily merciful about it."

Heat rippled off of Reese, filling Freddy and making him hard at the least convenient time. "Either way," he said, "you led and I followed. You taught and I learned. And now you're telling me to step back?"

"You can still save yourself," Reese argued, his gaze dropping to Freddy's lips.

Freddy slipped an arm under his still unbuttoned coat and around his waist, pulling Reese flush against his body. "If you think that, then you haven't been paying attention," he said, his voice a low purr. "I love you, Reese Howsden. In spite of your high-handed ways and your reckless belief in your own invincibility."

"It's not high-handed if I know what's best," Reese replied, a rakish tilt to his lips and a spark in his eyes. "If left to your own devices, you'd be homeless and lost, without an estate or a penny to your name."

"True," Freddy said, letting his hand slide down to caress Reese's backside. "And without me, you'd be beholden to a blackmailing bastard, your money draining away to keep your secret."

"Not to mention the fact that I'd be pining away for want of you," Reese added in a breathless voice. He circled his arms around Freddy's waist under the concealment of Freddy's coat, digging his fingertips into Freddy's back.

"Which makes us even at last," Freddy said, bringing his lips close to Reese's. "Neither of us is truly happy without the other. I still reserve the right to resent your management of me, but in the end, we balance each other."

"We do," Reese said, leaning into Freddy, the heat between them crackling.

"So how could you possibly think that I might want anyone other than you?" Freddy asked.

"I don't know," Reese breathed before closing his mouth over Freddy's.

In spite of everything, the kiss came as a surprise, but a welcome one. Freddy closed his eyes and gave into it, moaning softly as their lips parted and their tongues danced. He would never get tired of the taste of Reese or the pulsing need that the press of Reese's hard cock against him raised in him. But it was more than the fiery demand of lust that begged to be satisfied, more than the bodily urges that turned his mind off and made him want to meld with Reese. It was the love that ran so deep within him it joined his soul to Reese's. Yes, he wanted to tangle his naked body with Reese's and feel Reese inside of him, but even more, he wanted to sit across the breakfast table and talk about inconsequential things, argue over petty disagreements, snuggle in front of a fire with him on cold, winter nights, and grow old with him. He wanted everything.

A discreet throat-clearing from the parlor's doorway shattered the tender moment, sending ice water through Freddy's veins. He and Reese leapt apart from each other, red and panting, trousers tented far too obviously, and whipped toward the door. A lone, blushing footman stood watching them.

"I beg your pardon," Freddy blurted out, hurriedly closing his coat to hide his erection. He couldn't bring himself to look at the footman, or at Reese, for that matter. Reese had turned away from the young man and was frantically buttoning his coat with shaking hands.

"It's all right, my lord," the footman said in clipped tones. He glanced over his shoulder into the hall, then said, "I've been standing guard to make sure no one saw what they shouldn't."

Freddy swallowed hard, blazing with the heat of lust and embarrassment. "But you saw," Freddy said softly.

"I did, my lord." The footman nodded and glanced down awkwardly.

"We're terribly sorry," Reese said, standing as regally as he could and heading for the door. "I trust we can rely on your discretion?" he asked the footman with a wince.

"Certainly, my lord," the footman answered with a confident nod. "Our sort have to stick together, after all," he added with reluctant slowness.

Freddy's brow shot up as a relief like nothing he'd known filled him. "That's certainly right," he said in a hoarse voice. "We do, Mr.?"

"Ivan," the footman said. "Ivan Logan, my lord."

"Thank you, Ivan," Freddy said from the bottom of his heart.

He and Reese attempted to continue on, but Ivan stopped them with, "The man you're looking for, my lords."

Freddy froze, eyes going wide. "The man in the bowler hat?"

"You know about him?" Reese added.

Ivan nodded. "He's a nasty one, Mr. Fordyce is."

Freddy almost shouted in victory. "Is that his name?"

"It is," Ivan answered with a nod. "We all know about him. Our society, that is. The Brotherhood." He spoke the name with a slight question, glancing to Reese.

Reese broke into a smile and let out a breath. "Yes, of course. I don't know why I didn't think to ask their help from the start."

"The Brotherhood?" Freddy asked.

"I told you that there are numerous fellowships of men like us throughout England," Reese said. "The Brotherhood is just one. A unique one," he turned back to Ivan, "as it is made up of men from all social classes. I've attended a few gatherings myself by special invitation."

"Gatherings?" Freddy arched a brow, assuming he knew what that meant.

"It's all above board," Ivan reassured him. "Just friendship. Not like some of those other clubs. Though that's not to say more hasn't come out of it from time to time." He blushed furiously.

A thousand questions jumped to Freddy's mind. He felt as though he'd only just pulled back the corner of a curtain to gaze in at an entire world he knew nothing about but was destined to be a part of. There wasn't time for questions, though.

"Mr. Fordyce," he said as a way to move their immediate matter forward.

"Makes his living blackmailing our lot," Ivan went on in a rush, sensing the urgency. "I saw him here tonight. He came in through a window in the library and left the same way. He must have bribed someone in the house to let him in."

"That bastard," Reese said, energetic once more. "Do you know where we can find him?" he asked.

"He has a flat in Rupert Court, near Leicester Square."

"Then that's where we need to go," Reese said, starting for the door.

Freddy hesitated. "If you know where he lives, why hasn't anyone gone after him before?"

"Not everyone knows where he lives," Ivan said, his face turning redder. "It's just, I know a bloke who he paid to pose for photographs," he swallowed, "and some other things. He was sworn to secrecy on the threat of having those photographs exposed. He'd lose his place for sure, you see, and not be able to get another one."

"Fear," Reese said. "The man makes his living by fear."

"And he's just as much of a hypocrite as I thought," Freddy sighed, bubbling with hatred for the man. "If we fail tonight, at least we'll know where to send Jack to finish the job."

"But the photographs, my lord," Ivan asked, looking suddenly terrified.

"They won't ever see the light of day," Freddy promised. "Not if we have anything to do about it."

He nodded to Ivan, then to Reese, gesturing for him to head out. The two of them marched back through the hall and out the front door. The danger was still there, perhaps more than it had been before, knowing how many other men's lives they held in their hands. But that only meant it was more important than ever for them to catch Fordyce and destroy him.

CHAPTER 19

*R*eese had never been a violent man. He had always enjoyed the finer things of life and appreciated culture more than brute force. But as the carriage he and Freddy borrowed to take them to Rupert Court slowed at the end of the street to let them out as covertly as possible, he was ready for blood.

"Ivan didn't say which building was Fordyce's or which flat," Freddy said, studying the buildings as though planning a military campaign.

"We'll find him," Reese vowed, clenching his hands into fists for a moment before striding forward.

Rupert Court walked a line between the respectable businesses to the north and seedier enterprises of the Seven Dials area to the south. It was the perfect place for a man to live if he wanted to appear respectable while still wallowing in the muck. The tall, uninteresting buildings had an air of something not quite presentable covered by a respectable façade. Several shops and pubs occupied the ground floors. The weather was fair, so several patrons from the pubs spilled out onto the street, laughing a little too loudly as they drank their beer and spoke to women who were dressed adequately, but who were likely whores.

Reese threw whatever caution he had left to the wind and approached a couple outside of the nearest pub. The man, who had been leaning against the wall with a mug in one hand, chatting up a woman, sent an irritated look Reese's way and stood straight when he realized he was the focus of Reese's stern stare.

"I ain't done nothing," the man said before Reese could open his mouth.

"I didn't say you did," Reese replied, then sped on to, "Do you know where Fordyce lives?"

The man's startled, defensive expression flattened to a knowing sneer. "Oh. Him." His lip curled with disgust. "What'd you want anything to do with him for?"

Reese's chest squeezed. He'd miscalculated. Judging by the way the man was sizing him up, the locals not only knew who Fordyce was and what his business consisted of, the man was painting him with the same brush.

He opened his mouth, but before he could think of something to say, Freddy strode commandingly up behind him.

"Scotland Yard," Freddy said, his entire demeanor as commanding as any soldier. "We've heard reports of unscrupulous activity, and we're here to investigate."

The man snorted and exchanged a look with his female companion. "It's about bloody time." He pushed farther away from the wall and nodded to the upper floors of a building across the street and a few doors down. "He lives over there, number fourteen. I don't know which flat, thankfully."

Freddy nodded, snapping to attention and executing a military bow for good measure. "Your help is greatly appreciated," he said before turning sharply and crossing the street, gesturing for Reese to follow him.

"That was bloody brilliant," Reese murmured as they stepped up on to the opposite curb.

"It could have backfired tremendously," Freddy said, sending Reese an anxious, sideways look. "I believe Fordyce's neighbors know what he's up to."

"Which automatically throws suspicion on us for looking for him," Reese finished the sentence.

Freddy hummed in wary agreement, then stepped ahead to push open the door to Fordyce's building.

There was nothing inside the building that marked it as exceptional in any way. The dim front entry was clean, but that was the best that could be said for it. The walls held no adornment and the floor had no carpet. The thing on the doors that marked one flat apart from the others were painted numbers.

"One step closer, one step farther away," Freddy sighed, rubbing a hand over his face.

Reese shook his head, marching to the end of the downstairs hall, checking each of the doors that led to the ground floor flats. "Ivan said he had a friend who had been to Fordyce's flat for photographs and other things."

"I think I can tell you what those other things were," Freddy grumbled, following Reese to the end of the hall and then back again. They started up the stairs to the first floor. "The man is the very worst kind of hypocrite."

"He is," Reese agreed, keeping his voice low as he checked the doors on the second floor. "But the very fact that he lures young men to his flat or pays them to come means that his door must have some sort of distinguishing mark."

"Or not," Freddy argued. "You'd think a man like that would go out of his way to be as anonymous as possible. I mean, you've seen the way he can blend in and out of a crowd without being noticed."

"Yes," Reese agreed, reaching the last door on the hall and deciding they still didn't have the right floor. He gestured for Freddy to follow him to the second floor. "But instinct tells me he wouldn't go handing out the location of his flat to just anyone either."

"True," Freddy said as they reached the second floor.

"Which means there must be another way for the flies to know which flat is the spider's web," Reese finished.

Freddy huffed a humorless laugh. "I find that metaphor disturbing."

"I find this whole thing disturbing." Reese glanced over his shoulder to Freddy with a sour smirk. The deeper they went into Fordyce's muck, the more he hated the man.

No sooner had the thought taken hold in his mind when he reached the door at the end of the hall. Along with the number 22, it was marked with a small, blue stroke of paint with splotches beneath it. To anyone who wasn't looking, it might have appeared as though someone had spilled or splattered paint by accident, but Reese instantly saw more.

Freddy saw it too. He stepped up behind Reese and whispered, "Is it just my imagination or does the man have an erect phallus painted on his door?"

"My thoughts exactly," Reese said, tempted to laugh.

"So much for subtlety." Freddy reached past him to knock lightly on the door.

They waited, but heard nothing. No one came to answer the door and there wasn't so much as a peep from behind it. Reese's nerves bristled.

"Do you think he's just hiding or genuinely not here?" Freddy asked.

Reese glanced to him. "It's possible we could have beaten him home. He might have had other errands to run after threatening me."

"Well," Freddy said, pushing up his sleeves and speaking somewhat louder. "I haven't come all this way to walk home, scratching my head."

He tested the door handle, and when the door proved locked, he raised his leg and kicked the door so hard Reese flinched. The wood around the lock splintered, and the door swung open. Reese's heart pounded as Freddy stepped into the flat.

"If we weren't in the middle of a delicate operation, I would be extraordinarily aroused by that feat of strength," he said, tempted to laugh.

That temptation died a moment later. The flat was small, with no more than a front room and a bedroom leading off of it. The entire place was hung with photographs in various stages of production. It smelled strongly of photographic chemicals as well. One side of the main room was draped with a sheet of some sort, a chaise standing in front of it, with an empty tripod arranged as if the space were a studio. Reese caught sight of several alarming accessories on a table to the side, from leather straps to marble phalluses, as he followed Freddy across to the bedroom.

Aside from a rumpled bed, the corner of the bedroom was hung with thick, dark fabric, as though it served as a darkroom when needed. More photographs hung on the walls, most of them staged and grotesquely pornographic. The sight must have upset Freddy, because he took one look and dashed back into the front room to catch his breath.

"Hypocritical and perverted," Reese said in acid tones, following Freddy out of the bedroom.

"How do we even begin to destroy all of this?" Freddy asked in a hoarse voice. He moved toward one wall that was entirely covered with photographs, mostly candid, like the ones of Reese and Sebastian. Freddy's eyes went wide. "I know several of these men. I didn't know they were...." His words faded.

Reese didn't need him to finish the sentence. "You'd be surprised by who does what behind closed doors," he said, marching up to Freddy's side and setting to work taking down the photographs. He lingered over one photograph, tilting it toward Freddy. "This one, for example. He's not a homosexual, he just likes his cock sucked, and he's not particular about who does it."

Freddy made a sound that was either acknowledgement or disgust and joined Reese in pulling down the photographs. "I suppose we can burn these in the grate," he said, still hoarse.

"Burn them," Reese said, "tear them up, soak them in water. There are a hundred different ways to destroy a photograph. It's the equipment and the negatives and plates we should really worry about."

They took down every photograph from the wall. Freddy continued tearing down the others scattered around the room while Reese built a fire in the grate, using handfuls of photographs as kindling. There was so much to destroy, though, and they had hardly begun when a startled grunt came from the hall, followed by Fordyce dashing into the flat, his eyes wide.

"What are you...how did you...get out!" he shouted, more panicked than demanding.

"Mr. Fordyce, how nice of you to join us," Reese said, seething with hate as he threw the last handful of photographs into the fire and stood.

Fordyce's eyes grew wider. "How do you know—"

"A man like you makes enemies," Reese said, approaching him with fists balled. "Many enemies."

Fordyce stood where he was for a moment, mouth hanging open in shock, trembling slightly. It came as no surprise at all to Reese that the man was a coward when identified and called out. And it shouldn't have come as a surprise when Fordyce turned and darted from the flat.

"Stay here," Reese called to Freddy as he darted for the door. "Destroy everything as fast as you can." There was no telling if Fordyce had anything stored outside of his flat, but the quicker they were able to get rid of what he had, the safer they all would be.

Fordyce was halfway down the stairs when Reese dashed out into the hall and descended after him. The relative quiet of the building shifted to opening doors and curious stares as Reese chased Fordyce down.

"What's all this?" a middle-aged woman called after them as they tore through the first floor.

"Stop that racket," a man shouted from the ground floor as Fordyce hurled himself out the door.

Reese ignored them, praying they would simply go back to whatever they'd been doing instead of raising a fuss and calling the police. He chased Fordyce out into the street, gaining on him quickly. The man might have been a clever sneak, but he was in poor shape compared to Reese and barely made it halfway down the block before Reese grabbed the back of his collar and yanked him to a stop.

"You bloody coward," Reese growled, spinning Fordyce around to face him. "Hypocritical bastard."

He grabbed the front of Fordyce's coat and threw a punch out of sheer rage, landing it against the side of Fordyce's face with a sickening crack. Fordyce flinched to the side but managed to stay on his feet. That was fine, as far as Reese was concerned. It allowed him to throw a second punch, growling with all the years of frustration and anger that had built up in him over the way society made him hide who he was and whom he loved. He punched Fordyce a third time, turning his nose into a bloody pulp, for every man who risked his life every day for the chance to live and to love that was denied them.

"It's none of your concern," he roared, shaking Fordyce as hard as he could. "You ruin lives for money, but what have we ever done to you? You could have left us alone, but no."

He wanted to punch the man again, but instead, he let go of him, pushing him back. Fordyce spilled to the ground, whimpering and moaning as he covered his head. He pulled himself into a ball, as though he expected Reese to kick him.

"Oy! Get him!" a deep voice shouted from the pub across the street.

Panic flooded Reese, and for a moment he thought the half dozen men charging across the street were about to attack. He raised his fists defensively, wishing that Freddy were there to either save him or go down fighting with him. He was determined not to be as cowardly as

Fordyce, though. If he was about to die for who he was and whom he loved, then so be it.

But instead of attacking him, one of the men shouted, "Kick 'im! Kick the bloody fag while he's down."

Reese's stomach turned. The men didn't know. To them, he was one of them, one of the blokes, on the right side of the fence. He had the sickening feeling that they would cheer him on until he killed Fordyce in front of them, and then they would likely buy him a drink and laugh about destroying vermin. Bile rose in Reese's throat, knowing that at the drop of a hat, he would be in Fordyce's place.

He straightened, tugging at his coat, which he'd never had a chance to remove in Fordyce's flat. "My orders are to bring him in for questioning," he lied. "The man is wanted on several counts of gross indecency." Using the very law that was designed to destroy him and men like him as a way to save Fordyce from death turned Reese's stomach, but if he let the mob rule, he would be no less of a hypocrite than Fordyce.

Instead, he bent over, grabbing Fordyce's arm and wrenching him to his feet. The coward whimpered and wept, blood streaming freely down his face from his nose, as Reese tugged him back toward the flat. He stumbled along, moving like a child who had been caught by his nanny and knew punishment couldn't be avoided. The crowd that had been watching the scene didn't lift a finger to help him. They turned back to their beer and other amusements as if nothing had happened.

By the time they returned to the flat, the whole place stank with the acrid smell of burning photographs and chemicals. Freddy had swallowed whatever revulsion he felt to empty the bedroom of its photographs. He crouched by the grate, watching the corners of the pictures curling and melting as the images burned, but at the sight of Reese and the bloodied Fordyce, he jumped up, eyes going wide.

"You caught him," he said, shoving his handful of photographs into the flame, then coming to meet Reese in the center of the room.

"I told you I wasn't going to let him get away with this," Reese growled, glaring at Fordyce.

"Please," Fordyce begged him in a soggy, nasal voice. "Let me go. I'll give you whatever you want. Those photographs? They're yours. And I don't need the money."

"Oh, no," Reese said, panting with the force of exertion and fury. "You're not getting out of things that easily."

"I assume there was a fight?" Freddy asked, towering over Fordyce and pushing up his sleeves threateningly.

"Please," Fordyce wept. "Spare me. Spare my life. We...we're the same, you and I," he swallowed hard, darting a glance between Reese and Freddy.

"We're nothing at all alike," Reese spat.

"Where are the rest of your photographs?" Freddy asked with menacing calm, narrowing his eyes.

"They're here," Fordyce stammered. He pulled out of

Reese's grasp and stumbled to a bureau on one side of the room. "They're all here. I have everything you could possibly need. Great and important men in compromised positions." He pulled open a drawer and began piling its contents on top of the bureau. "You could make a fortune off of them."

Reese glared at the man, then exchanged a look with Freddy. Fordyce was lower than vermin, but the way he threw open drawers, offering them photographs, made Reese think that perhaps his entire store of blackmail items really was all in the flat.

"Or more entertaining pictures," Fordyce went on, opening another drawer and pulling more photographs out. "I've got every pose to suit your fancy, young men and boys. These sell for a pretty penny as well. You could be rich, you could both be rich."

"Burn them," Freddy growled, advancing on Fordyce and making the man cower. "Burn them all. You are going to destroy every last incriminating item in this flat."

"But...but they're worth a fortune," Fordyce wept.

"They're kindling," Reese said, striding to the bureau. He picked up a handful of filth and thrust it at Fordyce. "You're going to destroy it all, and we're going to watch to make certain you do."

"But I have nothing else," the man continued to snivel, messy with blood and tears and snot. "It's all gone to paying off debts. I have no money left."

"That is not our problem," Reese said. "Burn them."

Fordyce blubbered and protested, wept and pleaded,

but in the end, he thrust every one of the photographs and negatives in his flat into the fire. It took more than an hour, which alarmed Reese to no end. Just when he thought they had seen the last of the filth, Fordyce produced more and more and more. The sheer volume of evil the man produced and fed into the fire—each new stash more disgusting than the last—shocked Reese. He wasn't completely certain everything Fordyce had was destroyed until the man's weeping took on a whole new, pathetic character and he sank to the floor in utter despair.

"You win," Fordyce moaned pathetically. "I'm ruined now."

"Just as you sought to ruin us?" Freddy asked, arms crossed, not a trace of sympathy in his expression.

"It was...it was nothing personal." Fordyce glanced up at him. "It was just a way to make money. I started out legitimately enough, taking and selling dirty pictures. But then I saw what those pictures could do in the right hands."

"Destroy lives," Reese said, too tired to shout anymore, even though he held nothing but contempt for the man.

"But not your lives, never yours," Fordyce insisted.

Freddy snorted, crossing to the bureau where two cameras sat. "That's a lie if ever I heard one." He picked up one of the cameras, and without a second thought, smashed it down hard on the top edge of the bureau.

"No!" Fordyce yelled as the fragile contraption shattered. "Not my cameras."

Freddy dropped the splintered pieces of the camera to the floor, then picked up the other one and shattered that as well. He then disappeared into the bedroom. The sound of shattering glass and more splintering followed. Fordyce slumped to his side, sprawled on the floor, weeping so pitifully that Reese was tempted to kick him after all.

"That's it," Freddy said as he marched back into the main room. "All the photographs are burned, every last piece of camera or developing material is destroyed. I even dumped the bottles of chemicals on this bastard's bed for good measure."

Fordyce moaned, but Reese didn't have a shred of pity for him. "You will leave England immediately," he told Fordyce. "I don't care where you go, the continent, the orient, Australia, just go. Never show your face here again."

"If you do," Freddy added, "or if you decide to delay your departure, just know that we are close personal friends of Assistant Commissioner Craig, and by dawn, he will have given your description to every police officer in the city."

"And judging by the reaction of the men from the pub," Reese added, "you won't have many friends to hide you."

Freddy shook his head and sighed, pushing a hand through his hair. "You could have had friends," he said.

"You could have had men help you to build a life." He glanced to Reese, a tired smile softening his face. "We have friends, whether I knew it at first or not. Just because we have to be careful doesn't mean we can't live perfectly happy lives with those who care about us and want to see us safe and happy."

Reese smiled. He wanted to go to Freddy and embrace him, not for any carnal purpose, but just to hold him and tell him he was right, they were not alone. But Fordyce didn't deserve to see a display of affection like that. Not when he had worked so hard to destroy it.

"Let's go," he said instead. "Let's leave this bastard to his fate."

He headed for the door, turning to glare at Fordyce one last time in warning before nodding to Freddy and leaving the flat. A weight lifted from his shoulders as they descended through the now quiet building, side by side. They'd kept each other safe, and that was more than he ever could have asked for.

CHAPTER 20

*I*t was late by the time Freddy and Reese made their exhausted way back to Howsden House.

"I should really go home to Henny's," Freddy said as he and Reese dragged themselves through the front door and past the bleary-eyed footman who had stayed up to see them home.

"No, you shouldn't," Reese said, sending him a grin that invoked every manner of mischief, in spite of being just as worn out. "I've got plans for your night yet."

Freddy caught his breath, nearly popping a button on his coat as he undid it to hand to the footman. He sent a significant glance to Reese, darting his eyes sideways to the distracted footman. Reese, in turn, shook his head and shrugged out of his coat with a lopsided grin. Freddy was no expert at reading Reese's expressions yet, but he took the look and gesture to mean that the footman knew all and wouldn't tell.

That still wasn't enough for him to ask openly what Reese had in mind or to return Reese's increasingly heated grin. He was glad he'd kept his expression neutral when Lenore popped her head out of the parlor halfway down the hall.

"There you two are," she said, walking fully into the hall. "I've been beside myself with worry."

Behind Lenore, Henry and Mr. Garrett stepped into the hall.

"There, you see?" Henry said. "I told you that they'd be home before midnight without a scratch on them."

"It's twelve-thirty," Lenore told Henry with a frown. That frown didn't last, though. She was smiling again within seconds as she paraded up the hall to meet Reese and Freddy. "How did things go?" she asked with a knowing arch of her eyebrow.

"The matter is taken care of," Freddy said carefully. He glanced past Lenore to her father, then went ahead and stepped close to Lenore, resting a hand on her arm and leaning in to give her cheek an affectionate kiss.

"Smart man," Lenore whispered, her eyebrow flickering up and her mouth twitching into an impish smile. "Papa was concerned," she said slightly louder, spinning to the side to hook her arm through Freddy's and hug it. "I told you, Papa, Freddy and Reese were called away to help a friend in dire need. And it appears as though everything is well now?" She glanced to Reese for confirmation. Or perhaps to be certain he was in on the ruse.

"Completely well," Reese said without missing a beat. "And once again, I apologize for dragging your fiancé away from your engagement party."

"It wasn't really our engagement party," Lenore insisted with a laugh. "Perhaps we could throw a party of our own soon?" She batted her eyelashes at Freddy.

Freddy laughed. Life certainly wouldn't be boring during the time it took for Lenore to establish herself in London society and to find a real husband. "Whatever you want, darling."

There was nothing fake about the affection he bore for Lenore or his smile. Which was probably for the best as Mr. Garrett seemed to be studying the two of them closely.

"Very well," Mr. Garrett said at last, letting out a tired sigh and starting forward. "You've proven your point, sweetheart. And now I think it's well past time for you to go to bed. Me too, come to that. I've got a boat to catch in the morning."

Lenore skipped away from Freddy and took her father's arm, walking with him upstairs. "I'm going to miss you terribly, Papa," she said as they ascended. "You will smooth things over with Mama, won't you? I'll write a letter for her before I go to bed and give it to you before you leave tomorrow. You can all come over for the wedding, as soon as we settle on a date." She glanced over her shoulder and winked at Freddy before whisking her father on, around a corner, and off to the guest rooms.

Freddy shook his head, sending Reese a knowing look. Henry seemed to know exactly what it was all about. He approached them with a wry grin and thumped Reese on the shoulder.

"So you really have taken care of that problem of yours?" he asked, a hint of genuine worry in his eyes.

"More than taken care of," Reese said. "The man who was blackmailing me, Fordyce, has been completely thwarted."

Freddy inched one eyebrow up. He shouldn't have been surprised that Reese would tell his brother everything. Henry knew about the two of them, after all.

"We found out the location of his flat," he reported to Henry. "It turns out the bastard had hundreds of photographs that I do not care to describe and hope I forget as quickly as possible."

"The bastard made his living on blackmail," Reese continued the story. "You would be horrified at the sort of photographs he had."

"But they're gone now?" Henry asked, looking more alarmed.

"Burned," Freddy said. "We burned them all."

"And Freddy here destroyed the man's cameras and developing equipment," Reese said.

"Right before Reese told him to leave the country or else he would sic our friend, Jack Craig, an assistant commissioner at Scotland Yard, on him."

"I've never seen such a big coward in my entire life." Reese shook his head in disgust.

"At least he's gone now, and with his photographs and equipment destroyed, he won't be able to hurt anyone else," Freddy said.

"And I do believe he'll be out of England by dawn," Reese finished.

Freddy paused, just realizing that Henry's smile had returned and was growing by the second. He glanced between Reese and Freddy with an almost maudlin look of joy.

"What?" Reese asked.

"Nothing," Henry said, laughing.

"Don't give me that," Reese said, grinning. "You look like you're watching two children being adorable."

"I'm just happy for you," Henry said, letting out a tired breath. "I can't help but remember a time, several years ago, when I had made the decision to give up everything for Ellie, when you told me that the man you loved didn't even know you existed. And now...." He let his words fade, but thumped Reese on the arm again.

"I did so know you existed," Freddy said, the heat of sentimentality warming him, even though he was convinced it was silly. "How could I help but notice you?"

"You could have fooled me," Reese said, starlight filling his eyes as he gazed at Freddy.

Freddy let out a breath and shook his head. "From the moment I met you, Reese, I knew my life would never be the same. Everything made sense and I knew what I wanted. Well, until I convinced myself that wasn't what I should want."

"To think of all the time we've wasted," Reese said, his voice softening.

"And with that," Henry said, suddenly loud, stepping away, "I think it's best if I take myself off to bed." He turned to head up the stairs as fast as if something had stung him.

Freddy laughed, his face heating as he watched Henry go. "I suppose it is just a little too much to carry on like that in front of him, even if he understands and approves."

"Probably," Reese laughed. "And to be honest, I rather like keeping things just between the two of us."

Freddy hummed in agreement, shifting restlessly where he stood, no idea what to do next. He didn't very well want to leave. Not after Reese had hinted that the night wasn't over. But Reese didn't move either and didn't say anything. He merely glanced up the stairs in the direction Henry had gone, a mysterious smile on his face.

"What are we—" Freddy started.

Reese shushed him, lifting a finger to his lips. A moment later, they heard the distant thump of a door shutting.

"All right, now," Reese said, reaching for Freddy's hand.

He surged forward, drawing Freddy with him. They

climbed the stairs as silently as they could in an old, creaky house. Freddy's heart pounded against his ribs, knowing full well what Reese had in mind. When they reached the top of the stairs, he didn't need prompting to turn left and head down the hall containing the family bedrooms. He kept his mouth shut—though it was an effort, considering how badly he wanted to laugh at the madness of what they were doing—in case the spare family bedrooms were occupied.

As soon as they reached Reese's room and slipped inside, closing and locking the door behind them, he let out his laughter. The sound only echoed through the room for a moment before Reese reached for him, slanting his mouth over Freddy's.

It was pure heaven. The taste of Reese's lips coupled with the aggression of his sudden embrace sent Freddy's head spinning. He moaned deeply, clasping his arms around Reese and lowering one hand to his backside as the cares of the world slipped away. He wasn't anxious about whether he was doing things right or whether Reese would be pleased, he just followed what his heart and his body told him to do and thrust his tongue alongside Reese's, drinking him in. It felt so good to kiss him freely, passionately, without judgement or danger that within seconds, he was so hard the constriction of his trousers was almost too much.

"Let's get rid of these," Reese panted between eager kisses, fumbling with the buttons of Freddy's jacket.

Freddy hummed in agreement, raising his trembling

hands to Reese's jacket while also trying to shrug out of his own once Reese had him free. He was so desperate to be naked with Reese, to feel his body sliding against Reese's, that it made him clumsy. He wanted their mouths to stay joined and made effort after clumsy effort to keep kissing Reese as they made a mess of trying to remove half unbuttoned clothes.

In the end, laughter overtook every other emotion, and Freddy let his arms drop, giving up his efforts. Reese dissolved into laughter as well, and the two of them sagged into each other, giggling like mischievous school-boys attempting to play a prank. Reese's waistcoat was unbuttoned and his jacket hung off of one arm while Freddy's shirt was untucked in the back and his waistcoat was tangled in the arm of his half-removed jacket. They stood there, laughing with each other, foreheads pressed together, trying to catch their breaths.

"This is off to a chaotic start," Reese said at last.

"I'd wager the best thing we can do is to each calmly and carefully remove our own clothes," Freddy agreed.

Reese stood straighter, meeting Freddy's eyes with a teasing smile. "Where's the fun in that?"

Freddy's heart fluttered wildly in his chest. He wriggled enough to free himself from his jacket and waistcoat, letting them drop carelessly to the floor. "Would you rather we get naked quickly or waste time trying to be sensual?" he asked.

"Always waste time being sensual," Reese said with fire and humor dancing in his eyes.

He proved his point by tugging Freddy's shirt the rest of the way out of his trousers and sliding his hands up the bare skin of Freddy's belly and chest as he removed it. Freddy sucked in a breath, shuddering at every tantalizing sensation and raising his arms so Reese could tug the useless shirt up over his head.

"God, you're gorgeous," Reese said breathlessly, raking his hands back down Freddy's body once the shirt was discarded. "I could look at you for hours."

"We don't have that kind of time," Freddy panted in reply, grabbing Reese's jacket as it dangled from his arm and pushing it off.

He followed that by removing Reese's shirt in much the same way Reese had done away with his. Before it even hit the floor, Freddy fumbled with the fastenings of Reese's trousers, opening them and sliding his hand inside to caress his cock.

"Yes," Reese gasped, tilting his head back slightly as Freddy stroked him. "I love your hands on me."

"That makes two of us."

Freddy had the unaccountable urge to laugh as he fisted Reese's prick, rubbing his thumb across the sensitive tip, already damp in readiness. It had taken so much for them to come to this point, but now that they were there, it was as though he were soaring through the skies.

He wanted more. With one last stroke, he moved his hands to push Reese's trousers down over his hips. He was ready to drop to his knees to take Reese's cock in his mouth, but before he could, Reese reached for the fastenings of his trousers.

"I can't have all the fun," he murmured, pushing Freddy's trousers down and reaching for his balls.

Pleasure shot through Freddy so hard that he worried he would go off too soon, ruining the whole thing. Whether Reese could sense that or whether he had the same worry, he moved his hand away, sliding an arm around Freddy's waist and drawing him in for another long, sensual kiss. Their hips met, the hot spears of their cocks trapped between them as they mated with their mouths, kissing and circling their arms around each other, touching, fingertips dug into flesh, as though they could meld into each other if they tried hard enough.

"I love you," Freddy panted between kisses. "I don't ever want us to be parted again."

"We won't have to be," Reese said, jerking awkwardly against him. Freddy realized with an amused twist to his lips that Reese was trying to step out of his shoes and trousers without using his hands. "We'll find a way," he went on. "We will be together."

"I believe you," Freddy said, trying to step out of his trousers himself. They were the last, ridiculous barrier keeping the two of them apart.

They were not easy to negotiate without hands, though, and with one false move, Freddy tipped dangerously to the side. He caught Reese as he fell, and the two of them spilled to the floor in a pile of limbs and laughter. Freddy lay on his back, trying hard to swallow his laughter so as not to raise further suspicion after the noise they'd just made.

"Do you think anyone heard that?" he asked.

"I doubt it," Reese laughed, rolling off of Freddy to reach for his one remaining shoe and remove it. "Everyone, including Henry and Ellie, are on the guest wing at the moment."

"Thank God," Freddy sighed gratefully, lying with his arms stretched out.

Reese finished with his own shoes and trousers and moved to tug Freddy's off. When he was done with that, he crawled over Freddy's legs, closed a hand around the base of Freddy's prick to hold it straight up, and closed his mouth over the tip, all before Freddy could catch up to what he was doing. He gasped and tensed at the sudden jolt of pleasure, then let out a long, appreciative moan as Reese worked his tongue across his swollen tip. He tried to find words to express how good it felt, but all that came out were erotic sighs of pleasure.

Reese moaned briefly, then lifted his head, panting. "Those sounds," he ground out. "You could make me come just with those sounds."

"I'm making those sounds because I'm about to come," Freddy said, laughing once again.

"Not yet," Reese said, his grin turning downright mischievous. "Definitely not yet."

He rocked back to his haunches, offering Freddy a hand. Curious about the change in pace, Freddy took his hand and let Reese help him to his feet. As soon as they were standing, Reese crashed into him once more, their mouths meeting in a kiss that involved their whole bodies, not just their lips and tongues. Bone-deep need pulsed through Freddy, making his cock throb. He didn't want the pleasure and the need to end, not soon, not ever.

"You're in luck," Reese said at last, breaking their kiss and nudging Freddy toward the bed.

"I think that goes without saying," Freddy laughed. A shiver went through him as the back of his legs hit the side of Reese's bed.

Reese shook his head, his expression downright wicked, and shifted to the side. He bent toward the small table beside his bed, opened the top drawer, and took out a blue glass vial. Without a word, he held it up, biting his lip.

Freddy knew exactly what it was and what it meant. His heart thudded in his chest so hard it made him dizzy and his entire groin tightened in anticipation. "Fuck," he said, both an exclamation and a request.

Reese stepped closer to him, and it was all he could do not to let his knees buckle under him. "Turn around," Reese said.

Freddy did more than that. He turned toward the bed, leaning forward and bracing himself against the coverlet, hips raised. He let out a sudden sound of need as Reese nudged his legs apart, then gasped so hard he nearly jumped out of his skin as a trail of cool liquid slipped down the cleft of his arse. That was followed by

Reese's fingers as he spread the slick liquid across his opening.

"Relax," Reese ordered him, which only made his groin tighten harder. "Relax," Reese repeated. "The more you can relax, the better it will be."

"It's going to be good no matter what, because it's you," Freddy said, sentimentality blending with hard, carnal need.

Reese answered his statement by pressing a finger slowly inside of him. Freddy gasped, then growled and tightened, drawing Reese's finger in farther. It felt surprisingly good for an act he'd always seen as humiliating for the one on the receiving end.

"Do you like it?" Reese asked, his voice rough with desire.

"God, yes," Freddy told him, forcing himself to do as he'd been told and relax.

As soon as he did, Reese slipped a second finger into him, causing him to tense and growl with pleasure. Reese worked his fingers in and out, stretching and teasing him. The strange, new feelings were amazing, but Freddy knew there was more. He wanted to be completely filled, wanted Reese to hit that spot he'd heard so much about that would send him to heaven.

Reese added a third finger, but Freddy growled, "Cock, Reese. For God's sake, use your cock."

"Whatever you say, love," Reese growled.

But instead of ramming into him, like Freddy expected, indeed, wanted, Reese grappled with him, flipping him to his back. For a moment, Freddy stared curiously, almost angrily at Reese. His legs hung off the bed at awkward angles. At least for a moment.

With a swiftness that could only be born from experience, Reese lifted Freddy's legs, using his shoulders to fold them back until Freddy felt like a frog. The position opened him wide, though, and before he had time to worry about how it might feel, Reese was pressing slowly into him.

Freddy let out a breathless cry as every inch of Reese sunk into him. It was glorious, intimate, perfect. He hadn't dreamed that they could be together that way face to face, but there they were. Reese watched him with a passion-hazed grin as he moved faster, deeper. Just knowing his every expression was being watched, that Reese could see the pleasure-mad distortion of his features as he fucked him was irresistible. Being able to see Reese's grin fade into aroused abandon was everything.

It was good on so many levels, and then it got better. The warm pressure inside of him grew fast, turning into something he never could have anticipated. It felt as though a volcano had awakened within him that grew hotter and closer to oblivion as Reese pumped harder and faster. It was there, the spot he'd heard whispered about. He threw back his head and made wild sounds as Reese brought him closer to the edge.

"Yes, Freddy," Reese gasped, moving harder still.

"Beautiful Freddy." He reached for Freddy's cock, closing his hand around it as he thrust.

That was all it took. Freddy tensed as his body hurled over the abyss, then cried out as he came, harder than he'd ever come. He erupted as if the sunlight inside of him had to get out, spilling over Reese's hand and his own belly.

Reese made a gorgeous, carnal sound moments later as he thrust hard, spending deep inside Freddy, then gradually rocking to stillness. His energy seemed to drain as he pulled out, then collapsed on top of Freddy. Their sweating bodies tangled together, but they were both too exhausted to move to a more comfortable position.

Only after several long minutes did Reese manage to raise himself to look down at Freddy and ask, "So?"

Freddy blinked up at him for a moment, completely overcome with a love so deep he wasn't certain where his soul ended and Reese's began. Then he laughed. Reese laughed with him, and before long, collapsed onto him again. This time, they found the energy to shift themselves the right way around on the bed, climbing beneath the covers.

Once they were snuggled close, Reese asked again, "What did you think? Did you like it?"

Freddy laughed once more, then twisted to face Reese. He rested a hand on the side of his flushed face and leaned in for a lingering kiss. "I loved it," he said at last in a warm purr. "And it wasn't remotely like what I thought it would be."

Reese grinned, kissing him back lightly, his eyebrow twitching up. "I thought you'd be surprised by doing it that way. I mean, the way I'm sure you've seen it done, from the back, is fine too, but, God, the look on your face when you came." He growled as he spoke, and Freddy felt the distinct twitch of Reese's cock against his leg.

"I only have one question," Freddy said, sliding his arm around Reese's back and reveling in the heat of their bodies against each other.

"Anything," Reese said, brushing his fingers through Freddy's hair.

"Next time, can I be the one inside you?" The twist of anxiety that his question brought came as a surprise to Freddy, but the question wasn't as simple as it sounded.

Reese let out a long breath, smiling. He nudged his knee between Freddy's legs and stole a kiss before saying, "Darling, there are no rules. We're here for each other. I rescue you, you rescue me. I lift you up, you keep me from getting carried away. And when you fancy a fuck, I can take the lead or you can. We're in this together."

"Together," Freddy repeated, reaching for Reese's hand and twining their fingers together. "Forever."

EPILOGUE

*C*hristmas at Silverstone Castle was a jolly affair for the first time in years. Mr. Taylor and Mrs. Ball were overjoyed to be able to hire a full contingent of staff in the first place, and even more delighted to have the extensive house cleaned, aired out, and decorated to the rafters with holly, ivy, pine, ribbons, and every other trapping of Christmas cheer. But they were most excited about having young Harry and Ricky in the house to add a youthful burst of festivity to the season.

"I think Mrs. Ball is in love," Freddy commented to Reese as they stood near the massive Christmas tree, now strewn with opened gifts and the remnants of wrapping around the base.

Reese chuckled as he turned to watch the house-keeper, who sat on the floor in a shockingly undignified manner, helping Harry and Ricky connect the last bits of track from the massive toy train set Harry had received from his beloved Uncle Freddy. Reese wasn't sure which warmed his heart more, seeing Harry so blissfully happy or knowing that Freddy had been accepted as one of the family without so much as a question on Harry's part.

"Auntie Lenore, you must join us," Harry called over his shoulder to Lenore, putting a slight dent in Reese's smile.

"Must I?" Lenore glanced up from the conversation she was having with Henrietta and Fergus—a conversation that mostly involved her cooing over Henny's newborn son with stars in her eyes.

"Yes, of course," Ricky told her. "Leave baby Fred to Mama and play with us instead."

Lenore whispered something to the baby before handing him back into Henny's arms, then leapt up, crossing the room to plop down to the floor, as the boys had requested.

Mrs. Ball stood with a reluctant sigh. "I'll fetch tea, if you'd like," she said, smiling fondly at the familial scene around her.

"Yes, please, Mrs. Ball," Henrietta answered, playing hostess for the moment.

Mrs. Ball left, leaving only the family in the room.

"You know," Freddy turned to Reese with a laugh, "people need to stop naming babies after their brothers. It's going to be confusing in a few years."

Reese's mouth pulled into a lopsided grin and he thumped Freddy's back. "I can't think of a better name for a boy than Frederick."

"Neither could we," Henny said from the sofa where she cradled baby Fred.

"All right, it's a fine name," Freddy conceded, though his cheeks burned pink.

Reese laughed at him and nudged his arm in a way that turned into a far more intimate touch. That only made Freddy blush harder. Their family, Lenore included, knew everything about the two of them and the commitment they had made to each other, but Reese had the feeling Freddy still wasn't comfortable with showing affection in front of them. That was fine with him, when all was said and done. Discretion would always be key to staying safe in a world that continued to punish them for the crime of loving each other, but the sharp edge of danger all but vanished when they were among people who cared about them.

"I'm worried about Lenore," Freddy said, lowering his voice so that only Reese could hear him.

"Oh?" Reese blinked in surprise. "She seems happier than I've ever seen her." He nodded to where Lenore was discussing the merits of the different sorts of toy engines the boys had been given for Christmas and regaling them with tales of the train that had taken her across America from Wyoming.

"She's the happiest woman I've ever known," Freddy agreed with a grin, then shook his head. "But you've seen the way she dotes on baby Fred. She's going to want babies of her own, and soon, I'd wager."

"You aren't holding her back from finding someone who can give them to her," Reese reminded him.

"No," Freddy conceded with a nod. "But I can't help but be anxious that the quicker she calls off our engagement, the more suspicious it will seem."

"I'm not calling anything off anytime soon," Lenore spoke from the floor without looking up at the two of them.

It was Reese's turn to flush hot with embarrassment. "So we aren't being as quiet as we thought, eh?" he asked.

"No." Lenore glanced up at them and smiled. "But I could see the worry in your eyes when I was holding Fred." She paused, pointed a caboose at Freddy, and said firmly, "Don't worry. I haven't even met someone I want to throw you over for yet."

"Because she's having too much fun teasing half the confused, young men in London," Fergus added from his chair, which was parked beside the sofa where Henrietta sat.

"English men are delightful," Lenore said with a giggle. "Especially the young ones." She reached over to tousle Harry's hair, prompting a short protest before the three of them went back to playing with their trains.

"English men are delightful," Reese agreed, slipping his hand into Freddy's.

When Freddy accepted his touch, twining their fingers together and inching closer to him, Reese dared what he never would have just months before. He leaned toward Freddy and stole a quick kiss, even though the family was all there and Henrietta was watching them out of the corner of her eye. She smiled at the gesture, though, and cooed at baby Fred.

"Do you like babies?" Reese asked once everyone had resumed their activities and conversations.

"Of course," Freddy said. "Everyone likes babies."

Reese's chest squeezed tight. "Would you like to have one?"

Freddy turned to him, his brow shooting up for a moment before he dissolved into laughter. "Darling, I think you fail to understand how the reproductive system works. Yes," he added, lowering his voice to a barely audible purr, "we've been going at it as though trying to set a record these last few months, but I doubt the end result will be a child."

"I know that," Reese grinned, heating at the very mention of how physical he and Freddy were with each other behind closed doors. "But there are other ways, you know."

Freddy arched an eyebrow at him.

"It's been brought to my attention that one of my tenants at Albany Court has an unmarried daughter who has found herself in the family way," he whispered, excited to finally be sharing the idea he'd been contemplating for the past fortnight, since the farmer in question had come to speak to him with concern. "As I understand it, the circumstances of the conception were harrowing, criminal." A pinch of anger filled Reese's chest.

"That's awful," Freddy whispered in return, squeezing Reese's hand.

"And as such," Reese continued, "neither the young woman nor her family wishes to keep the baby once it is born. The reminder would be too painful, or so my tenant says. He came to me, asking if I knew of any institutions that would take such a child." He paused for a moment, his heart beating faster. "What would you say if we were that institution?"

Freddy's eyes went wide and he turned to face Reese fully. "You mean that we should adopt the child?"

Reese nodded, practically holding his breath in anticipation.

"Together?" Freddy asked, his voice pitching higher.

Reese nodded again, his smile widening. "It couldn't be official or legal, of course," he rushed on. "For appearance's sake, I would take the baby on as a ward. I don't believe it would be questioned too thoroughly, considering the tenant in question and his family have been associated with Albany Court for generations. It would likely be seen as an act of charity. I could use the excuse that Harry needs a playmate, and since I have no intention of ever remarrying...." He glanced to Freddy, hope filling him.

Freddy continued to gape at him, his expression bright with surprise and possibility. At last, he blinked rapidly for a moment then blurted out, "All right. Let's do it. Provided this is truly what the young woman wants."

"I believe it is," Reese said with a rush of joy. "You

can speak to her yourself to be certain, as soon as you'd like. She's due in May."

"May," Freddy said. He let out a breath and brushed a hand through his hair. "I'm going to be a father," he laughed, shaking his head.

"And a damn fine father you will make," Reese said.

He peeked to make sure the rest of the family was thoroughly occupied with their own affairs, then slipped his arm around Freddy's waist, leaning in for a kiss that sealed the love between them. He didn't care what the world said, Freddy was his heart, his blood, and his soul. He was family, and in spite of the odds, he would do everything to make certain that family grew and flourished.

I HOPE YOU HAVE ENJOYED REESE AND FREDDY'S story! It's a story I've wanted to tell for a long, long time. Particularly since there are so many misconceptions about what life was like for gay men in the 19th century. It's a fact of human nature that we tend to look at the past through the lens of the present and to assume we know what life was like for people, but when it comes to the history of homosexuality, in my experience, most people get it very wrong.

Yes, it's true that, up until 1861, homosexual acts in Britain were punishable by death. The last execution for homosexual acts took place in 1835, however, and I find it very hard to believe that no men were caught in the twenty-six years between those two dates. And yes, the Labouchere Amendment to Britain's criminal law code in 1885 introduced the idea of "gross indecency", which enabled men to be arrested and imprisoned or fined for homosexual acts, even those committed in their own homes, in private, there is overwhelming evidence that men who were caught out, like Sebastian Stone, were by far the exception, not the rule. In fact, there was a deep, thriving secret community of gay men throughout the Victorian era. Author Graham Robb writes extensively about this community in his book *Strangers: Homosexuality in the 19th Century*, which I highly recommend for anyone interested in this topic. The greatest protection that the gay community had in the 19th century, something that might be hard for us to imagine today, is the mere fact that the majority of the population didn't even know what homosexuality was. The term "homosexual" wasn't even coined until 1869.

When most people think of Victorian homosexuality, they think of Oscar Wilde and the Aesthetic movement. They also think about Oscar Wilde's trial for gross indecency and point to that as proof that homophobia was rampant and even mighty men were brought low because of it. But historical record is pretty clear on the fact that Wilde went to trial because his lover's father had a bone to pick more than because of any general public outcry. In fact, the transcript of Wilde's trial makes very clear that he didn't take the whole thing seriously, never imagined he could be found guilty and sent to prison, and therefore joked and teased while on the witness stand... until he realized, too late, how serious the situation was.

The point being that, while we might be tempted to think that Freddy and Reese and men like them would have been forced to live haunted lives, always worrying that the fist of the law would come down on them, and that they were a few, lost souls with no society to help them out or give them comfort and camaraderie, the reality is that few people would have questioned a strong friendship between two men during the Victorian era. In fact, intimate male friendships in the Victorian era were so common that it is incredibly difficult for historians to sort out which relationships were sexual and which were platonic. It truly was a different era.

ANYHOW, I COULD SAY MUCH MORE ON THE subject...and I'm going to. Soon! Are you wondering what might happen to Sebastian, once his secret is exposed? You'll find out soon in book two of an all new series, *Tales from the Grand Tour*. You'll meet Sebastian again in *Rendezvous in Paris*. You might also meet another, far more sinister character again, one who was forced to leave England. Will he get his just desserts?

AND WHAT ABOUT LADY NATALIA MARLOWE AND Dr. Linus Townsend? What was going on between the two of them during Lady Katya's party? Find out this spring in *The May Flowers*, book five, *When Lady Innocent Met Dr. Scandalous*.

AND BY THE WAY, IF YOU'RE INTERESTED IN READING the story of how Mr. Charlie Garrett met and married his wife, Olivia, I've written that book! It's called *Trail of Aces*, and it's part of my *Hot on the Trail* historical western romance series.

I'VE ALSO WRITTEN THE ENTIRE STORY OF HOW LORD Henry Howsden and Ellie met and fell in love. That book, *A Passionate Deception* is free when you sign up for my newsletter!

Click here for a complete list of other works by Merry Farmer.

ABOUT THE AUTHOR

I hope you have enjoyed *The Earl's Scandalous Bargain*. If you'd like to be the first to learn about when new books in the series come out and more, please sign up for my newsletter here: http://eepurl.com/cbaVMH And remember, Read it, Review it, Share it! For a complete list of works by Merry Farmer with links, please visit http://wp.me/P5ttjb-14F.

Merry Farmer is an award-winning novelist who lives in suburban Philadelphia with her cats, Torpedo, her grumpy old man, and Justine, her hyperactive new baby. She has been writing since she was ten years old and realized one day that she didn't have to wait for the teacher to assign a creative writing project to write something. It was the best day of her life. She then went on to earn not one but two degrees in History so that she would always have something to write about. Her books have reached the Top 100 at Amazon, iBooks, and Barnes & Noble, and have been named finalists in the prestigious RONE and Rom Com Reader's Crown awards.

ACKNOWLEDGMENTS

I owe a huge debt of gratitude to my awesome beta-readers, Caroline Lee and Jolene Stewart, for their suggestions and advice. And double thanks to Julie Tague, for being a truly excellent editor and assistant!

Click here for a complete list of other works by Merry Farmer.

Made in the USA
Coppell, TX
21 November 2021

66165411R00173